DEDICATION

My books will always be dedicated to my wonderful husband Duncan, great friends, and my family, but above all, to any woman who has faced betrayal.

Right now, my 1950's sisters face betrayal after betrayal by the government put in place to protect their rights. They will never cease to have my admiration and respect for their continued battle against the injustice that has been perpetrated against them by a 'Not so Great British Government.' Every book I write will continue to be dedicated to them till we have justice.

Still, they Rise and may their daughters and granddaughters rise after them.

Deeds Not Words

Grateful thanks to Hazel Marina Dorie Bell and Lynne Cage for their massive help in getting this edited.

Rhia's Walk: ©Dee Kearney 2020   Publisher: Elsworth Creative

CHAPTER ONE

Old Endings
Rhia 1995

At what small moment, insignificant, unnoticed, does the past start to destroy a future. Is it a progression of moments that we follow relentlessly without regard for what we may bring down upon us? Or is it truly fate – a slight deviation from the norm that sets us on a path of destruction...

Rhia sat silently. Through the thin material of her skirt the damp earth clawed at the flesh of her thighs. She sat in quiet regard as the mountains, calm, majestically white capped and unbelievably beautiful, beckoned her on even higher.
She had a choice to make... Would she make the right one, or become a pawn at the hands of fate, her own destiny?

How does the end of a life start? Is it a slow realisation? A state of panic? Or just plain tired of the game. What brings someone to the point where it no longer really matters? And they opt for death with an almost que sera attitude. She rested her chin on her hands and her elbows on her knees, lost in the reasoning.

The evening drew on and with it the cold. All she had to do was stand up and walk down the mountain, or not... She looked at the snow laden roofs of the town below illuminated by a mixture of early streetlights and oncoming sunset. Musing on the scenario's that were likely being played out right now by those seemingly intelligent and reasoning people living under those nouveau-riche, cosmopolitan, cuckoo clock homes.

Such games, such twisted, bitter, and selfish games. Games with no humanity. Games for the sake of games, from sheer boredom and with no regard for damage done. Revenge without reason. Manipulation for the sake of ego. In short, to break the mediocrity of their lives.

It seemed to her that overall, people were just facades, and few of them worthy of trust or even simple regard. This much she had learnt. It had been a slow process starting early. |A gradual peeling away of faith, and in its place a growing cynicism and despair. Each small event chipped away at something innocent and beautiful, till all that remained was the woman sitting quietly and still, awaiting the end of her day.

The stillness of the approaching evening crept insidiously over her, and with it the cold intensified. Yet she felt nothing, for a half smile slowly warmed the face that had recently started to line with the years of pain and longing. The veiled but visible sadness that hovered in the once lovely eyes lifted, and it was as though all had been a mere moment that could be easily forgotten, like some small insignificant memory. Wiped away as once more, she sought sanctuary in a place of ancient times and distant music…her eyes sparkled with some overwhelming and joyous emotion…Certainty.

The first opening chords of massive attacks 'teardrop' echoed through her mind like a distorted overture on an ageing piano and she was no longer on the hillside in Switzerland.

Breathing deeply and quietly the air of the mountain that should have been her last living memory. It was instead the strong musk of his skin she remembered, telling its own story of their lovemaking that she inhaled, tasted, and once more she was years ago, on a red wine scented April evening… trembling, mouth on mouth with an intensity of passion that she had thought only soulmates could create. Immeasurable…what I feel for you…' The words of a poem she had written for him drifted through the memory and she was lost to the present and all its pain.

Certainty

You are my second skin,
A kind of opiate washing over me,
erotic and gentle,
giving me so many moments to savour
Your mercury eyes, fluid with passion draw me in until nothing else matters
The salt taste of you on my tongue,
The subtle musk of your sweat,
drawn from every moan of pleasure you draw from me.
Sweet, sensual man, never doubt how you make me feel,
I wear you, feel you, and try very hard not to love you..

CHAPTER TWO

New Beginnings – Rhia (2014)

The river moved slowly as if sensing the heat of the day and the need for quiet. Little could be heard but for the occasional bird passing overhead. Insects buzzed around the edges where the water lapped gently over the pebbles and sand. All else was still. It was an uncanny silence brought on with the need for nature to take shade.

The woman moved quietly through the trees, her movements careful and stiff with age. She carried a duffel bag across her shoulder, and she would stop and pick the occasional blackberry from the brambles that threatened to overrun the narrow path and popped it into a plastic bag within as she walked.

She was tall and strong boned, but age had softened her skin and the flesh of her arms, which, though brown with the sun, was wrinkled and peppered with age spots. She wore a battered old Stetson over shoulder length loose white hair and a long Indian cotton skirt that brushed the tops of her ankles with old slip-on trainers. A sleeveless vest topped the outfit and had seen better days. From a distance you might have mistaken her for forty but on closer appraisal, it was clear she had seen many more years and was likely an old hippy.

Behind her trotted an old collie cross. Her deep red coat also peppered with the white of age around her mouth. These two were a match, the dog, and the woman. Walking slowly in the sunshine to the river's edge, she stood for a moment and breathed in the sun warmed air as the dog paused beside her awaiting instruction with a wagging tail.

Slipping off her shoes and letting the skirt slip to the ground, she stepped out of it and carefully made her way across the stones and into the water. The dog followed on her cue and the two waded in until the water released them from gravity and age, and they were young once more in the cool of the river.

"Dammit!" she muttered as she paused to take off the hat and throw it to the bank. It landed by her shoes to settle in the still of the afternoon as the woman and the dog swam quietly on. The dog circled the woman in its excitement as she floated quietly on her back, her white hair circling her face like a dandelion clock. She had always been a good floater, she mused, large breasts you see. Unfortunately, their former glory had been lost over time and they had flown south for the winter several years ago and never returned.

Turning to follow the direction of the dog she smiled with affection for the friend that was always close. The peace was immense and the river calm and safe. It was not always the case. She had often seen it a raging torrent as the early autumn brought rain and it cut its path through the valley with a force that was fearful and fast flowing.

She floated gently in the natural pool that had been carved from the valley sides and looked up through the trees that were shielding her eyes partially from the sun. The dog had swum to the bank and was splashing in the shallows. This was her cue for home. Turning over, she swam towards her companion and carefully waded out. Her old bones protested as they started to bear her weight once more and trying to stand and walk through the shallows affected her balance. This was the risky time where she could no longer rely on her strength to keep her upright and a nasty fall now would not be good. Age was such a betrayal of spirit. Drying herself with her skirt, she dressed slowly and then called the dog to her side.

"Come on Clucy old girl, time to go home."

Ten minutes later she pushed open the gate to a single-story dwelling that by some miracle had remained distant from the growing village nearby. Extracting the key from its hiding place inside the greenhouse that was just about clinging to life, she walked through an overgrown, but once beautiful garden and opened the front door letting the early afternoon light stream into the small hallway. The room she entered was large but sparse in furnishings, but what furnishings there stood out as statement pieces. For an older woman, it was unexpected, with large low white walls filled with art mainly in peacock blue/greens and the occasional reds. At one end stood a large work that stood six foot high in blue and purple metallics. It was of a woman with peacock feathers for a dress and a peacock mask over her eyes. In her hand she held a shallow bowl and in the bowl were words, faded with the years. It was a stunning piece, and you were immediately drawn to it.

Her home was to all intents and purposes, a studio, and despite its lack of normality it was otherwise comfortable and colourful. The artworks around the walls echoed the atmosphere and an easel stood in front of a large window on a cotton sheet that was paint spattered with years of creation. The window echoed its pattern in a way that demonstrated the energy of the artist and the apathy of the housekeeper. She gave the current canvas a cursory glance and made her way through to the kitchen to pour herself a large glass of water and replenish the dogs bowl.

Returning to the room she sat wearily in the armchair and sipped the water. The heat, even after her swim, had quickly drained her energy and she was ready to rest. The canvas that faced her chair was a landscape under development and she stared at it critically noting every brush stroke. For a moment, her eyes filled with tears but soon closed as fatigue overcame her. She slept and she dreamed.

CHAPTER TWO

Mack (2014)

Mack hovered slightly back from the shopkeeper as he showed him how to work the till in the village shop. He was saving up to go to University in London and despite the owner's grumpy reputation, he had managed to secure a couple of shifts at the weekend. Low pay of course, but beggars could not be choosers in this small village where the work was scarce. As the man continued his tuition, hE Surveyed the small shoP. THE supplies were basic, but the local farm produce was fresh, and most people could survive on the provisions from this shop on a day-to-day basis. This was rural France where the towns were spread out and although reachable, it was a chore to travel between them unless you had a car. So, this was the easiest option for employment.

English by birth, he had grown up in France when his mother and father, after several holidays to this part of Brittany, had decided to take the plunge to change their stressful lifestyle back home to one of peace. His bilingual ability made him an attractive addition to the shop when dealing with the many British tourists, but in culture he was French, just not by birth.

His mother had been an insurance consultant and his father a freelance robotic engineer and with just the occasional trip to update their skills, they could work pretty much anywhere.

They had bought a tumbledown property with its own small patch of land on a whim for just five thousand pounds in 2002 and three years later, bought a caravan spending another three painful years rebuilding the ruined house and extending it to a standard they were happy with. John, his father, was a natural talent in design and had the practical skills in building to back it up. However, he was lacking in finishing power and would often deviate to something new, which always provoked a row. One thing was certain, the results once achieved Were stunning and the frustrations forgotten. It was small, but it was perfect.

His mother had much preferred her new rural life to London and as the equity from the London house had bankrolled them for the new life here, she soon downed tools preferring to manage the land and property whilst her husband flew off round the world on various contracts. It suited them and Christina was happy enough with her only son for company. In between business, John, her husband, and she would tackle some new project on the house. They had gradually built and landscaped their new home until it gave them the quality of life they had craved.

For Mack as an only child, had never much had the company of youngsters and was a quiet and serious boy, a quality that had got him the job here. The shop owner couldn't abide selfish teenagers, but he needed a strong pair of hands for the lifting nowadays. Mack's quiet and polite demeanour when he had shopped here previously had been noted.

The lad wasn't a natural mixer, preferring his own company, but was friendly to all he encountered. The outside world was something he had little knowledge of, but he had experienced it online through Google Earth and YouTube and he was longing to get to London, despite his natural shyness to explore a new type of life. He was determined to save every euro till he had enough to travel and live comfortably whilst he undertook his Information Technology degree.

A good-looking boy, if a little gangly, his accent and behaviours were French. The girls in London would be climbing all over him, his mother had thought when he had surprisingly announced his intention to study in England some months ago. She had mistakenly thought he would be content to stay close to home, but she had been wrong. The boy was starting to seek new horizons and she would be left without his company soon. It was a sadness, and she wasn't looking forward to her own company going forward, but he was growing up and it was only natural.

Content that his new employee had grasped the basics, the shop owner left him stacking shelves and went into the back room to make himself a coffee, leaving instructions to call him if he had any problems. Mack whistled to himself quietly until he got into a rhythm and the afternoon passed quietly with just the odd customer pulling up outside buying only a couple of items and leaving him to get his bearings without being stressed.

Armand, the shop owner, had realised quickly that he had employed a capable lad and took himself off to tidy the outside store. Mack worked steadily on and was glad of the shade within the small shop and the rows of fridges cooling the air. It was certainly a hot one.

A shadow crossed the door and Mack looked up to see an old woman enter the shop. It took a moment before he recognised her as the English lady who was reputed to be a bit mad. He'd seen her often enough walking her dog down by the river but like most youngsters he had kept his head down rather than attempt a conversation with a stranger.

She seemed taller than he remembered, and he stood up from his chore and turned to greet her.

"Hello," he smiled, and she smiled back quietly as she meandered around the shelves picking the odd item and examining it. Some she kept and placed in her basket, some she put back unceremoniously. A few minutes later she approached the counter, and it was his signal to return. He hoped he remembered how to use the till.

He spoke in English as a courtesy, and she acknowledged him with a smile. He knew she was fluent in French as he had heard her previously, but he thought she might welcome hearing her mother tongue and he liked to use his with someone other than his parents.

"€10.80 please."

She took out a small, beaded purse and he watched her as she counted out the money. Her hair was caught back in a ponytail, and she had large peacock blue glass earrings dangling from the ears. She wore a blue smock with knee length cut off denims and the Stetson sat firmly on her head. 'Quite modern for an old dear' he thought with the dismissiveness that only the young and sheltered could achieve.

"You're the Aspinall's boy, aren't you?" she asked taking the change from him.

"I am, yes," he replied.

She didn't enlarge on the question. It was more of a statement to acknowledge what she already knew.

"Can you put a card in the window for me?" she said.

"Certainly." He took the card and glanced at it "Oh, you need a gardener?" he asked.

"It appears I do...Old age is a terrible thing. Why do you know one?" she replied with a wry smile.

"Well, I might be able to save you the notice fee. I'm looking for work. Do you need an expert, or a general labourer?"

"No skills required. I just need someone trustworthy who can take my direction...but you're working here are you not?"

"Oh yes, but only a couple of days a week and I am saving to go to Uni so I would appreciate the work."

"What would you want paying?" she questioned.

"Same as here. It's fair enough. Nine euros an hour." He knew he was under selling but he needed the work.

She studied him for a moment, and he felt embarrassed at her scrutiny. She was a surprisingly assured old bird for someone her age, pretty cool really and she intrigued him.

"Tomorrow then? Ten am? We'll start with a trial and go from there. I'd need you a day a week, but a couple of days this week to break the back of it, how does that sound?"

"Sounds great, thank you!"

"I take it you know where I live?"

"Oh yes everyone knows where you..." He coloured with embarrassment, and she raised a quizzical eyebrow.

"Indeed?" she said "10 am then… and don't be late."

"I won't, and thank you!" he stammered, hardly able to believe his luck. Two jobs in a week, 'awesome!' he thought.

Picking up her shopping and placing it in her duffle bag she turned to leave. Suddenly she paused and turned back.

"I expect you have a name?" she enquired.

"I do!" he said, then feeling immediately stupid "It's Mack... short for Mackenzie."

"Different... I like that. My name is Rhia. Sorry, I should have said earlier. I'm losing it!" She smiled and made for the door. Mack couldn't help but be impressed. She didn't talk like an old person, and she hadn't called him 'young man' once.

Ten am prompt the next day, he knocked on her front door and a minute later it opened, and she greeted him with a satisfied smile.

"Good time keeping, I like that, a rare quality in the young. Come on, let's get to it!" Swinging open the door with enthusiasm, she walked past him giving him no time at all to respond. He followed her round to the side of the house, and she showed him briefly where the garden tools were and then took him on a tour of the garden.

It was clear from the strange selection of sculptures that she had placed around the garden that she had intended it to be an experience for those lucky enough to be invited in. It was also clear that the labour required to keep on top of such a garden was starting to defeat her. Her greenhouse still held vegetables and fruit plants on its shelves and there had once been an allotment type of area that had been discarded and was now bare. She had obviously been a keen gardener in earlier times.

"How good are you at building planters with wood?" she asked.

"Pretty Good, my dad's a brilliant carpenter and he always taught me things."

"Good," she said, "because I want you to build me some raised beds where my old vegetable plot is. My back can't stand the bending nowadays."

He paused for a moment wondering if he had bitten off more than he could chew with the woodwork, but his dad would always help him if he struggled. He took a leap.

"I can do that I expect."

"Very good," she nodded, and leaving him a list of where to start first and showing him where the tools were, she went back inside the house.

The house was low level with lots of windows and had been externally lined with a cool blue slate. Not at all like the rest of the properties around here. He wondered if she had had it designed and built for herself or whether she had just stumbled on it and bought it. It was certainly unlike any other house of its age around here.

Wisteria and Jasmine tumbled across the walls breaking the severity of the stone but was in danger of taking over the windows. This was one of the first items on her list. "I must have my light," was all the reason for urgency she had given.

The garden would have once been spectacular, he could see that. Had she done it all herself? There were structures built from rock and wood with seats in and crystals and chimes hung on strings from the trees. It would have been glorious at its best and it engaged his imagination.

Mack worked first on the lawns that surrounded the house and though his back cried out for mercy by lunch, he was very pleased with the results. It was amazing the difference taking control back made. She brought him fruit juice and bread and cheese at noon and exclaimed with pleasure at the progress he had already made. It was clear she was pleased but she seemed distracted and left him to go back inside as though something called her. Sitting on a low wall as he ate lunch and looked at this once stunning garden. It really was a work of art. Each new foray into the undergrowth had delivered something interesting in his mornings work and for someone into computers mainly, it had engaged his imagination, and he was curious to discover more. It was hard work but a pleasant way to earn money for someone strong.

After lunch it became clear as to why she was so keen to go back inside. As he took the pruners round to the rear of the house and approached the large windows at the back to commence pruning, he saw her standing at a large easel inside. She was wearing an old white shirt many sizes too big and was close into a canvas with her back slightly towards him and unaware of his presence. It was clear that whatever she was painting had her completely absorbed and for a moment he watched her, fascinated.

She had to be about sixty-five, but in front of this easel it was as though she was much younger, so intense and animated all at the same time, that he couldn't help but watch. Picking up the pruners he started to clip away at the overgrown climber around the window whilst keeping an interested eye on her, but she never noticed. Eventually he became absorbed in his work and forgot her for a few moments only to be completely surprised when he turned back In her direction to find her at the window, brush in hand and staring out at the skyline beyond the trees. A single tear spilled down her face and it was clear she did not see him. She was somewhere else entirely and he stepped back out of sight so as not to embarrass her by his presence.

A couple of hours later she came out with a drink for him and exclaimed on how hard he'd worked.

"I forgot to tell you; the bathroom is inside the hall to the left. I think you have done enough for one day. Same time tomorrow?" He smiled and thanked her as she paid him for his labours. He didn't mention that he had been forced to take a pee behind her tool shed earlier.

"Yes, great!" he said as he drank thirstily and as he started to tidy his tools; she surveyed his work. She looked sad, he thought. Whatever she was painting wasn't making her happy.

CHAPTER THREE

Sophie (2014)

Sophie examined the contents of the rucksack one last time and then hid it under the bed. She also counted the money she had been hiding and trembled as the realisation of what she was about to do hit her. The pop-up two-man tent and sleeping bag was stashed in the bottom of the wardrobe and she had retrieved her passport and birth certificate from her mother's 'official drawer.' Her hand went guiltily to the debit card she had lifted earlier from her mother's purse before she left for evening work at the supermarket with not a word of goodbye to her daughter, such was the rift between them. She was seventeen and ready to run.

Placing it back in the pocket of her jeans, she hoped her mum had a couple of hundred left in her account. Her mother had never given her pocket money, so she considered it several years dues. Most of their money went down their necks and the flat around her spoke clearly of the neglect of someone with a drink problem and there were two of them here.

He, as she referred to her stepfather, was down at his local getting pissed no doubt and she knew she had to be out of here before he returned, and the thought of his imminent return caused her stomach to churn in fear.

It had started slowly, little touches and lascivious looks, until bit by bit he had crossed the boundaries and to the evening a few weeks ago that had left her traumatised and in terror. Things had reached that point where it was impossible to stay a day longer and his previous apologies and remorse were now starting to be forgotten. Every day he watched her more and more and she knew it wouldn't be long. She had tried to tell her mother, but she had all but clapped her hands over her ears. Her mother refused to believe her as it meant she would have to act and as the woman hadn't the courage to go to the police against her husband, running was Sophie's only option. Her mother's refusal to acknowledge what he had done to her daughter had all but given him carte blanche to repeat the abuse and for Sophie, which had been the line drawn in the sand.

She had the brains to know that she would find no life around here, it had to be far and somewhere they wouldn't even think of. All she could remember was having the most wonderful time on a school trip at eleven to France and so she had focused all her will on making that journey once more. She studied French language CD's secretly and was determined she would go fully prepared. Her teacher at the one school she had managed to stay at for more than a few months, had said that besides her art, she had a flair for languages and that had always pleased her.

She wasn't a dishonest girl normally, but desperation had driven her to stealing small amounts from her mother's purse and his wallet of course. He never knew exactly how much he had but he always had a wad of cash in there. Late at night he would stumble in, fumble in his beer-stained trouser pocket and would carelessly throw everything on the sideboard on his return from the pub. Unaware of how much he had spent, the stupid bastard didn't even question if anything was missing because he didn't know.

She would sneak downstairs when he slept and lift a fiver here and a tenner there. She had amassed over three hundred quid over a period of weeks without him noticing...what an idiot. This, added to the small amounts from her mother who had less cash because she usually used her card, totalled three hundred and eighty-five. She would have one chance only tonight to steal from her mother's account. After that she wouldn't dare, it would point them to the direction she would be taking, and she couldn't risk it.

The house was quiet now and she checked her things nervously one last time. She had two changes of underwear, a bikini, two summer dresses, a jumper, shorts, and a lightweight anorak. A small beach towel, a toothbrush, and some toiletries. She had bought a camping water bottle along with the tent and that was her limit. She had to travel light. She carefully opened the bedroom door and tiptoed down to the kitchen to raid the fridge for anything to eat on the journey. Satisfied she had everything, she had got her bike from the shed and ran back in for the rest of her things. She left her phone turned off as she'd seen enough detective series and didn't want anyone tracking her. She would get a new 'pay as you go sim' at the first opportunity, it would be like a burner phone criminals use. The thought, so ludicrous, was the first thing about this that had made her smile. There were no real friends to say goodbye to as they were always moving from place to place, and she had just left the last school after attending only a few short weeks.

With the last-minute addition of a cap to hide her face, she strapped everything on the bike and kicked off from the curb. Terror was in every bone, but the adrenalin pushed her onwards. A quick stop at the cash machine realised the two hundred she had hoped for, but she knew that the withdrawal now made her officially a thief and it was not a good feeling.

She headed for the train station and bought a ticket for Dover. Having done all her research, it just seemed all too easy. She arrived at Dover around 11pm and wasted an hour in a cafe at the end of the promenade. She considered it safer getting an early morning ferry and arriving in France in the light, so she got another coffee in the town and then cycled up to the port and bought herself a ticket for the 3am ferry to Calais. Knowing she looked older than her age she was not surprised that no-one batted an eyelid, she just looked like any other student going on a cycling holiday. Life had given her experiences and a demeanour that were for the first time useful.

She chained up her bike below decks and headed upstairs to watch the white cliffs disappear as the boat pulled out of port. It was still not light and so no-one saw the tears that streamed silently down the girl's face. She had left her home and the so- called family she despised behind and was truly alone for the first time in her life.

She considered going to the cafe but decided she would stay on deck and curl up for a nap on the bench. The boat purred its regular rhythm as it crossed the channel. She must have slept up there on the deck because she jumped as the boat's revs changed and she felt it slow and turn.

The run into Calais called her to the railings and she watched the nearby beaches pass by and couldn't help feeling the first stirrings of excitement that she had chosen her path and was moving forwards hopefully to a better life. Anything would be better than what she had left behind her in Tottenham.

CHAPTER FOUR

Mack was there bang on time once more and received a smile of approval from Rhia. He had to admit he was stiff this morning from yesterday's efforts, and he'd begun to appreciate how hard she must have worked to keep on top of a garden like this one as long as she had.

Today she pottered alongside him with her dog at her side as he worked, occasionally giving him a word of advice. They went to measure up the raised bed area and she talked of the satisfaction of growing her own food and how frustrating it was to be unable to do so under the current conditions. She was excited like a child at the prospect of having a more manageable vegetable garden. The dog must have picked up on her excitement and was having a mad half hour racing round before she flopped in the shade panting.

"I know how she feels," laughed Rhia and Mack was glad she seemed in better spirits today. She had piled her hair on top of her head with a pin and was in battered linen pants and a long cotton tunic and he thought that she had a style all her own. The Brits weren't renowned for it around here, but she was the exception.

Later, she wandered back in with the promise of preparing lunch and soon enough she called him to the house. Directing him to the bathroom to wash up, she went back to set up the table out on a small veranda that had no air, but some shade. He opened the bathroom door and was amazed. It was a huge utilitarian shower room with the only difference to style being two large artworks made from mosaic tiles where the shower fell in the corner, which met the deep-sea blues of the floor in a continuation of the ceramic tapestry. The rest was left simply decorated yet unique, with slate lining the wall. There was no mirror over the sink, just a basket-work drawer with towels stacked on top and a laundry basket. It should have been luxurious, but it was as though it had been started but unfinished.

He followed her voice till he found himself in the huge living room that was more a gallery, and he paused in awe at the strange and wonderful abstracts that adorned the walls. The only difference to comfort was the low stone fireplace and open fire in addition to the radiators and a very comfortable L-shaped leather sofa strewn with colourful blankets. Art books lined the walls one side and videos another. She obviously like her films.

"Wow! Are all these paintings yours?" he asked.

"Guilty as charged... Come get some lunch," she answered as she beckoned him to a small table that had obviously given her pleasure in dressing.

"Sit yourself down. There's wine and juice, just help yourself to whatever." She moved back into the kitchen and brought back rolls and fresh butter. He got the feeling she was enjoying the company; she must be lonely out here on the outskirts of the village.

"I like my own company...and Clucy's of course, but occasionally it's nice to have someone to prepare a meal for." She must have read his mind. He quickly pulled out a chair and sat as she seated herself opposite him. The dog followed to sit nearby hoping for scraps and put on her most soulful dog expression in the hope someone would succumb.

"Eat, eat, don't be shy," she laughed, and it was a pleasant sound. He liked this lady; she was different to most people.

"It's very kind of you, thanks," he mumbled shyly as he spooned paté and chutney from the main plate. There was balsamic and olive oil to dip and freshly sliced huge tomatoes. Soon the food and the surroundings worked their magic, and he lost his self-consciousness.

"So, is that what you did...paint I mean...for a living?" he presumed she was retired.

"Still do... I was lucky enough to get an agent who worked hard to promote me, and he keeps me busy enough to this day, sometimes too busy! And you, what do you want to do?"

"I want to go to uni in London in the autumn to do a degree in IT, but I haven't got enough saved just yet. Mum and dad will help me, but I want to earn enough to enjoy the city whilst I'm there and travel a bit."

"Good for you, there's a lot of beautiful places in England but a lot of poverty also. Choose your visits with care. Edinburgh Festival is a must, Tate Modern, Stratford! You haven't lived till you've seen Shakespeare performed at the Swan and the replica Globe Theatre in London of course. Then there's the lakes... although I suppose you will have your own preferences." She petered out realising her tastes may not be what he had in mind.

"No, those are great suggestions, thank you. I'll keep them in mind," he said politely.

She watched him eat, thinking that here was a boy who had that little bit more about him. He felt her scrutiny and coloured up.

"Would you show me your artwork and tell me a little about it?" he asked as their meal came to an end.

"I will, but you must form your own opinions on it first. It makes it much more exciting for me. Come along, no time like the present!"

She stood up and he was obliged to follow, and she led him to the first wall where there were several thickly layered 'impasto' paintings. The colours were jewelled landscapes, and each horizontal layer of paint had several vertical layers of paints laid into them by scooping up lines of colour from different areas of the picture. It was fascinating how many different colours were in there and he realised it must have been a painstaking technique and not the usual one of someone painting with a palette knife.

"This must take you forever to do," he exclaimed as he went in closer to look.

"It certainly does, well spotted. Not many people are observant enough to realise that." She was pleased he had appreciated the time and effort in each work.

They then moved to a more spiritual range which was at odds with the others. She explained as she saw him looking at them.

"Those are Tarot, just my particular take on them. She preempted him.

"I was wondering, they are very different." They weren't his taste, but he found them fascinating.

"I think I've always had a split personality artistically speaking. I started off as a scenic designer, so these are miniatures for me really. I was used to working to a brief, so I developed several styles which isn't always a good thing for an artist. I guess I was just lucky that the styles I chose became popular." Mack had stopped dead in his tracks as he spotted the large metallic painting on a wall of its own.

"Wow!" He moved to it inspecting from different angles as the light changed the colour of the metallics.

"She's my Cre-Angel, the guardian of my work," came the reply as she followed him over to the large canvas.

"It's fabulous!"

"Thank you, Mack. That's so lovely to hear from a young person."

Mack had turned to her latest canvas and couldn't resist asking.

"This is your latest. What's it about?"

"It's just something from memory, nothing more." Somehow a light had left her eyes and he felt sad for her.

"Is it anywhere I know?"

"No, just the place where this house should have been built...Shall we get back to work?" It was clear she wanted to end the conversation, so he followed her lead and freed her from the thing she obviously did not want to discuss. Why would she have built the house here then and not where the picture depicted. It was a mystery he was determined to solve. That it made her unhappy was clear, but still she was clinging to that memory regardless. Where was that place?

By the end of the third week, they had an easy friendship if he didn't ask her too many questions. Little by little he gleaned bits of information. That she had worked in theatre mainly when she was younger. Then a little bit of TV and film, but that her love was really her art. It was pure chance that she worked on a shoot for a renowned agency, and it had brought her some hot introductions that had moved her art career on. She had been married briefly when she was very young, but it had been a mistake that took her years to get out of and she had been determined never to marry again.

That she was quite well known was no surprise to him when he Googled her later and he found many posts referring to various aspects of her career. A couple of images had her pictured with famous people but nothing much about her private life apart from that she was somewhat reclusive as most artists aspire to be. She had been a real babe In her younger days, that MuCH was obvious from the few photos he found.

The summer was a hot one and often she would disappear with her dog and return later with wet hair. When questioned she would just smile and say, "The river beckons me always." He worried that she would have an accident and when he voiced his concerns, she brushed him off saying, "I float well, always have, it's my therapy. The day I can't swim is the day I die and besides Clucy has to have her exercise, don't you old girl?" Clucy would come and sit at her feet with a look of adoration, and he knew he had been dismissed.

Weekends Mack still worked in the shop, and it suited him fine. Armand was used to him now and trusted him to run the store efficiently. On the days Armand left him to go to the local town to meet friends for a beer. Mack would play his favourite music quietly to ease the boredom of the chores he knew now like the back of his hand. At lunch, he would help himself to something from the counter at Armands behest and sit outside the shop in the shade chatting politely to the odd passer-by.

It was such a day that required shade that he was sitting outside with a cold drink and a sandwich when he saw the girl leading the bicycle down the street. Her movements were stiff and weary, and she was sunburnt. Clearly not happy, she pushed the bike with its baggage along the street till she reached him.

"Hi," he said, "having trouble?"

The girl looked at him suspiciously. Three weeks of riding through France without finding work and fending off various cons and advances had drained her spirit as well as her money. She had managed a few days on a campsite near Le Touquet at the beginning, cleaning the showers whilst the regular cleaner was off sick in return for her site fees and had hoped to stay a bit longer whilst she searched for more permanent work. That had ended abruptly when the manager had made a pass at her, and she had fled.

Moving further south she had found no work and not much of a friendly reception wherever she enquired for work and her heart was starting to plummet. In desperation she had boarded a train heading to Brittany having spent days cycling and job-seeking to no avail in the hope she might be able to find farm work. The last town had frightened her so much. She had been accosted by a shady looking character in a I who was asking far too many personal questions and looking too intensely at her. At the first opportunity she had headed off into the night as fast as she could pedal. Terrified and suspecting he was a pimp and too frightened to wild camp, she cycled through the night till she found a camp and paid for site fees with the last of her funds. She had hoped she might be able to find further cleaning or work there, but they had said she wasn't fluent enough in the language to deal with differing nationalities. Now to add insult to injury, her bike chain had come off and she had taken a tumble and grazed her knee, and she hadn't got a clue what to do next. All options and money appeared exhausted, and she was beyond tired and desperate.

"You're English?" she questioned.

"Sort of. Do you want some help with that?"

"What's the catch?" she scowled, wiping the sweat from her brow.

"No catch, just help if you want it." He smiled disarmingly and she regretted her tone especially as she really needed help.

"Thank you, yes I would, if you can, do you have a loo I could use?"

"Through the door on the right of the counter and on the left."

He pulled her bike towards him and squatted down to examine the problem. It wasn't so bad. He had the chain on easily and was just going back into the shop when he caught her stuffing cheese and olives into her bag.

"You know if you're that desperate you only had to ask. I'd have given you something..." She reddened more than the sunburn could disguise.

"I'm so sorry. I didn't mean to, but I ran out of money a couple of days ago and I'm just so hungry!" She looked about to cry.

"Shouldn't you have brought more with you before coming on holiday?"

"I'm not on holiday, I'm trying to find work, but no one will hire me!" It was all too much, and she burst into tears. "I've been cycling round for three weeks and nothing!" she sobbed and then snatched back her breath and Mack felt immediately sorry for her.

"Then can't you go home?" he suggested.

"I can't! So go fuck yourself!" The anger with which she lashed out surprised Mack and he fell silent whilst she searched for something to wipe her eyes. It was clear that she was in some kind of meltdown so Mack being a kind person went inside a got her a pack of tissues.

"Look I'm sorry, I didn't mean to upset you. Haven't you got someone you could call at all?"

"No...no one." She was sobbing now, and Mack felt at a loss what to do. He hadn't expected to be dealing with this and he had certainly never dealt with a blubbering girl before, so it disarmed him completely. He cracked a cold can of orange from the fridge and handed it to her. It had a better effect than any verbal comforting and with a hiccupped 'Thanks' she stopped crying to drink thirstily. She had gained a measure of control by the time she had drained the can.

"Do you know anywhere I can camp safely around here? I can't pay for a site anymore," she hiccupped, regaining some composure.

He thought for a moment. "Give me a minute," he said, fumbling in his pocket for a phone and dialled.

"Hi mum, can I bring a friend home tonight? She's got her own tent but needs somewhere safe to pitch it. Can we help."

He listened for a moment and moved away slightly and Sophie could hear a quieter conversation, obviously about her. She had reached a point of fatigue that she just prayed that they would let her stay somewhere safe for a night so she could sleep without fear. She had reached her limit after weeks of constant stress and disappointment.

"Right, you can stay at ours tonight, but if you nick anything from my family I'll call the police myself! Mum says you can have a shower and she's making a meal for us when we get back." His voice was firm, but kind and it was almost the undoing of her, and the tears started to spill over once more.

"Thank you…really. I didn't know what I was going to do…I'm sorry I shouted at you." She dabbed the tears from her cheeks and managed a half smile and Mack thought she could be quite pretty with a tidy up, with her long dark hair and large eyes. Obviously, she had been washing in the sea and wherever she could for a couple of weeks and that wouldn't help her appearance. The strain was clearly showing on her face and her hair. He reckoned that this girl desperately needed some respite from whatever she had been dealing with. He had told his mum as much and on hearing that the girl was crying, his mum stepped up to the plate and told him to bring her home.

His mum was a lover of all things animal and people and was renowned for her kindness. She had once found a large Polish man the size of Hagrid from Harry Potter lost on the road in the freezing cold and rain one night and setting aside any common sense, had taken him for petrol for his broken-down car. Giving her husband a near heart attack when she had rung to tell him what she was doing, he had made her promise never to take that kind of risk again. A desperate young girl was up her street and hopefully a less risky option.

He made the girl a sandwich in the shop and put some money in the till for what he had used, sitting her outside in the shade to eat whilst he finished his shift. Sophie ate hungrily and looked about her at the sleepy street on the outskirts of Josselin. She found it hard to stop the butterflies that had been a constant in her stomach for the last few days as her money had run out, but the food was helping and as she sat there, she felt herself calming a little. The fact the boy had rang his mum had made her feel better about accepting his help. In truth she had no choice, and this was a small miracle in a frightening time. She suddenly felt so very tired, and her eyes started to close in the heat of the day. By the time Mack had closed up, he saw that she was nodding and obviously exhausted.

The walk home was fifteen minutes and Mack wheeled the bike, whilst she carried her rucksack. She asked him about himself, and he told her of his ambitions to go to London, but on the subject of herself she was determinedly reticent and would not be drawn on anything but her experience of the last weeks in France. She was nearly eighteen and liked studying languages, that much he knew, but apart from her name, little more.

His mum had set three places at the large kitchen table by the time they arrived as John was away on business and she greeted the girl warmly to put her at ease. The girl was very subdued, and Christina chatted away to Mack but had the wisdom to refrain from any questioning. It didn't take much to see that this wasn't a worldly young woman, rather the opposite. There was a story behind the girl's journey she thought, but questioning her would tempt her to flight, so Christina observed instead and restrained her suspicions. She smiled at Sophie.

"I expect you might appreciate a soak in a bath?" she asked.

"Could I? Oh, thank you so much." The thought was heaven.

"Come on, I'll show you where everything is. Mack can pitch your tent in the garden while you're having a bath and there's an outside loo and sink under the veranda at the end of the house. I'll get you a couple of roll up camping mattresses and a proper couple of pillows...make you a bit comfier." Sophie shyly handed Mack the tent to pitch with mumbled thanks but clutched the rest of her things to her. She was obviously frightened they would go through her bag and discover something.

Mack cleared the table and went outside to pitch her tent as his mum came down with an armful of things to make her stay more comfortable. She sent Mack off for a fold up chair and camping lights from the garage. By the time Sophie came back down in fresh clothes and out to where they were the tent was up and there was a table and chair nearby. A couple of bottles of water and some chocolate biscuits and fruit were on it in a cool box to keep off the flies and Christina had even strung some solar lights from a nearby tree to make the coming night less eerie for the lone girl. The bed had been made up in the tent and Christina had taken a sniff of the grubby sleeping bag and replaced it with a fresh one of theirs and an extra blanket just in case the night got cold.

After taking the girl's sleeping bag to wash, she returned with a couple of magazines and some basic toiletries and tissues. She looked up, satisfied with her efforts as the girl approached.

"I expect you're going to need a good night's sleep so we will leave you, but if you're worried about anything please knock on the door. Don't be out here frightened, OK?" Christina put a hand on the girl's arm and gave her a little squeeze accompanied by a kind smile and Sophie welled up with tears as she was so weary and unused to kindness.

"Thank you," was all she could manage without embarrassing herself once more.

"You're very welcome. Sleep well and come in for breakfast in the morning. Don't be shy, whenever you're ready. I'm usually up from 7am."

"Night Sophie," said Mack and followed his mum back into the house. As they closed the door he turned to his mum.

"You know it's only 8.30pm mum?"

"Yes, I do, son, but that girl is exhausted and probably needs a good cry, I expect she'll feel better tomorrow after a night's rest, poor thing."

"I guess so…thanks mum."

"Don't tell your dad if he rings!." She added grinning, the Polish man was still fresh in John's memory. Mack laughed and turned the dishwasher on.

	Mack lay later his bed wondering about the girl and why she was travelling alone. A couple of times he had gone to the window to check on her in the garden below. The tent was in darkness and eventually he conceded his mother was right, the girl was exhausted and probably fast asleep.

Sophie was asleep finally; she had spent the first half hour sobbing out her grief as quietly as possible till fatigue overcame her. As she calmed down and looked at the comforting colours of the fairy lights glowing gently through the material of the tent, she realised that the joy of a soft pillow was something she had previously taken for granted and snuggled down. With the roll mats to soften the hard ground it was heaven by comparison to the last few nights and she found peaceful sleep for the first time in three weeks.

CHAPTER FIVE

Mack rose early and looked out the window to find the tent flap thrown back. He jumped out of bed, pulled on a T-shirt and jeans and hurried downstairs to see if Sophie was all right. He shouldn't have worried because he found her washing her clothes in the kitchen sink whilst his mother sat at the table. There were two cups of coffee half-drunk, so it appeared they were getting on amiably enough.

"Morning," he said brightly.

"Morning son. Grab a coffee. I'll make us breakfast soon. Sophie is going to stay a few days, just till she gets her strength back a bit and who knows, we might even be able to find her a bit of work if we ask around." His mum looked at Mack and she all but winked. 'Didn't you just love her?'

"Great! Sounds like a plan. You ok with that Sophie?" He looked at the girl who had half turned from the sink and smiled at his mum.

"That would be so great," she said with a young girl's enthusiasm. His mum had worked her magic as usual and made the girl feel at home. She never pushed. He noted that his mum could have taken her clothes from her and put them in the washing machine, but she had cleverly offered the sink instead to hand wash them so that she would have time to put her at ease and talk.

"I'm off to Rhia's today mum, will you be ok?" He felt he should ask. She waved him away.

"Absolutely fine son. Sophie and I will do a little exploring in the town later and she can have some time enjoying France instead of pedalling round it. We'll see you later." She was giving him permission to go.

They ate a quiet but companionable breakfast and as he left, Sophie was stacking the dishwasher under instruction from Christina as she had never used one previously. It gave Christina an inkling of her family background, they either didn't approve of modern facilities or they couldn't afford them. Little things often gave more away than direct questioning and Christina was content to bide her time.

Mack was feeling good that he had done something kind as he walked the small distance to Rhia's house. The sun was coming up strong again and it was going to be another hot day. He had taken to wearing a cap on Rhia's insistence. 'Young enough to get skin cancer started for when you're older' she had said pointing solemnly to a couple of visible scars on her chest as she handed him and old battered trilby. He had brought his own today to save him the embarrassment of looking like an extra from an old movie.

Mack was pruning the trees down the side of the house today and had amassed a large bonfire pile. It was too hot and dry now to risk lighting it, so it would have to wait till a spell of damp weather. The garden was starting to look beautiful now and it was clear it was bringing joy once more to its owner. He was fast realising that everything in this garden had a reason, be it artistic or sentimental. The resulting eclectic mixture of planting, sculpture and strange items that had been incorporated into its grounds as art, was fascinating. Rhia's past life was a secret, but her creativity was on display for any lucky individual privileged to be allowed in this garden to see it. He had uncovered a wildlife pond that was almost swallowed in the undergrowth and on further examination he found a mosaic path that was a work of art in itself. As he had cleared and scrubbed it, he was awed by the patterns and designs within it, and it became an addiction to follow it to where it led.

Rhia came outside to greet him with the dog in tow. She was off for her morning swim before the heat of the day kicked in.

"Morning Mack, I'll be back in an hour. Help yourself to drinks," she shouted.

"Ok Rhia, enjoy your swim." He waved his brush in the air, and she returned the salute.

An hour later and despite the shade, he was sweating profusely but proud of his morning's work. The path had led him into the trees to a swing made from wood that hung on an old rope thrown over a large branch of the tree above. On it had been nailed a planter and forget-me-nots had gone to seed in it and spread around the ground below. The wooden planter was crumbling, and Mack thought it might be nice to repair and repaint it. He pulled it free from the base of the swing and then couldn't resist the temptation to have a go. Miraculously it held his weight and he hoisted himself up onto the makeshift seat and swayed two and fro examining his earlier gardening efforts.

His eyes strayed to the bark of the tree where it was crusted and old except for one part that had been stripped and carved into. Curious, he jumped down and went in close till he could make out the word 'Certainty.'

What did it mean? It dawned on him that he could hear Clucy barking some distance away. They must be heading back. So, he picked up the planter and brought it back to his workbench in the shed and then went in search of liquid to quench his thirst. Rhia would be home by now.

He went around the side of the house and through the open veranda windows but neither the dog nor Rhia could be seen. It worried him and he glanced at his watch. She had been gone way longer than her usual hour. He could hear the dog barking still and followed the sound down towards the river road. There he found her hobbling towards him using a branch for a crutch. He ran towards her, and she brushed his attempts to help her off with a wave.

"I'm OK, I just cruckled over and I've sprained my damned ankle. I'll be all right when I can get it raised and strapped up. Clucy shush! There's a good girl." The dog was obviously as concerned as Mack and wasn't being dismissed easily.

"You really shouldn't go down there on your own, it's rough territory," he said.

"What would you have me do, curl up in an armchair and wait to die like those old dears in the nursing homes...I don't think so!" There would be no telling her, she was a law unto herself. That much he had quickly learned.

"Well at least lean on my arm and throw that branch away. We'll walk at your pace."

He took the branch from her and threw it to the side of the path. The dog chased after it and tried to drag it back to them and they looked at each other and laughed.

"Here was me thinking she was being protective, she just wanted a stick all along, bloody traitor!"

Slowly they made the painful walk for the last few hundred yards till he got her sat comfortably in a chair on the veranda. Fetching a cold compress and bandages on her instruction he wrapped them round the swollen foot. He also brought her a drink which she gulped thirstily. She was a tough old broad, but she had an unhealthy disregard for her own safety. At least he was here to keep an eye on her, but what about when he went to university? She worried him, he would have to ask his mum to look in on her.

Suddenly as he sat there chatting, a thought popped into his head. What about Sophie? Perhaps he could help them both. He made up his mind to speak to his mum and Sophie on his return with his idea. In the meantime, Rhia instructed him to get her a broom and pad it with some materials and gaffer tape so she could use it as an impromptu crutch. 'Damn the woman,' he thought, she didn't know when to give in. The dog sat at her side, occasionally trying to rest its head on Rhia's bad foot, which she did not appreciate.

He left her with a sandwich and drink on the sofa and fed the dog for her. He also filled a glass jug with water and put it with a glass on her bedside table. He was uncomfortable going into her private space, but he hoped she trusted him enough by now to see it as a kindness.

By the time he arrived home his mother was unloading shopping into the cupboards and Sophie was chopping potatoes and leeks. The difference in the girl was quite amazing. She had a happier face and was completely at ease with his mother.

"Can I help?" he enquired.

"I don't know about you, but I fancy a glass of wine. What about you Sophie?" said Christina.

Sophie coloured slightly, not used to being treated like a grown up.

"Yes please, if that's all right?"

"Why shouldn't it be honey? Right let's get this chicken on and then we can sit outside and watch the world go by for ten minutes."

Mack went and pulled a bottle of the local red from the rack and grabbing a tray he put glasses and the bottle on it to take outside. His mum and Sophie followed, and he couldn't help but think his mum had herself some female company at last and was particularly enjoying it. He pulled up a couple of loungers and they sat in the evening sun savouring the wine he had poured.

"So where did you two get to today?" he asked of the girl. She looked up animated, her face had lost so much of the stress of yesterday.

"We wandered around Josselin, and your mum showed me the Château grounds and then we had coffee on that hotel veranda overlooking the river facing it. It was lovely!"

Christina added to the conversation. "...and there might be a chance of some waitressing work there, so all in all a good day." Christina took a sip of her wine satisfied that she had achieved.

"Well, I've had a thought, but I decided I'd better run it by you first Sophie. You know the old artist lady I work for, she's fabulous, but she's hurt her ankle and is struggling at the moment, so I thought of maybe asking her if she might employ you to help for a while...what do you think...she's not 'old ladyfied', she's really quite cool when you get to know her."

Clearly enthusiastic, Mack hadn't seen his mum's smile of humour at her son's ageist remark. Kids rarely saw the elderly as human beings with personalities and dreams. This woman must be doing him some good, she concluded.

"It's worth a try Sophie" said Christina "...and she will be struggling with shopping and such like so she might appreciate a hand for a few days. You could always do a bit of both if you get the waitress job. Our house is only small, but we have a larger tent we could put up for you that would give you a bit of privacy and you could stay for the summer or until you get on your feet...what do you think?"

Sophie looked at them both and she was full of an unknown emotion. No one had ever been this kind to her. She so wanted to belong to this family.

"I think you're the nicest people that I've ever met!"

That evening, inspired by more than one wine, they ate al fresco and played music as they put up a larger five berth tent that gave Sophie a sleeping compartment and an open space to use as a living area. Christina had great fun kitting it out with things that would make it more homely for their young guest and Mack ran an outdoor power cable and extension from the workshop so that she could have light and music from an old radio and bedside lamp he had also found. He also discovered and old fold up bed frame and dragged it out of the workshop so that Sophie wouldn't feel the cold through the ground when the temperature dropped at night.

Satisfied with their efforts they sat out till dark, lighting the firepit and chatting happily. Sophie inspected her new tent with satisfaction. The bed, now padded with a couple of old quilts for a mattress, was quite the comfiest bed she'd had in weeks and by the time they parted to go to their respective rooms Sophie was feeling like she was on holiday for the first time. With these good people, her life had suddenly and dramatically taken a turn for the better. She couldn't believe her luck.

The next morning Mack arrived earlier than usual at Rhia's bearing fresh croissants, expecting that she wouldn't be up to a trip to the patisserie. He thought she might need some help if her foot had swollen more overnight. He was right as she was nowhere to be seen. He wondered for a moment if she stayed in bed normally when he wasn't due, but she didn't seem the type somehow. Going round to the back where he knew the veranda door would be unlatched despite his recent lectures on security, which of course she dismissed, he entered quietly so as not to frighten her.

"Rhia?" he called quite loudly so she would know the intruder was only him. She answered on the second call in French 'un moment!' which was unusual for her as she always spoke English with him. She must have been asleep.

He went towards her voice as she opened the bedroom door dragging on a gown over a short nightdress that exposed her badly bruised foot and she limped painfully forward flustered at his arrival. Sensing her embarrassment, he lifted the bag of croissants for her inspection.

"I thought you might like breakfast… Where's your crutch?

"Oh that…It's in the bedroom…The blasted bristles kept pricking under my arm!" She stepped gingerly forward. And his instinct was to stretch out his arm to help her. She almost refused but on putting her weight on the injured foot she thought better of it and conceded.

"You should get it looked at, it could be broken," he admonished gently.

"No, I've had broken before, this is not broken." She limped to the kitchen with him as support and he sat her at the large wooden table with the magnificent marble top that must have cost a fortune. She looked at him and smiled the most beautiful smile and for a moment he caught a glimpse of how vivacious she must have been in her younger years.

"You're such a kind boy. Could you let Clucy out she's hopping about like she's ready to burst." She said, and Mack felt himself blush.

"Where's your coffee live?" he asked to cover his blush and turned to the cupboards behind him.

"Above your head," she responded, and he looked up and opened the cupboard door to find all things beverage. Taking two cups from the bottom shelf, he started to prepare breakfast under her directions.

"Rhia, I hope you don't think I'm being rude..."

"That sounds ominous, should I worry?" her ankle might have failed but not her quick wit.

"No! It's just that I have a favour to ask."

"Go ahead." He noted her tone was slightly wary. She hadn't known this young man for long. Was he about to disappoint her?

"We have a young British girl staying with us. I found her a couple of days ago with no money and in a mess. Don't get me wrong, she seems like a nice girl, but something's gone on that has made her run away from England. We've let her pitch her tent in our garden and she's just shy, but she really needs work to get her back on her feet.
I wondered if you might like some help for a few days whilst your foot heals?"

Rhia's eyebrow lifted. "Are you saying I can't manage?"

"No, not at all, just that it might make things easier for you. She could do some housework or whatever..."

"I don't like many people, Mack. You are an exception to the rule." Mack persisted as he hadn't received an outright no.

"I think you'd like her, and I think you would be good for her. She looks like she's had the stuffing knocked out of her and I think you might be the person to put it back... and it would help you while your foot gets better." Mack's intelligence and gentleness was his best asset when dealing with Rhia, did he but know it. She paused for a moment whilst she looked about the kitchen that she knew had recently got away from her. The oven, though quality, was greasy and the shelves and cupboards had a layer of dust.

"I don't like people much, I admit, but there's one thing I dislike more and that's housework...most women do you know. I like a nice home, don't get me wrong, I just dislike the mundanity of getting it that way!" She smiled wryly. "Give me a paint brush and I can work all day but give me a broom and suddenly I feel old!" She laughed at her own quip.

"What do you think then? I mean, you might not be able to afford it, I didn't mean to push."

"Yes, you did, and yes, I can, so you tell this girl to come nine am tomorrow and we'll see how she does. I won't pay her the same as you till I'm satisfied that she can do the job reliably. I don't like fly by nights...but if she fits in, I'll consider it."

Mack grinned broadly "Thank you Rhia, you're a star!"

"Mmn," she replied, "Just don't make me end up feeling like an old gullible woman."

Next day, true to his promise, he arrived at nine am with Sophie in tow. The girl looked terrified, and he'd had to jolly her all the way saying that it would really be ok. His mum had rooted out of all things a crutch from the garage that John had had when he had broken his ankle. He had carried it like a wooden soldier all the way through the village and even goose stepped to get Sophie to smile.

He knocked and entered calling out Rhia's name and on hearing her distant response beckoned Sophie to follow him. Rhia was in a knee length white kaftan embroidered with delicate gold thread that was quite beautiful and her white hair was brushed and around her shoulders. She was reclining on the long leather sofa with her bandaged foot up like an old Cate Blanchett and was the epitome of regal. He could hear Sophie's intake of breath as she entered and saw the long expanse of walls with her artwork. She was star struck and fearful all rolled into one.

"Come forward you two, I won't bite." Rhia summoned them with an elegant arm with fingers clad in modern silver rings.

"Would you like me to make you a coffee Rhia whilst you talk. Oh, and by the way my mother sent you this." He held the crutch aloft triumphantly as he asked, eager to remain near enough to overhear any conversation.

"Oh really? That's so kind of her. Would you thank her for me? Coffee would be very nice Mack, thank you. Now Sophie, come sit with me and tell me what you think you might be able to do for me. Can you type?" Mack paused on his way out relieved she hadn't said 'Tell me all about yourself.'

He heard Sophie say she was pretty good at IT and then had to reluctantly leave the room to make the coffee. By the time he returned Sophie, though still nervous, had seemed to have calmed a little and even had a shy smile on her face.

"Oh, coffee, just at the right time. Now Mack, Sophie is going to come in for the mornings and help me for a week and then we'll review it. How does that sound?" She looked directly at him, and he felt she was doing him the favour by allowing someone to look after her. He grinned broadly.

"That sounds absolutely fantastic, thank you Rhia."

"She's going to stay today and get used to the place and then she can walk home with you and won't have to worry about finding her way back to yours later." Said Rhia.

"Splendid! I'll crack on in the garden. The wood is coming today for the planters by the way," he replied enthusiastically.

"Well! An auspicious day all round then, Sophie have some coffee?"

Sophie glanced at Mack's retreating back as she took the cup and prayed that she wouldn't do anything to embarrass him.

Two hours later Mack was close to completing the first of the raised planters. He had another five to do but he was pleased with his efforts so far. Rhia hobbled out on her new crutch and was delighted to see it coming together and then hobbled back in to try and paint.

When Mack came in for liquid refreshment, he found Sophie cleaning the kitchen and for a young woman unused to housework, she was doing an excellent job and had made a difference. Later, Rhia had her sort through her old artworks that were stored in one of the rooms with the intention of photographing and cataloguing them on a database. Sophie was so delighted with the artwork that Rhia found herself telling the girl about them individually and Sophie suggested that they do a paragraph of Rhia's explanation on the database. The afternoon went by so quickly that even Rhia was surprised when Mack came in and said, "Are you ready to go home Sophie?"

'Home' thought Sophie. There was a word she had never been able to use in context with her life before. Rhia had almost seemed disappointed to see them go, and Mack promised he'd come back tomorrow without pay to continue the planters so that Rhia would have them sooner and he saw her perk up visibly. He had to admit that he was becoming very fond of this Grand Dame.

Later that evening as they sat with Christina under the shade of the veranda, they talked about the day and Sophie seemed genuinely taken with Rhia and her art and enthused most of the evening. Mack looked at the girl and thought that she had more about her than he had first thought. He was glad finally to have someone he could consider a friend.

"Your dad's home Friday by the way." Christina dropped the bombshell and Sophie looked stricken. A man in this equation was an unknown and she visibly withdrew into herself.

"Great, He's been gone ages this time!" Mack replied oblivious.

Christina was not unaware of the girl's reaction, and she wasn't sure if it was John coming home to an unknown guest that put that wary look in Sophie's eyes or whether it was because he was a man. She filed the reaction for later and stepped into ease the girl's tension.

"Tell Sophie what your dad's like Mack," she said.

Mack laughed. "My dad's a teddy bear, he likes a grumble now and then but he's dead kind and clever. He does tend to fall asleep over his laptop a lot though!"

Sophie smiled, but it didn't reach her eyes. Christina thought it was time.

"Do you have a large family back home Sophie?" she asked.

"No, there's no one I'm close to."

"That's a shame. I was an only child and so's Mack, so there's only really us. When we moved here it was a big leap, but we loved it. We have friends here now but at first, I was quite lonely and missed my friends at home so badly." She relaxed back in her chair and left a gap in the conversation for the girl to fill. Mack raised an eyebrow towards his mum but stayed silent. She had cleverly covered the question and normalised it by talking mostly about herself.

"I didn't have many friends...We always moved around a lot." Sophie let her guard down ever so slightly.

"That's a shame. Was it with your parents' work?" she pushed.

"Not my parents, my stepdads. He was always looking for new work and my mum just went along with it. I don't think I ever stayed at a school more than a year, so I had no-one special." She subsided into silence once more.

Three pertinent points in a couple of dragged-out sentences thought Christina. The girl had a stepfather, he didn't provide stability and the mother was a pushover by the sound of it. 'Enough for now,' she thought.

"That's a shame, Mack's suffered in that respect. There weren't many kids around here of his age, so he had to find his own amusement. I'm pleased you two have met up and I'm personally very glad to have another female around here for a change. More wine?" Christina knew when to stop digging and she turned the conversation to Mack's exploits as a child and watched the girl gradually settle once more. It was a start.

The evening continued with easy banter, mainly between Mack and his mother. Sophie smiled but Christina could see she wasn't quite with them. Something had destroyed this girl's trust in people, but it was too soon to jump to conclusions. Hopefully, she would eventually open up when she felt she could trust them.

CHAPTER SIX

The next morning dawned as bright as ever. They really were having a run of extreme heat. When they arrived at the house Rhia was already having a coffee on her veranda her crutch propped up by the doorway and she welcomed them warmly.

"Sit and join me for a while," she called to them.

They did as she bade, and she seemed excited about something. She waited till they had helped themselves to coffee and then she began.

"My agent called me last night. He has got me an art book deal on the Tarot range, and they want me to hold a retrospective of the work alongside the launch around August. It won't come to fruition until next year, but it just seems bizarre that only yesterday we started to catalogue the work. So, it seems you and I will have to work a little faster as they want it crated up ready to send to Paris for photography by the first of next month!" She positively glowed and Mack realised that was all she wanted, for her art to be recognised and appreciated. Sales were good, but a book that would sustain her in history was something else. Even Sophie, who had been very subdued on the journey, was enthusiastic.

"We must finish all your descriptions especially, they will probably want to use them," she said with a smile.

"Indeed, my dear, we certainly must." For a moment she had forgotten that Mack had come to help her with her beloved planters in his own time. The garden had come second to her art on this occasion, and he found himself 'Billy no mates' for the morning as Rhia and Sophie worked their way through the numerous artworks with a renewed sense of purpose. The only company he had all morning was Clucy who dozed in the shade of the potting shed.

Rhia sat on a chair with a laptop whilst Sophie carefully sorted the artwork under her instruction. Between them they had set up a database that could include pictures and be easily converted to a shipping list or catalogue. Sophie was impressed that Rhia had a firm grasp of IT and Rhia was impressed that she was so methodical for one so young. It seemed like a perfect partnership. The trial continued beyond the week with no mention of the work ceasing.

Mack very soon realised that he had brought together two complete opposites by the merest chance and created a perfect working team. Who would have thought it? The strong-minded veteran artist and the shy young girl. Sophie idolized Rhia and before three weeks had passed Sophie had shown so much interest in art that she was invited to sketch alongside Rhia on a couple of afternoons a week. She seemed intent on learning and listened attentively to everything her new tutor had to say. Rhia had now thrown her crutch aside and was once more on two feet and eager to progress.

It had come about one afternoon when Sophie was housekeeping quietly around the house as Rhia painted the large canvas that currently held her captive. Sophie brought her a coffee and stood behind her as she wiped the paint from her knife.

"Rhia, can I ask you something?" she said.

"Go ahead, as long as you don't comment on this picture." Rhia placed her knife down and gave the girl her full attention.

"How do you know what you're going to paint?"

Rhia smiled. "Ah… Often I don't, I just have a flash of something comes in and I start to lay paint on the canvas. It usually develops from there. Some artists are very measured in how they prepare but that's not my way, I prefer the freedom of letting something flow naturally. My old mentor David, when I first was invited to paint with him, had me paint a mandala on the canvas and just start by throwing random paint at it. He said the mandala would draw my concentration in and something would take over my hand and the painting would in fact 'become'." She emphasised the point with a rounded hand gesture. "I tell you what, tomorrow bring some old clothes and I'll set you up with a larger canvas when you've finished your work in the morning, and you can paint with me. It's better to show you than to tell you, but it will be messier than the work you've done so far."

Sophie looked thrilled. "Really? Oh, I'd so love that... but I haven't got any old clothes...I haven't got any clothes really, I was travelling with just a rucksack." Rhia noted that the mention of earlier times had brought a shadow across the girl's eyes, and she had also noticed the lack of diversity in her clothes.

"No matter, I have plenty, we might have to give you a belt to hold the pants up, but we'll find something." She smiled at the girl noting her petite frame and Sophie couldn't help but smile back.

"It must be so fantastic having your work recognised Rhia?"

Rhia paused and for a moment she looked past her current canvas and beyond the trees that surrounded her beautiful garden and was thoughtful.

"I have just two things I wish for when I leave this earth, lovely one. That despite everything, it was a life well lived and that someone will miss me, all else means nothing." Her smile faded slightly and she looked sad. Sophie couldn't help but ask. For a reclusive artist she didn't seem to have anyone around to miss her, was that why she was sad? Mack had mentioned that he had seen her crying and Sophie felt for her, she knew what it felt like to be lonely and on the whole, alone. Perhaps that was why they had gelled; each had recognised something familiar in the other. A hidden pain perhaps?

"Why despite everything Rhia?" she probed, and the artist glanced once more at the landscape she was working on and then back to Sophie. She raised a hand and cupped the side of Sophie's left cheek.

"That's a story for another day sweetie." She then laughed and the sadness left. "Now look, I've covered you in paint!" She reached for the turps and a clean cloth and cleaned the cerulean blue from the girl's skin. "Now go wash your face, you don't want to permanently smell of turpentine like me, do you?" Sophie walked away thinking perhaps she did.

On this particular morning, Mack was feeling proud of himself. He had finally completed all the raised planters and had them filled and ready for Rhia's inspection. She came outside with Sophie following on with a tray of sandwiches and juice.

"Oh, how wonderful! We must go and buy some seeds and start our vegetables for autumn," she cried in delight. Rhia busied herself about the planters and then she started to look about the garden.

"You must show me what you've done Mack, now that I'm back walking normally," she smiled, and they sat down at a nearby table to eat. Mack pulled up a crate as there were only two chairs and he balanced precariously.

"I was thinking," continued Rhia "That we should have a drive into Josselin to do a little shopping tomorrow. I need some bits and I think Sophie if you are going to become my PA that we should get you some suitable wear… it's ages since I've treated myself or anyone else and I'm in the mood. Mack you're welcome to come if you are up for it."

Mack politely declined; shopping was not his forte. He did wonder how they were going to drive into Josselin however and asked her so. She waved a hand in the direction of an outbuilding on the other side of the road on the approach to the house.

"I have a car of course; did you not think I could drive? Why I used to drive wagons in my younger days in theatre Mack...besides its time Delilah had an outing."

"Delilah?" questioned Mackenzie.

"My Megane convertible. I'll tell you what, do you drive Mack? "

"Yes, but I don't have a car. I occasionally borrow mums."

"Then how about this afternoon, you get her out, wash her and take her for petrol and tyre check as it's been a while."

"If that's what you want…?" he looked a little unsure.

"I'm 67, not dead or senile yet. I'm perfectly capable of driving my own car," she said wryly.

"Of course you are," he reassured, but had to admit to himself that he had concerns.

"So that's decided. Now Mack, let's see your progress." Sophie hadn't had much chance to intervene, so she just nodded a little still absorbing the information that Rhia had just promoted her to PA. Rhia stood slowly and started to make her way round the garden with Mack and Sophie close behind. She paused when she reached the little path Mack had uncovered recently and then followed it. Winding through the trees she encountered the swing and gasped in distress. Mack was taken aback, he thought she would be pleased.

"The planter on the swing, where is it?" she asked Mack urgently.

"It was rotting so I took it..." he didn't have chance to finish.

"You haven't thrown it away, have you?" She was clearly distressed.

"No Rhia, it's just waiting to be repaired. I've put it by the shed till I get round to it." She sighed visibly and was clearly agitated.

"I'm sorry for being sharp, it's just that it has a special memory for me. You haven't taken the plants out, have you?"

"No, but the soil is just dust, I was going to replace it with fresh and replant. It was just some Forget Me Nots. I didn't think they were important." Mack felt a little put out that she had reacted so strongly, but it piqued his interest.

"The smallest flowers should never be forgotten. Leave it to me, I'll do it," she said, her eyes suddenly brimming with tears. Her hand felt its way along the bark of the tree till it touched the smooth area with the word carved in it and her fingers brushed the word lovingly and then she pulled away.

"I'm sorry, I should have told you to go with caution in this area. No harm done." And with that she turned to retrace her steps leaving Sophie and Mack to look towards each other with a shrug of Mack's shoulders and a raised eyebrow from Sophie. More mystery.

Sophie and Mack discussed Rhia all the way home. Sophie was still reeling from the implied promotion but had been told nothing concrete, and Mack was intrigued about her earlier strange reaction. Perhaps Rhia would enlarge on it tomorrow on their trip to Josselin. The summer was past halfway now, and Mack was saving hard. Sophie had also started bringing home small treats for the family as Christina would not take a penny in board.

John had returned and very soon Sophie had seen that here was a man that was equal in kindness to his family, and she started to relax. John had also been given the background and Christina's thoughts on what might have driven Sophie from her family in England and he was careful not to be anything other than circumspect. Over the first days he saw her visibly relax until soon she had become as at ease with him as the others.

That evening they had their first thunderstorm for weeks and the heat gave way to the relief of rain. The scent of it hitting the warm earth and vegetation was intoxicating and they dined on the veranda just for the thrill of it.

John was bringing up the subject of Mack's impending departure for Uni at the end of August and in turn it brought up the question of how Sophie would be housed in the autumn. She could initially have Mack's room, but it would only be a temporary measure as he would need it when he came home in the holidays.

Sophie's stomach started to churn at the thought of having to move out from this warm-hearted family to the unknown, but at least now she had the promise of a regular wage and a possible semi- permanent job with Rhia. That night listening to the distant rumbles of the storm that thankfully hadn't breached the sides of her canvas home, she fretted on what to do and sleep wasn't forthcoming. She thought about Mack's departure and was sad. He was her only friend here. Most girls had romantic ideas at her age, but she couldn't bear to think of anything like that. Mack was so kind, but she had nothing to give. It had taken her most of her courage just to consider the idea that she could have a true friend. She closed her eyes and tried to block out the memories that threatened to invade her happiness, but some things could not be erased, and she cried, for the loss of innocence, for the loss of the mother who did not believe her and for the happy family life she never had.

She had experienced six years of fear, starting at eleven years old and those six years had separated her from any idealistic dreams she should have had at her age. It had been a dark, cynical, and lost young woman that inhabited her shell. The last few weeks had brought in light and the notion that there could be something joyful out there, but she was far from reaching faith in people just yet.

The morning sun rose and the increase in heat set aside any need of an alarm clock. She let herself into the house quietly as it was the weekend and tiptoed to the shower room downstairs. By now she was used to going alone to Rhia's. Some days Mack came along for an hour or two just for the hell of it and others he'd stay home working on some IT project he had set himself. He was a strange combination of computer geek and outdoor man, not often seen.

Today was his shift at the shop and she cast her mind back to several weeks ago when she had arrived on his doorstep close to starving. Here she was, new clothes, new life, new job, new me! She thought and left the house with a skip in her step that morning. She walked along the lanes with a smile to anyone she passed and even greeted one or two in French. A different persona entirely from the frightened girl she had been. Rhia was in her shower as she let herself in and she called to her through the door. "Une cafe Rhia?"

"S'il vous plait" came the response as Sophie headed for the kitchen. The space was bright and clean as the many weeks of an enthusiastic young pair of hands had worked its magic. She had even polished the copper pans that hung above the oven. Looking about the kitchen she could see that everything was of a fantastic quality, yet the layout seemed unfinished somehow. It was clear that Rhia had had an eye for hand-built cupboards, but it was though they hadn't quite been finished...as though the builder had gone off the boil somehow. It was not short of colour; the ceramics were cheerful and bold and there was always light in every room.

The house, she had learned whilst working consisted of the massive lounge, a small snug and office, three bedrooms and the bathroom. Two of the bedrooms housed wrapped artwork that Sophie longed to take a peek at, but she felt it would be disrespectful to do more than she had been invited to do, and so she restrained her curiosity. The kitchen was built around a central island which for its age must have been very forward thinking at the time. It had to have been done many years ago by the look of the appliances that were fitted.

She put the coffee on the veranda and left the doors open to let the fresh air and garden scents in. Rhia came in combing her shoulder length hair and Sophie was drawn once again to the incredible whiteness of it.

"Did you design this kitchen, Rhia?" she asked.

"Of sorts, yes," she answered. "It was a kind of joint idea, but yes, I guess you can say I designed it… and built all of the house." Sophie wasn't expecting that, and her mouth dropped open. How capable must this woman have been.

"How on earth did you manage that?" she replied, astounded.

"You forget I spent eighteen years as a set designer. One type of design is much like another once you grasp the concept. I was going to have help… but that didn't materialise, so in the end I just got on with it myself and brought the trades in only when I needed to. It was many years ago and I was younger and stronger then."

That's what she had noticed. It was home built and by Rhia herself! What a feat of achievement.

"It's so fantastic that you did it for yourself. I wish I were that talented!" said Sophie.

"You are that talented my sweet. I have watched you create your art and the way you support me in business, so what's to say you couldn't, you are no different now than I was at your age. Each experience is a learning lesson, some lessons hurt us, and some develop us, but there is always something to be learnt."

She sat gracefully down at the table in white linen pants and a khaki man's shirt. Her toes were painted and in silver sandals that corresponded with the thick man's bracelet around her wrist. Sophie noticed she touched the bracelet a lot as though it calmed her. She suited a masculine style, and it certainly stopped her looking like a twee old lady.

"So, Sophie, what have you learned so far in life?" she enquired but it was a probing enquiry that set Sophie in an uneasy position.

"Come on, put away your shyness and just say the first thing that comes into your head my dear, it's an experiment." She pushed and Sophie thought 'What the hell.'

"I've learnt that not all people are bad."

"What else?" came the response.

"I've learnt I can take control of my life even if it might go wrong occasionally."

Rhia took a sip of her coffee.

"Well, that's two massive pieces of life learning already."

Sophie picked up her coffee and grinned.

"What about you then? What have you learned from living?"

Rhia swallowed and thought for a moment.

"I have learnt that even with a bad start in life I had the potential to rise above it and put the past behind me." She placed her cup back on the saucer satisfied with her answer.

"One more...I did two." prompted Sophie.

"Oh well... I learned that not all perceived true love works both ways and when that happens you must then learn to love yourself first and foremost, however hard and however painful it may be. That ability is real strength."

"That's very cryptic Rhia" said Sophie whose interest was now truly engaged.

"Cryptic comes with life's complications, lovely one. You'll learn that as you grow."

"How old were you when you built this house Rhia?" asked Sophie.

"I was in my early forties, and I had just escaped death." She said it with a smile, but it didn't reach her eyes. "It focused my mind somewhat and not long after I threw myself into building this house as a means to keep my sanity." Sophie was shocked.

"But how…?" she was prevented from enquiring further by the rise of Rhia's hand.

"One evening, when its winter and we have nothing better to do I will tell you, but will you tell me one thing? What made you run away from England with just the clothes on your back. Did someone hurt you?"

Sophie wasn't expecting such a direct question and her mouth opened and shut several times before any sound came out and then her pretty face crumbled.

"It was my stepfather...he raped me!" Suddenly it was as though the flood gates had opened, and the girl put her head on the table, and she wept violently. Rhia moved quickly round the table and turned the girls face towards her and Sophie flung her arms round the old woman's waist and wept as though she would never stop. Rhia crooned to her as a mother would a child and then when she was satisfied, she was done, she reached for a tissue from the shelf nearby and started to dry the young woman's tears. Sophie was surprised to see that Rhia had cried with her and gradually her sobs slowed as she started to gain a measure of control.

"There ,my sweet, it's ok, it's ok...The one thing I will tell you is that though it may never quite go away, you will reach a point where you can put it aside. He won't win. You will, because you have youth and great promise of life on your side, and he is getting old and is an ugly soul. Those types never do well."

"How do you know that? I see him, smell him, all the time!" Sophia started to cry again, and Rhia took her firmly by the shoulders.

"Listen to me, I know because I had a paedophile for a stepfather and I lived in fear for years, just as I expect you have done. It started with small, nasty little moments when he would let his hand linger on me, wanting to dance with me at events and making me feel grown up, when all along he was cultivating me, making me feel special. I was ten when he asked me to sit on his knee when my mother was at church and I still till today cannot remember what happened next, it's a blank. I just remember there were different coloured strip lights, he was an electrician you see and the ultraviolet was something really innovative then. There was just darkness and him in his dressing gown and these lights. It was an old-fashioned dressing gown...wine and cream coloured coarse wool with one of those twisted cords and to this day I cannot bear to see or touch that kind of material. I was young but something in me knew I had to get away from him. For years he tried to get me on my own or opened bathroom doors that unsurprisingly, never had locks, when I was in the bath, pretending it was a mistake. By fifteen I it was all out war between us, and I hated him. So many rows, which my mother put down to me being a teenager. My mother never made me feel I would be believed if I told her and so I said nothing. I was lucky, he died of cancer when I was seventeen. So, you see. It never goes away...but have I let it destroy my life? I wouldn't give that worm the satisfaction and you mustn't too, do you understand?

You have everything before you and he has nothing, so you have already bettered him my dear."

Sophie stared stricken as Rhia spoke. Not once had she said, 'We must call the police.' Her own story mirrored Rhia's words and slowly and painfully she let the words come until the burden she had carried for what seemed like a lifetime was lifted.

The older woman had pulled her chair to face her and held her hands as she spoke. When there were no more words Rhia quietly refilled her coffee cup, put an extra sugar in and bade her to drink, which she did. When she had finished, she looked at Rhia.

"Why are men so awful?"

Rhia shrugged gently. "Not all, but I think they don't all have the self-control emotionally that women tend in general to have more of, and it's that ability that is the difference between a good man and a weak one. Believe me, you can still be aggressive and weak at the same time. Women shoulder a lot of emotional pain in their lives, and I think we carry it more... oh what's the word…Formidable!" She lapsed into French to find the right meaning she wanted to convey. Rhia examined the young girl closely to ensure she was past the worst.

When she was happy that Sophie was passed the worse, she smiled at her reassuringly.

"I knew you were meant to come here, we can help each other," said Rhia. "Now shall we carry on with the catalogue if you are, ok?"

"Yes, I think I am Rhia, thank you, but don't tell Mack or anyone will you?" she added the addendum quickly.

"You will tell Mack when you are ready and you will do it without fear," was all she said as she rose from the chair a little more stiffly than when she had sat down.

"I'm not ready to tell anyone else just yet. I'm not sure I ever will be." Sophie sighed and fumbled to put her tissue away to pull herself together.

"That's only natural, it will take time."

Although Sophie was quiet throughout the day, she felt calmer, and the work helped her put aside the memories she had had to face. Rhia went through the Tarot series methodically and explained her thoughts on each of the painting's elements so that Sophie could type it all into its appropriate box on the database and the repetitive work helped push all negative thoughts away.

After lunch they continued, and Rhia brought out the poetry she had written for each of the Tarot cards to express its meaning. Sophie had uncovered her favourite painting of a stunning dark-haired woman in a decaying dress walking through the woods and she exclaimed in pleasure, Behind the woman stood a white horse watching her progress through the trees that were morphing into imps and gargoyles. The whole picture was beautiful, but dark and she was captivated by it. Rhia let her absorb the picture and then handed her the poem that was its meaning and Sophie sat to read quietly.

Rhiannon's Walk

Step and square, a stranger's dance, circles like a shaman
Rattles tails and fatalistic chance, myriad the reasons
Earthly bound and spirit drawn, ever change of season
To follow paths Rhiannon shows, draws me back, then on,
and away
Scattered seeds amidst her tread, dictate the fall and sway

Moving through a living forest, barefoot breaks the leaves
She wears her dread and dark decay like a satin crinoline
Sinuous and molten, fluid hope and hopeless cause
Pained with lust and lily white, stretched in the longest
scream

Silken moths suspended in a flame, kiss the air around her
crown like gossamer, a veil
Forgetful wind that brushed her face, memories enslaved
Barest breath, a rise and fall, unearthliness, and pale

A moon, moments in a bottle, fights against the wave
She is love, she is low, she is nowhere else to go
She leads the white horse in unending mystery and pain
And we follow on like children
Captive in her unending turmoil and beauty…

"Oh Rhia, this is beautiful, what does it mean?" Sophie looked up wide eyed.

"What do you get from it and the picture?" Rhia was standing very still, waiting for her response.

"Just despair, hope, all of it, as though she is being called on relentlessly and the white horse follows...am I right?"

"There's no wrong, but yes you have some of it. There are parts that are mine that no one shall have or understand, but she is essentially the fate card, The Fool's Journey, and to some extent she is me. The horse signifies wisdom. Fate calls most of us onwards and wisdom naturally follows, observing from behind usually, don't you think?"

"That is so what the painting shows, but it's like the woman is gradually dying from despair, but she goes onwards..." Sophie stopped and looked swiftly to Rhia as the words she had spoken had echoed back and the veil fell from her eyes. Poor Rhia, this was her spirit woman, with all its pain still trying to find a path through all the trees with their distractions and demons. Suddenly she knew this woman had suffered greatly and she had poured all her suffering into creativity and trapped it there in order to go on. There was so much more that this artist had experienced than a bad childhood. The story went much deeper. Rhia stood quietly and her eyes sparkled with unshed tears and Sophie welled up and her heart and throat hurt with the emotion she was holding back; it was as though they were one.

"This picture will be yours one day and hopefully by then you will appreciate all it means to me. I would like you to have it." She swallowed and for a moment Sophie thought that she might say more and then a shutter came down over the pain in her eyes and she turned away on the excuse of looking at some other work to bring her emotions under control. For the first time in her young life Sophie felt real sorrow on behalf of someone else, she was starting to grow up.

"Rhia, you must include these poems in the book, they are all part of your art!" she exclaimed as the thought occurred.

"You think so?"

"I know so, you must, they make the artwork all the more interesting." said Sophie in awe.

"Well, I guess that's just what we might do then. Here's all the poems. They are labelled with the pictures title. Do you think you could write them correctly into the database and in a separate file as a backup. It's important that the are written up exactly as I wrote them… I might have a little rest before I paint. I'm a little tired."

"I can do that this afternoon" she answered, noting that Rhia had lost a little of her sparkle today.

"Good girl, thank you. I'll see you later and you can bring me up to speed with what you've done," and with that she left the room and Sophie was left feeling sad for her rather than her own situation so recently revealed.

CHAPTER EIGHT

Rhia was sleeping deeply, but in her dreams, she was back at the beginning. It was 1992 and her career was on the up.

"Here Rhi! Grab this toolbox, we're up in the top floor studio until they give us a schedule." DB slid the box along the ground, and she grabbed the handles at both ends and walked into the back of the tall Victorian building that was going to be home for the next three days. The smells and noises of back street Liverpool assaulted the senses and a low buzz of excitement started inside her. The prospect of her first breakthrough role as an Assistant Art Director for one of the country's top PR companies was about to enhance her CV with a vengeance, not to mention paying a few bills, it held her on a high.

This was her first big break crossing over from Theatre into TV. When they had landed the internet contract for a large company, she knew it was a great start on the media ladder. At thirty-one after retraining following her divorce, she had left it late to start a career in an area that was known for its cut-throat, nepotistic and ageist attitudes. She was good at what she did, but the

market was flooded with hungry young hopefuls who producers knew were all eager to get a foot in the door and would work for nothing. Now at forty-one, work was hard fought and scarce. She never undervalued the luck that had brought her this opportunity, and she was keen to excel.

The high profile of the company she was contracted by required she dress the part and she was suited and booted as the sophisticated Assistant Art Director, if only for the initial introductions and till she got down to the real work, which was often dirty, laborious and far from the glamour she portrayed at this moment.

Sliding the box in the goods lift she returned several times to fill the cage with props and costumes. Walking out into the rear car park again to lock her car, DB was pulling the remnants of his set dressing materials out of the boot. She waited patiently knowing he never moved fast but was excellent at his job. The combination of his knowledge and attention to detail coupled with her efficiency made for a talented team but Dawson moved at his own pace, and she had learnt to accept this as the norm. It did make him thorough in all things.

The purr of a blue estate car attracted her attention as it pulled into the yard and slid to a stop alongside. The door opened and a guy with white and meticulously spiked hair climbed out. The driver slid out the other side and made his way round to the back, opening the boot.

"Hi' she called 'you here for the shoot?"
"Yeah."   London crew obviously from the accent she thought.
"I'm Rhia and this is Dawson Bain, DB for short – Art Director."
"Jonathon – photographer and this is my assistant Sean."

A hand raised in greeting from the back of the car and then carried on unloading.

"I'll send the lift back down when I unload in a minute. We're stashing everything on the top floor studio until the PM gets here. There's a canteen as well, they said to help ourselves."

Jonathon nodded and Rhia and Dawson made their way upwards. The smell of old oil and cardboard permeated the air as the goods lift clanked and creaked it way to the top of the building giving glances of what looked like a furniture store on each small, windowed outlook over the three floors as they ascended.

'Strange place for a studio shoot of this calibre?' mused Dawson.

They had been told the exec team were across at the stadium on last minute negotiations and decided to just start setting up for the first shots. The storyboard Rhia had seen hadn't exactly inspired her, but she presumed that they knew what they were doing and started to unpack the gear.

One of the assistants from the store approached her and told her there were extras arriving and the production manager had told them to have them wait in the street. Hardly kind on a cold March morning, but not her area to make decisions so she thanked the girl, said unfortunately it wasn't her call and continued towards the canteen to put the kettle on in the hope of giving them a hot drink whilst they waited. The guy who had been unloading the photo equipment passed her in the corridor and said 'Hi' to which she smiled but was passing so quickly she didn't take much notice. Making her way to the loo's she stripped off and got into her work boots and army pants and vest ready to commence rigging and painting the backdrop. Scragging up her long blonde hair on top of her head she emerged back into the studio. She had a talent for covering herself in paint and had learnt the hard way.

The studio area was small and the ceiling low, so rigging the heavy cloth was going to be easier than she thought. Turning to unload her paints she encountered the guy from the corridor again. For some reason as she smiled, he stopped in his tracks and did a double take. Then he grinned and offered help rigging the cloth which she accepted. He paused stretching up to clip the first edge of the cloth onto the bar.

"What did you say your name was again?" he asked.

"Rhia," she replied.

"Sean," he responded and smiled warmly, and he held out his hand to shake hers. Such a small moment and insignificant to anyone in the room including herself, was how it began.

Two days later they were firm friends and when questioned he grinned and admitted the double take was because he thought the sophisticated woman he first met and thought was management was attractive, unapproachable and in truth a bit snooty, but he had thought the scruff in the paint stained army pants and steel toe capped boots was gorgeous. The double take, he said, was when it occurred to him that he was looking at one and the same person. He followed the admission with that crinkled charming smile that had started to endear him to her, but even then, it never crossed her mind that within two weeks they would be lovers.

People in this business networked, that's how they found out about other jobs. Two days later, cards exchanged, and goodbyes said, Rhia climbed in the car, waved to Sean, never expecting to see him again. She reached round for the seatbelt and as it snapped in, she caught Dawson looking at her.

"You want to watch him," he said soberly.

"Why?" she asked.

"Just be careful," was all he said.

She grinned "Nah, we're just friends. We got on really well that's all." Engaging first gear she drew away, threw one last glance with a wave, as Sean turned to load his own vehicle, and pulled out of the yard. That was the nature of the business…ships passing in the media night.

Two weeks later she was hanging from a tallescope putting the final touches to a backdrop for a performance of Blue Remembered Hills at a local theatre, when her phone started to ring. Struggling to *handle the paint pot that was hanging from her arm and hold on to the ladder she manoeuvred the phone to her ear.*

"Lady up a ladder so make it quick," she said.

"Really? Hi," he said. "I'm on my way back to London from Cumbria, just done a shoot for an art mag. I've got a gig in Huddersfield tomorrow on route and wondered if you and DB wanted to go for a drink? Oh, and do you know any bed and breakfast local to you? You're only half an hour from Huddersfield so we can have a drink and I won't have to drive till morning."

"Well Dawson is abroad at the mo, Louis Vuitton shoot...I'm covered in green paint and finished about nine but if you don't mind a late start with a paint spattered woman we could get a drink. If you want, I have a spare room you're welcome to use... save yourself some money." She started to make her way down the ladder to stage level.

"Great, thanks," he said. "Tell you what. I'm still packing up here, so it will be around nine before I get there...If you want, I'll bring a couple of bottles of red, and we could just chill. I've got an early start, and it would be nice to just relax. I hate living out of hotel rooms."

"Fine with me. Come to the theatre and I'll stop painting when you arrive, we'll grab a bite to eat on the way home." As she clicked off the phone, 'couple of bottles' sort of registered, but not enough to worry her.

So it was that his scruffy but surprisingly attractive media persona unloaded an expensive kit onto her living room floor. He had walked into her home and slipped his boots and socks off to walk barefoot and it was as though he had always been there.

Later, the easy and friendly way he helped in the kitchen as though he were home and the gentle polite manner that bathed her in his tranquillity as they prepared the food and ate was a balm after a stressful and physically tiring day. She scraped the green paint off herself in the bath whilst he washed up and as she came back down the stairs in clean clothes, he had looked up from putting on a CD and she realised and there was suddenly an intimacy and awareness that they were alone. The mood had changed.

Two hours and a bottle of red later, they had talked themselves into silence. He sat cross legged on the rug as she stretched her aching back as she sat facing him on the sofa, the stretch continued to her toes, and she flexed her feet easing out the ache of being perched on a ladder painting for hours.

Leaning forward he caught hold of her right ankle and held her gaze. It seemed the most natural thing in the world to do as he started to massage her feet. Working slowly on the muscles of her calves he stroked downwards almost imperceptibly drawing her from the sofa to the floor beside him. He pulled her top over her head gently, and laid her face down before the fire, caressing her back with his delicate yet work roughened hands and enslaving her heart forever. That moment never left her. She lay on the carpet, her head on her arms, trembling, whilst his hands slowly worked her spine and up to her neck and the line of her hair. He knew just how far to run his fingers onto her scalp and withdraw for the maximum effect. Down again until his hands spanned her waist and then skimmed her buttocks and thighs until she could bear no more. Turning over, and covering her breasts in some belated sense of modesty, all she remembered were his grey eyes, like mercury in their arousal and the two words she heard herself say... 'kiss me...'

Until that moment in her life, she had never been kissed. Or at least it seemed so till then. He lowered his face to hers. The softness, the sensuality, and the infinite invasion of him until there was nothing else to *remember. **All she could think was… Forty-one years to reach this moment…***

Rhia jumped awake and went to sit up quickly. In her head and still part way in her dream, she was still in the body of the woman she was in her prime. Her weaker frame soon disabused her of that notion, and she groaned in pain, some part through arthritis and the rest emotion, as his name was wrenched from her lips. Slowly she sat up and looked about her.

She had allowed herself no pictures of him, the only one she had framed and put on her wall was one photo that he had meticulously taken of her as they had met one June for a few hours and picnicked in the middle of a cornfield. A brief moment of celebration for her birthday before he had hurried back home. He had arranged every stalk until he was satisfied, he had the shot. She needed no such picture of him, for in this photograph her eyes reflected all there was between them at that moment. She had always followed the principle that the only way she could allow herself thoughts of him was if they were transferred into something positive, like a picture. Did she but know it, this had held her more captive than if she had plastered his face across every wall in the house. For her artwork captured for eternity each moment of passion and pain and held the memory there fast. She had made herself his prisoner for all time and as she couldn't bear to part with the work, she had put her heart and soul into, there was no escape.

Rising from the bed she made for the kitchen hoping to find Sophie there, but there was only silence. She had slept longer than she thought, and Sophie had let herself out quietly so as not to disturb her. The house seemed too quiet somehow and added to the highly visual dream she had experienced; her equilibrium was dented, and she felt suddenly very alone. Those two young people had woven their way around her heart and when their chatter and laughter wasn't around the house, she felt somehow bereft. Clucy nuzzled her fingers as if sensing her sadness and she reached down to the old dog.

"Just you and me tonight old girl. Come on let's pull ourselves together and get something to eat."

She walked to the sink and filled the coffee pot and the dog trailed at her heels waiting for treats. Making herself a sandwich she took it to the veranda to eat and the dog sat on her feet throughout. The feeling of Clucy's warmth filtering through her fur comforted her and the emotion that hovered over her like a cloud started to disperse as the evening sun filtering through the trees spread its calm.

She set aside her plate and filled herself a large glass of white wine and strolled round the garden as she sipped it to enjoy the colours that were now coming through. Since Mack had been working through the borders to reveal all the shrubs and hidden gems, the garden had finally started to come to its full glory once more and now it was just a case of maintaining it. She pottered for a while by her vegetable planters and the growth that was appearing gave her much pleasure. It was strange how just walking through nature had such power to heal the soul where nothing else did. This house and her garden were the extension of her personality and there was always peace here. She found herself walking to the swing with its newly refreshed planter and she paused for a moment, reached for the word carved in the bark as was her habit and sent out love through her fingers in the hope it would reach the recipient. Then she pushed the swing gently as though rocking a cradle and stood for a moment with her memories.

"Enough..." she whispered to herself and turned back to the garden and the sunshine once more.

CHAPTER NINE

Mack, on his mother's instruction had invited Rhia to dinner with them that evening fully expecting her to refuse, but surprisingly she didn't. She had arrived in an olive-green satin blouse and white palazzo pants, with her white hair up in chopsticks looking quite the movie star. In her hand she carried a bottle of ruby port that she had learned was his dad's favourite and flowers for her mother in the other.

She had driven up in the convertible and so her hair was fashionably windswept and Christina opening the door couldn't help but be impressed. Even more impressive was the way she had settled naturally into their home and conversed warmly with his parents on many subjects as the meal progressed. There was no ill at ease moments that you would normally expect when entertaining a new guest, and the laughter flowed.

As Mack watched, he was really pleased that his mum and Rhia had taken to each other so well. Perhaps it was the start of a friendship that might bring them both comfort in the coming months as he left for uni. He worried about them both and here might be a solution.

Sophie had really started to come into her own since working with Rhia, she had seemed to come on in confidence by leaps and bounds. Painting regularly now, and changing by the minute, she had found a younger, but sophisticated style of dress that Mack was sure was influenced by Rhia's unique taste. It suited her and with her choppy modern hairstyle and her deepening tan she had become quite lovely. Mack had found himself staring at her more recently and realised that he was getting quite a crush, but Sophie seemed oblivious, continuing to regard him as a friend and he really didn't want to spoil that easy way they had with each other by saying anything stupid. Besides, anything more would be pointless with him leaving for Uni in three weeks. He wouldn't be back until Christmas so better left unsaid had been his decision. Still as she sat opposite him with her head thrown back in laughter at some quip his father had just made, and she drew his eye. He couldn't help but wonder if something between them could be a possibility. Suddenly the conversation drew him back to reality.

"Well Sophie, why didn't you say? You can stay with me...if you wish to, that is. You might not want the company of an old woman full time, but you are very welcome. We can move the paintings into one room, and you can have the other, what do you think?"

All eyes were on Sophie as Rhia presented the solution for her living arrangements after summer ended and sleeping under canvas would no longer be an option. Sophie coloured beautifully for a moment and then she smiled the most beautiful of smiles.

"Really Rhia? I couldn't wish for anything better! Christina and John have been so kind to me but everything decent around here is more than I can afford, and I've been struggling to find somewhere I liked…Could I? I would pay rent." she stammered.

"Nonsense lovely one, you'd be company for me, I don't need payment. It would be an absolute joy to have you. If we play our cards right, we might rope Mack into some decorating before he leaves. We'd have to order you a bed as that room has always been left empty and just become a dumping ground. Let's do it! I'm quite excited!" she laughed out loud and you would have never put her at near seventy as her face became animated and her eyes sparkled.

"I could help too," said Christina. "John's off to Canada on Monday for three weeks and I'll be bored witless!"

"See, it's all settled then. When Mack goes to Uni, you can move in with me, and we'll all help" said Rhia with a satisfied smile.

Activity started on the Tuesday after John left and Christina was embraced into the nucleus of the 'Famille Nouveau' as they laughingly had started to refer to themselves as. Rhia, watching the comings and goings from her position as supervisor wondered how she had survived all these years living in isolation. It gave her renewed creative energy to watch them turn the old bedroom into something quite lovely and then off she would go to produce joyous new abstracts that were a definite change from her recent artworks.

Christina had taken Sophie shopping and they had come back with bed linens and matching drapes and even a few extras to make the room homely. Christina was aware that Sophie had nothing to treasure and so she bought her a painted box to store all her new treasures in as a new home gift. Sophie's previous reservation left her, and she had thrown her arms around Christina's neck in genuine affection, and she was hugged back with equal care.

"I will miss you; you know. Don't be a stranger will you," whispered the older woman suddenly feeling quite tearful.

"I won't, I promise, you've all been so good to me."

One evening as the time for Sophie's departure approached, she sat quietly with Christina on the veranda. Mack had gone with his father to the pub in the village and there was a wonderful quiet about the place and she felt it was time. She owed this woman so much for taking her in as an unknown when many would not have taken the risk.

"Christina, I need to tell you some things...but can it just be strictly between us?" said Sophie.

"Of course it will." Christina braced herself as Sophie slowly and with great dignity, started the story of her young life, the betrayal, the fear, and the degradation of being subjected to the depravity of a man who could abuse a child. Throughout, she held back her emotions and just listened but by the end of Sophie's words her throat ached with the effort to keep control and the tears spilled silently down her face. Sophie cried silently also, but this time without the violence of her admission to Rhia previously, but with the genuine heartbreak of a young woman bearing a tragedy with great strength, who was learning to move on. Christina's heart was full for her.

"I am so proud of you Sophie. To tell me this took great courage and of course it will be between us. Remember this though, you will always have a place here, no matter what, so never be afraid to come back to us. If you ever want to take things further and give that monster retribution, you will have our full support, whatever it takes you just ask. Do you understand?" Christina stood up and so did Sophie and it was the most natural thing for them to meet halfway and cling to each other for comfort. Christina kissed the girl on the cheek and out her at arm's length.

"Whatever the past, it has brought you to the young woman you are now becoming, and I think you are going to be pretty formidable!" she said with absolute certainty.

"That's the word Rhia used, formidable!" smiled Sophie brushing her tears away.

"Rhia knows then?" questioned Christina.

"Yes, she got it out of me in that probing way she has." Sophie almost laughed and the mood lightened.

"Well, if she says formidable, that's what you'll be!" Christina hugged her once more for good measure and they each smiled. By the time the men had arrived home they were watching a movie, and nothing was noted.

By a week before Mack's departure Sophie was ready to move into her new home. They took down the tent and packed everything else away in the workshop once more. Sophie had started to accumulate more clothing and Christina had bought her a really good quality travel case to use, thinking that with Rhia's coming travels to Paris in the next few months it would be a good present. Sophie was thrilled. Rhia had announced her intention to visit Italy also in the spring before it got too hot and would require Sophie's assistance. The girl couldn't believe her luck.

The last few days before leaving for Uni, Mack shared out his time between home and Rhia's, eager to ensure he left her garden as perfect as he could and had reminded Sophie of her promise to keep on top of the lawns until he got back. For a young man he was surprised how fond he had become of the old lady, and he was even more acutely aware of how his feelings for Sophie had developed. Excited as he was to be moving on to an independent stage of his life, he felt sick at the thought of leaving this beautiful house and its occupants. On the day his mum and dad took the journey with him, they called to say their final goodbyes to Rhia and Sophie at the house. For the first time ever there was awkward silence as they finished their coffee before standing to leave. The unsaid was heavy in the air.

Finally, Mack stepped forward and hugged Rhia who surprised them by bursting into tears as she admonished herself with "Oh... take no notice of me I'm just a foolish old woman!" as she dabbed her eyes with a tissue. Mack himself found a lump gathering and he swallowed it down quickly.

"I'll ring often" was all he could get out.

"Make sure you do!" she responded, getting a little of her old self back. She picked up an envelope from the table and placed it in his hands.

"This is for the lakes and Stratford and the Globe, oh and anything you think will expand your horizons," she said.

"I can't take this Rhia." Mack was aghast.

"You can and you will young man! I underpaid you for your services and you never complained and so I put the rest away as a savings policy so don't argue" She tempered the tone with a watery smile, and he realised she'd finally called him young man. He hugged her again.

"I'll be back for Christmas, and we'll have a great time then." His statement encompassed Sophie and she stepped forward to hug him also. He was so much taller than her and so she only came up to his shoulder and was lost in his embrace.

"I'll miss you" he said and meant it.

"And I you, you be careful in London, not all parts are safe to walk around, so be safe."

"I will and I'll phone you too. Look after Rhia." He pulled away and he could see she was close to tears also.

"Goes without saying," she smiled.

He bent down to give Clucy one last fuss, and the dog rolled over for her belly to be tickled.

"Hussy," he said, and everyone laughed to break the pain of goodbye. They all hugged and promises of dinner on their return were made and within five minutes the sound of the car had faded away and Rhia and Sophie were left with just the sound of the dog padding her way back to the kitchen now that the excitement of visitors was over.

"I think you and I should go out for lunch today or we may just sit here blubbing," said Rhia. The tissue came out again and she dabbed a stray tear. "He's such a lovely soul, he reminds me of someone I thought I once knew."

CHAPTER TEN

The weeks between the start of term and Christmas had flown by for Mack. He had been so busy with all the fresher's activity that it seemed to go nowhere, and he was only just settling down to his coursework by the time it was Christmas break. Part of him wanted to go home to see all the people he loved, but the other half had only just opened himself to the cultural delights of London and a list of friendships that he was now forming.

Mack though quiet, was friendly, and it soon endeared him to a few like-minded students on his course. The fact he was tall, with brown eyes and a ready smile topped with a mop of thick dark hair brought him female attention that he appreciated but wasn't quite sure what to make of. He still had to admit that seemingly his heart was engaged in France, did the recipient of his affection but know it. Anyway, he was having too much fun just trolling about with a group of friends discovering all the local student haunts.

The course itself certainly wasn't going to be as easy as he had thought and a lot of individual research was required of each student, so his time was taken up. Each weekend he would faithfully ring home and to Rhia and Sophie, bringing them up to speed with all that was going on and his stories always left Rhia with a smile on her face. He texted Sophie every day, little snippets, just to remind her he was thinking of her, even if he said nothing of how he missed her.

Christina had become a frequent visitor to Rhia's since Mack had left for University and John was away on contracts and the three women would sit outside in the autumn sunshine and became as close as any three women of different generations could be. Sophie had slipped easily into Rhia's routine and Rhia had to admit that she found herself more inclined to venture out with the young woman for company. Life had enlivened slightly, and she was grateful for the social activity to break the creative when it got too heavy.

Sophie herself had taken to art like a true creative. An hour a day Rhia would instruct her on colour, styles, and general art history in a conversational way and then the agreement was that Sophie would work quietly and Rhia would have that time undisturbed to work on her own commissions. Some days Rhia would play an eclectic range of music, which she said helped her paint and

Sophie would enquire about the musician. What the young woman wasn't aware of was that she was having an extensive education on all things creative without even realising it. Her knowledge and confidence was growing daily. Rhia had converted Sophie to the genius of artists like Joni Mitchell and Fleetwood Mac and the noise of the music charts in England no longer held her attention apart from the odd artist which she in turn shared with a receptive Rhia and received a thumbs up or down accordingly.

She was now knowledgeable in all aspects of art marketing and was often now asked for personally by the companies responsible for the exhibition, rather than bothering Rhia. She was completely on top of it and very proud of herself on the quiet. Life was peaceful but never boring and that was all you could ask for really.

As the autumn wore on, the need to turn the heating on was becoming evident and Sophie would ask if it was ok to light the fire as she found it comforting. Rhia would read with her specs perched on her nose whilst Sophie sketched, or often they would look for an old movie. Sometimes she would choose and sometimes she would leave it to Sophie. This evening it was Sophie's turn, and she scanned the shelves of CD's looking for inspiration. Her suggestions would either get a maybe or a grimace from Rhia until they struck on one that they agreed over.

"What about this one?" she cried out pulling a case from the bottom of a pile. "The Bridges of Madison County" It's got Clint Eastwood in…?"

"No!" Came the sharp response. "Not that one." Rhia's eyes opened wide in shock. "I didn't know I still had that one..."

"But it looks good. It's got Meryl Streep as well."

"No... I really don't want to watch that one my dear. It has too many painful memories for me." Rhia took off her glasses and put them away. "You watch it if you want. It's a very good film. I think I might have an early night." With that she raised herself slowly from the chair and made for her room. Sophie was left holding the box and looked once more at it intrigued. Why would a film have painful memories that made Rhia run for her bed? She made sure Rhia was in bed and made herself a sandwich and a coffee and slipped the cd into the player to see what all the fuss was about.

Rhia lay quietly in her bed; the mere mention of the film had set off a thought process that was unstoppable. She had flashes of particular scenes from the film and with it, the rerun of the regrets that followed.

1992

Only hours after he had left for Huddersfield with one last kiss, she was back in the theatre working on the Blue Remembered Hills set. What a difference twelve hours could make to a life. She had designed a stage with a running stream, real turf, and bark to assault the audience's senses. Yesterday she had been so pleased with her sensory creation, but today all she could smell was the subtle musk of his sweat. She couldn't concentrate on the job in hand. Sitting on the edge of the auditorium and surveying her work, her head was full of him and the most intimate parts of her still pulsing from his lovemaking. He was all over her like a mist. There wasn't one part of her that he hadn't tasted or touched. There was just no getting away from the overwhelming feeling of him.

"Rhi!" A crew member called "The ponds level is down; it must be losing water!"

"Shit! How close are those wires running?" She strode to where Steve was pointing and crouched down, water and theatre electrics spelt potential disaster.

"S'OK," she said, crouching down to inspect. "It's these foam rocks absorbing. Keep topping it up, when they reach saturation the level will maintain," she said,

breathing a sigh of relief. As the moment of panic passed, her phone started to ring.

"It's me," he said. "I know it's wrong, but I can't stop thinking about you...I need to see you again babe." At that moment she was lost forever. The first irrevocable step had been taken and her downfall started to lay its erotic path before her.

The game was on. Many, many phone calls, all hours every day, singing to her on her birthday, the soft London accent lulling her in its smiling sensual tone. He was so far away, and they were both so busy and meeting up was almost impossible at that distance. The ache was strong.

There would be a phone call, a place. It started with a bedroom picnic in room 48 of a service station on the M62 and progressed swiftly and passionately from there. Leftover strawberries and chocolate for breakfast and snuggling down to watch 'I Dream of Jeannie' repeats between the languid moments of lovemaking that haled their parting the morning after. 'Moments in a bottle.'

Nine o' clock, Saturday evening, Manchester. The phone ringing...

"Come to Naaden with me?" he had said.

"Where?" she questioned.

"Holland... I'm booked on the channel tunnel at five am. You've got seven hours to get to Kent."

An hour later she was flying down the M1. Three hours after that she looked up at the stars through the supports of the Dartford Crossing and thought about the madness that her world had become and how close she now was to him as they made the drive to each other.

In the sleeping and darkened village near Canterbury and in the shadow of the church, with its rustle of trees and night sounds to stir the soul that was perfection for lovers, she waited and dozed.

Quietly pulling open the rear door of her car in the deserted car park of the Leather Bottle Inn, she jumped from sleep as he kissed her upside-down face, gently at first and then deeply as she started to come round. Then turning his attention to the breast that had strayed from her dress he caressed the nipple suckling gently and climbed into the tumble of sleeping bags... The saying, not knowing where one ended and the other began had never been truer. He was her soul, the love of her life. It was blind, joyous, and heartbreaking in its innocence and folly.

The tunnel crossing and the realisation that in thinking they were alone; they had furtively made love in the cab of the lorry he had hired for the contract to deliver a photographic exhibition. They were oblivious of the security cameras directly on them and initial embarrassment, was followed by laughter and thankfully no arrest.

Pulling off the road at a car park just ten minutes into the journey on the outskirts of Calais and into the back of the van, clothes frantically pulled aside against the wall of the van and then having to sleep for an hour to recover, wrapped together on sleeping bags like babes in the woods, amongst the boxes he was transporting.

Ten minutes later as he stashed the petrol receipts under the dash and stopped to watch her walk towards him with two coffees across the petrol station forecourt, her question 'What?' as he gave her that look was met with' I can't believe we made love half an hour ago and I want you again..!' She smiled wickedly, handed him the coffees, and climbed in stretching across to kiss him provocatively. This was the passion...the blindness.

The day progressed much the same and the journey slowly. Stopping at services every hour and parking up with no room hardly but for him to lift her onto a packing crate and stand on a toolbox to reach her. The frenzy, the smell of his leather jacket, the unending mutual desire. The dilated silver eyes as he murmured against her mouth "I'm crazy about you," and later in the hotel room where she emerged from the shower naked to find the room lit with candles he had brought, so un- male and so him. He lay in just his jeans, relaxing on the bed with a joint. As his eyes strayed to her silver belly chain with its delicate procession of tiny stars he sat up and pulled her to him. 'Fucking hell!' was all he could manage before he threw the stub in the ashtray and pulled her towards him. Rhia's walk had begun and with it, her life would never again reach a time of complete peace.

For six months the love affair continued, mainly in spirit and on the phone, as it was so hard for him to get away. It occurred to her that another woman was his main concern, but his assurances that his marriage was all but over, and he was there for his children only, gave her the excuse to blinker herself to reality. She was a romantic and romantics were fools when it came to true love.

Gradually the cracks began to show, the loneliness, the insecurity, and the knowledge that he was sharing his life with a family she had no part in, gradually began to take its toll and she started to question. They were a mystery that he would give her so little insight into. She never saw a picture of his wife, only his kids and her heart ached to have the connection of a child with him. Her early forties were hardly the time to start a family with a married man, still she yearned for something that was his and hers completely.

When tired he would sigh and say' "It's no bed of roses Rhi. If she found out she would make sure I lost my kids and besides, I don't want to be a part time dad. I want to be there in the morning when they wake and there to tuck them in at night. Do you really think I want to carry on living this grey half-life? I can't ask you to wait babe, maybe when the youngest one is old enough for university, we have a chance…"

Sometimes they would lie in bed when they were too tired to make love any longer and create the life they would want together, like teenagers playing a fantasy game. He would say "I can see you and me designing and building a house on the side of a hill in Switzerland or somewhere with a great view, all stone and glass," and they would grab a pen and sketch ideas on anything to hand till they would have an image of their future home. The game would end with him always saying "But for now babe, I can't offer you anything…This is how it has to be…"

A sadness would come over him and that would be all the promise she would have. There would then be a silence as he held her against his chest and then he would kiss her forehead gently and the lovemaking would begin again, but always tender at these moments and she knew he was fully aware of the sacrifice he was asking of her.

She wanted to say she had the strength, but the love for him was overwhelming and emotion was a frail yet passionate creature. She was never sure if she would have the will to endure this. Answering his kiss with her own, there would be an unspoken understanding between them that each knew the other's pain. The wait would have to be eight years.

By this time friends were telling her she had no life just waiting for him when all around her were happy couples. Good or bad the love she felt was just too deep to end it, and so this was how Rhia's long and painful walk continued…

When he wasn't with her, which was most of the time, she would imagine him there, the smell of him, his head on her stomach where he would settle sometimes, collapsing upon her after lovemaking. She would run her hands through his scruffy mop of brown hair with its flecks of grey and watch him drift to sleep, his hand cupping her thigh. He had a peppery scent that he gave off when they made love and she would recapture it, and in its comforting memory she would sleep...

***

Rhia, in the first light of dawn, finally slept, a fitful sleep full of memories and betrayal. When she awoke quite late, she felt old and unrested. Thank goodness she had Sophie to bring the sunshine back into her day. Soon Mack would be back, and they could look forward to Christmas. It was the best someone like Rhia could hope for. Why did her past hold her prisoner so?

Despite everything that had assaulted her faith these past years, he was, regardless of everything, in the deepest places of her heart, still a thing of beauty in her memory. No games, lies, denials or manipulations could ever taint those precious times for her. It was the only thing left untouched by the despair and self-disgust that encompassed everything else. How many years was it now since she had sat on that mountain and everything that followed it? The dates were getting lost in the fog of time. Twenty-one years, was it? and she still hadn't come of age and wisdom.

Sliding her legs to the floor, she took a deep breath. She had used her five minutes per day allocation of thought to Sean already and needed to put him from her mind. It was her survival technique that allowed her to live with some kind of equilibrium and if not joy, then tranquillity at least. She stretched and pulled herself up and spent a few minutes doing some simple yoga exercises to keep her mobility and balance. Slipping a thick robe on she felt along the bedside for her warm slippers. She really did not relish the prospect of winter and its limitations for her. The smell of warm bread drew her to the kitchen where Sophie was sat eating a croissant and jam and smiled warmly as Rhia entered.

The previous night Sophie had watched the film that upset Rhia and she struggled to see how it applied to Rhia. The woman in the film had two children, was a farmer's wife and fell into an affair with a travelling photojournalist. Still, something within the story touched Sophie and regardless of her confusion she had still cried like a baby at the beauty and tragedy of the lost but abiding love. Rhia looked strained this morning and so she thought it better not to discuss. Instead, she pulled a chair out and bade her sit whilst she made her breakfast and at Rhia's request "Tea for a change."

Rhia used to love Christmas, but the years and her aching back had lessened the need for a tree, besides there was only usually her, so she considered it pointless. This year however Sophie had never stopped mentioning how lovely the living room would look and that she would do it all. Rhia had eventually caved in and ordered one for delivery today.

Sophie was beyond excited. They had planned with Christina to share Christmas Eve together as Rhia's was the bigger house and she was already halfway through an enthusiastic shopping list for later that day. Rhia had humoured her because she had been so thrilled at the prospect of a family Christmas, and she had wanted to take the decoration on by herself. The tree was delivered and immediately after Sophie had made sure the fire was stacked and the heating on. Satisfied that Rhia was happy, she left her sandwich ready and was out the door and on the bus to Josselin.

Wandering around the town all muffled up against the cold she looked around at the festive shops and the families milling about. She waved to a couple of people she had come to know, and they exchanged season's greetings in fluent French.

There could have been no nicer place to spend Christmas than Josselin with its red and cream mediaeval buildings and cobbled streets. Everywhere you looked was characterful and garlanded for the festivities. The cafe bars were filled with last minute shoppers having a break before moving onwards for more. Her cheeks were rosy, and she had no idea of the attention she was attracting with her khaki wool cape borrowed from Rhia topped with a red scarf and black wedge boots, she was quite stunning. She stopped for a mulled wine and watched the activity.

"May I join you?" A youngish man with black hair and obvious confidence stood over her. It was the first time she had ever been approached by a man, let alone a very attractive one. She froze for a minute as panic set in, but she nodded "Certainement," and he pulled out a chair and sat down.

"Are you on holiday here?" he enquired.

"Non," was the best she could do as her throat had gone dry.

"Then why have I never seen you?"

"I don't get out much." She didn't get out much! she heard her inner voice squawk, and she lost the last ounce of courage.

"De dois vraiment y aller maintenant... Joyeux Noel," she muttered and gathering up her things quickly she pushed back her chair and fled. The man left sitting was surprised to say the least. He was not accustomed to being rejected.

Sophie scuttled round the corner and didn't slow her walk until she knew he was not following. Why was she behaving so ridiculously? Then it dawned on her, he was exhibiting attraction to her and that in itself was enough to put her to flight. She shuddered. Would she always feel this way? Like a frightened mouse every time someone showed her attention. This fog of fear that slid over her at the thought of a man and intimacy she needed to get over. Rhia, if nothing else in their discussions, had taught her the only thing to do about the past was to move on from it. She had mourned long enough. Head down she continued determinedly with her shopping.

Mack was over the minute his bag was unpacked and they drank mulled wine and toasted marshmallows on the fire whilst Rhia sat with a blanket over her feet. She watched them happily as they caught up with everything the other had done and they had missed. Rhia couldn't help but think to herself that they made a beautiful young couple, but they were still very young, and these things couldn't be rushed. Better that they were friends first and foremost, they had a long time for love if it ever developed from that strong foundation.

As if someone had waved fairy dust, the sky clouded over on Christmas Eve and as the light started to fade, the first soft flakes of snow started to fall as if to order. The fire was burning bright and decorated across the hearth with branches and baubles and the décor was mirrored by the tall Christmas tree that stood in front of the large expanse of window. With the snow falling behind outside the glass it was as though the tree could have been outside. Sophie had placed large candles around the room and decorated a table with Christmas sweets and wine. The soft lights enhanced the magical atmosphere she had created. She was a natural thought Rhia as she watched the young woman make the finishing touches. With the eye of a true designer Sophie had created something intimate and welcoming and Rhia appreciated the work that she no longer had the energy for.

Sophie had done pork in a cream sauce, garnished with salted roast potatoes and honey roasted vegetables from a recipe book she had found in the snug and was extremely happy with her efforts. When she opened the front door to Mack and his parents, they all had a dusting of white and spirits were high. John brandished the port. Christina had a fruit cake and cheese and Mack had the bag with the presents. It was a small gathering but a happy one. Around eleven they made their excuses when they noticed Rhia's eyes start to get heavy. They said their goodbyes and Sophie closed the door with a content sigh, feeling very festive she went to help Rhia off with her shoes and handed her a nightdress. She did not receive any rebuff so Rhia must have been tired, or it could have been the second large port. She wished the old lady good night and Merry Christmas and as Rhia rested her head on the pillow, Sophie leaned in and kissed her on the forehead.

"Thank you, Rhia, for all you've done for me. This is the best Christmas ever!" Rhia opened her tired eyes and caught the girls hand bringing it to her cheek to kiss the palm.

"Goodnight lovely one, not too early in the morning, eh? I'm an old lady, you know." She smiled with her eyes as her toes felt the warmth of the hot water bottle her young companion had put in the bed earlier and gathered it to her.

"You'll never be old to me Rhia." Sophie moved quietly to the door and blew one last kiss as the door closed softly.

That night Rhia slept instantly, with a smile on her face. Lovely times had been had tonight that were not tarnished with any thoughts of the past and there were no dreams to make her wake with regret. It was a Christmas blessing.

CHAPTER ELEVEN

Christmas day it was their turn to come to Mack's family and he picked them up for Christmas Lunch at one. The meal was a splendid affair and everyone including Rhia was stuffed. Mack had dragged Sophie out into the snow, leaving the parents to entertain Rhia and they walked across the fields with Clucy in tow as a reward for being on her best behaviour throughout the meal.

Presents had been saved for after lunch and Sophie was blown away by Christina and John's gift of six driving lessons. It had never occurred to her that it was possible to learn to drive, but apparently, they had planned it because Rhia had told her that she fully expected her to be chauffeur once she'd passed and would have the use of her car. Rhia had bought her an easel of her own and brushes, canvas, and paint. Mack had bought her graphic pencils and pens with a professional quality sketch pad, and she was thrilled.

She felt that by some crazy chance she had been given a second family, the one she had always wished for. As she gave effusive thanks for the presents, she also gave silent thanks as she looked around the room at these lovely people. Whatever had pushed this good fortune her way and saved her from something she didn't even want to think about.

The snow had stopped around midnight and a sharp frost had set in, leaving the ground crunchy underfoot. They walked to the old church and through the orchards before turning for home.

"Is uni really ok then?" she asked Mack as they trudged through the trees with Clucy running herself ragged in excitement around them.

"Yeah fantastic, love it, the course work's hard but the company's great. I've got a few mates already."

"So not missing us at all then," Sophie smiled wryly.

"Always missing you guys," he responded and stopped suddenly.

"What's the matter?" she asked.

"Can't miss an opportunity," he said and pointed upwards into the taller trees.

"Look up," he said. She did and in the tops of the trees were bands of mistletoe. As she looked back down it was too late and he had taken a step closer to kiss her. The suddenness of the move made her jump back and her arms went up defensively.

"I'm sorry, no!" was all she could muster, and Mack looked hurt and embarrassed. It was his first attempt to kiss anyone special.

"I'm sorry, it was only a Christmas kiss."

"Sorry, you just took me by surprise, that's all." The moment had gone, and Mack's courage had left him. He coloured with embarrassment and didn't pursue it.

"No problem," he answered, but on the walk back there was an awkwardness that neither of them could get past. The rest of Christmas Day went fine in the company of others, but something had changed for both and yet was left unsaid.

Mack was despondent and Sophie felt a fool for reacting so badly. It was clear the moment was not right for them and whilst they chatted casually with everyone. Each took a surreptitious glance at the other now and then to try to assess the damage they had done to their relationship.

New Year came and went and although they went through the motions and Mack still came to Rhia's to visit as normal, he had mentally backed off from Sophie, his young heart bruised. Sophie herself had several conflicting emotions. She loved Mack dearly, but she did not want to consider anyone boyfriend material. It just wasn't what she wanted right now. Her art and Rhia were the main focus of her life, and she was addicted to the new person that she was becoming over the last few months. She was also deeply attached to the woman who had become her mentor in all things and couldn't conceive of anything that would make her want to break the bond.

Like Mack, she had researched Rhia online and was fascinated by the glamorous persona she saw portrayed of the woman a couple of decades ago. The one thing she never found was any evidence of a serious lover. She had been clearly beautiful, so it seemed strange.

The woman she lived with even now had style but was also very grounded and caring, a winning combination. You would have thought that she would have attracted the right man somewhere along the way. Sophie had tried to glean something from Rhia's agent Bertrand in their discussions of the coming exhibition, but apart from that he had known her over twenty years, he remained tight lipped on the subject.

The day for Mack to leave came all too soon and after a brief stop off at Rhia's with Christina and John as they took him to the station. After hugs all round he was gone and Sophie felt bereft, like she had lost the chance of something more important than just the company of her only young friend.

"You miss him," observed Rhia shrewdly.

"I do," she sighed.

"He'll be back in summer break, if not before," came the reply.

"I know, it just seems like such a long time away."

Mack boarded the train at Nantes and watched the French countryside passing by as he thought of Sophie. By the time he reached Calais he had convinced himself that it was useless. She just didn't think of him in that way and not being privy to Sophie's past, he put it down to there being nothing between them. By seven he was back in his digs cracking a can with his mate Connor who was on the same course.

"Did I miss anything?" he asked.

"Only the best New Years Eve party ever mate!" Came his friend's reply, and he felt gutted. He should have come back sooner. He had wasted an opportunity to be in London on New Year's Eve to spend a few more days with Sophie... He wouldn't next time.

The new year brought heavy snow and apart from the odd trudge on foot to the local shop once a day, they were confined. The snow brought with it new opportunities to paint and both Rhia and Sophie took the chance to draw on the inspiration the 'white out' that the several days snowfall brought them. They worked silently together, and it was Rhia's rule that they did not view each other's work until finished. Even a small misunderstanding of body language of the viewer or a remark could imply criticism. That then might alter the artist's intention or confidence in the piece they were doing. Sophie understood and respected this.

Northern France was a pristine white, but London was grey, slushy, and wet and Mack, although deeply involved in his course work couldn't help but carry a mild depression. Winter weather in London didn't have the same serenity as his home in France. Still, it had its comforts. He and Connor had found an excellent student pub near their digs with an open fire and the atmosphere of a Dickens novel and had become regulars with others from their course. He found after the second pint that thoughts of Sophie receded.

His confidence grew daily and with it his attraction to the opposite sex. Mack had already kissed his first girl in a drunken night last week and by the looks of the girl a couple of tables away giving him the eye that Connors hefty nudge had drawn his attention to, he might well be on his way to a second. Perhaps things weren't so bad after all.

CHAPTER TWELVE

Spring was well underway, and Sophie sprang out of bed with it every morning, eager to do her work so that she could begin her painting. The agreement was three hours housekeeping and one hour PA work in exchange for her keep and one hundred euros per week. Today they were planning the trip to Italy, something that Rhia felt more confident doing now that she had stronger younger company. She hated acknowledging that age had been starting to limit her life until now, and Sophie was beyond excited which pleased her.

She had fired Sophie up with talk last night of the places she wanted to revisit, and they were wide ranging. A 'Grand Tour' starting in Venice, then Milan and the Opera, followed by Rome. Then they would have a week's rest in the Italian lakes and then on to the Amalfi Coast. Finally, they would head down to the heel to visit friends in the Bari region of Puglia, which Rhia had promised would be a feast for any artist's eye. They would spend ten days relaxing there before coming home. Rhia had promised them a driver for their stay there as Mino and Carole would find them a more sensible sedate driver to taxi them about, as she would not be subjecting Sophie's new driver nerves to the emotions of Italian driving.

She tiptoed through to the kitchen trying not to disturb Rhia as it was early. Putting on the coffee, she opened the veranda door onto a beautiful April morning which was unusually warm. Looking about the garden she noted it was short of some TLC and would have to tackle the lawns for a first cut soon. It brought Mack into her mind. He rang regularly but recently there was a distance that had not been there previously. He was obviously heavily into student life, and she hoped London life wouldn't drag him into anything that would destroy his lovely nature. Still, there was nothing to do but wait for his return in summer and she would see for herself if he had been living the life too wildly.

They had eight weeks to plan for Italy and the favourites had been printed off and an itinerary was underway. Currently they were laid out methodically on the large kitchen table so they could check the journey's progression which would take them just over four weeks. Rhia had said no expense spared as it might be her last big holiday and so the anticipation and ease of choice was fabulous as beautiful hotels were opened to them.

Rhia had told her June could be cool early on, so she would need a mix of clothes and to save some money to buy at least one special outfit in Milan, otherwise what was the point of going to Italy she had laughed mischievously. Drinking her coffee quickly and calling the dog quietly from Rhia's sleeping side, she put her lead on for their morning stroll to the boulangerie. The spring morning had prompted a few early risers, and she called her hellos to the locals as she strolled along the quiet village streets. French was easy for her now and on Rhia's advice she had started learning Italian. The difficulty was keeping herself from mixing the two into one language.

Sophie's artwork had really impressed Rhia, and the older woman was determined she would eventually promote her when she felt the time was right. Unknown to Sophie she had already spoken to her own agent and given him instructions that should anything happen to her prior, that he would set up a launch exhibition for the young artist with funds she had set aside specifically. Sophie was oblivious to Rhia's intentions and was blithely pushing forward with her artistic development, just happy to be under a mentor who had her best interests at heart.

Once a week they would go for lunch at Christina's and Sophie would be allowed to drive Delilah Rhia's convertible the short journey to improve her confidence. She had passed the driving test recently scraping through with thirty-six questions right but there was nothing like practical experience. Sadly, Rhia wasn't the calmest tutor and so the short journey to Christina's was the most of her new young friends driving she could tolerate. Christina was also sitting in with her and giving her additional support, so all in all she was improving daily.

At last week's lunch Christina had mentioned that Mack had said he wouldn't be home for the half term as he had a lot on. He would not see them now till summer break. Sophie was deflated and Rhia had seemed sad also. She had grown very attached to the young man in his brief time with her. Still, they would be in Italy before they knew it and then once back home, he would be there within a couple of weeks. Sophie let it go, preoccupied with all their exciting preparations.

After the meal Rhia told them both about her previous trips and what had made it so attractive to return. They were captivated with Rhia's tales of her travels as a woman alone. How once she had taken that first journey it had become an addiction to explore and she had saved every penny to take her wherever the urge directed. She had returned to Italy many times, but her love had been for New Zealand. Maybe next year if she were up to the long journey and Sophie was still with her, they could go. Sophie immediately protested that 'of course she would be' but Rhia had patted her hand and replied saying 'the one thing she knew in life to be true was that you could never rely on planning ahead. "Live for today, for tomorrow may take you on a different journey," she had said.

The weeks moved swiftly on, and with it Sophie's confidence had grown. Days outside in the spring sunshine keeping her promise to Mack to keep on top of the garden till his return had revitalised her faded tan and she looked healthy. She had a fragility about her that made her feminine but underlying that she had a determination that belied her outward appearance. Rhia had heard her conversing on the phone regarding the forthcoming events on numerous occasions and it left her in no doubt of how capable she was of looking after both her own and Rhia's interests. She had a pleasant, yet forthright manner that charmed and disarmed any opponent.

CHAPTER THIRTEEN

Rhia had sat with her to do the final checks on the journey and the bags were in the hall ready to leave. John was going to drive them to the airport, and did Sophie but know it, Rhia was as excited as the young woman she was nurturing to be going on this journey once more. She just hoped she had the stamina for it. If she could manage this, she would aim for New Zealand next year and that would be her last hoorah to her lost youth. After that she would travel more sedately as was expected of someone her age. But for now, in her head, she was thirty-something once more taking her first adventure alone to Italy. She felt alive and vibrant and couldn't wait to show her young protégé everything that she had discovered in her younger years.

Six hours later they had stepped off the plane into the sweet Italian air and Sophie buzzed with excitement at what was spread before her like a sumptuous feast. An appreciation of what this woman had done for her was beyond her almost nineteen years and the action of linking her arm through Rhia's as they came down the plane steps was born of genuine love for the old lady and not just a need to steady her descent. The looks they received from other travellers were not noticed, but they made an interesting pair. The elegant and modern older woman and the fresh and beautiful younger woman beside her.

Rhia had insisted on a private car to take them from the airport, so once they had cleared customs it was relatively stressless to track down the driver who waited for them with a sign calling for 'Señora Rhiannon Hart.' He was a cheerful and polite man with a good grasp of English, which helped Sophie's attempts at basic Italian immensely. He gave them a running commentary on the way to the hotel, leaving his car to transfer their baggage onto the vaporetto and escorting them to the desk of their hotel. She now knew why Rhia had said this was a necessity for a first-time traveller in Venice. She was very relieved that she hadn't been the one responsible for getting them there safely.

From the moment they approached the Piazza San Marco, till the moment she closed the bedroom door of her stunning room she had almost held her breath with the beauty of it all. Seeing Rhia settled in her room first she then gave in to the excitement of it all and let out a long low 'WOW!' Never in all her young life had she experienced such wealth and opulence. Rhia had been right when she had said Italy would change her outlook on life.

Throwing open the shutters on her window she looked out on the canal and the romance and noise and glory of it all was so overwhelming that she ran back to Rhia's room and threw her arms around the older woman. She was also standing in a similar position looking out of her veranda onto the activity below.

"Thank you, thank you for bringing me here!" Sophie clung to Rhia in a wave of emotion and Rhia found herself overwhelmed as she welled up and hugged the young girl right back.

"You're very welcome, lovely one. I will enjoy it twice as much through your new eyes...Now I am going to rest for a couple of hours and then we will see some sights, believe me! You come get me and be ready for dinner at about 7pm and we will go by gondola to a beautiful restaurant by the Rialto Bridge, I'm so excited!"

Sophie could not stay in her room and had a short foray out onto the San Marco square heeding Rhia's previous advice not to sit down there in any cafe unless she wanted an obscenely priced coffee and cake, so she made for a small cafe back by the hotel just to test her Italian safely. She watched in awe as the gondolas jockeyed for position with motor launches on the Grand Canal and was like a child in her excitement and the furthest from sophistication that she could be.

Rhia had watched with quiet joy as her companion's eyes had opened like saucers from the minute the Vaporetto had approached the landings at St Marco until the moment she had left her to rest with yet another hug of gratitude and a loving kiss on the cheek promising to return in time for their outing later.

When Sophie knocked dressed in her best, Rhia stood in an elegant trouser suit and silk blouse. She loved her satins and silk and Sophie admired how her companion hadn't given in to age. With a style that was classic and yet modern, she looked superb. Sophie had chosen a short white dress and piled her hair on her head to make herself appear older and more sophisticated than she actually felt. Rhia had handed her a beautiful yellow ochre coloured pashmina, saying she would need it later when the evening chill set in and she accepted it gratefully. Feeling very grand they walked through the Hotel lobby and to the jetty to board the Vaporetto to Rialto Bridge. The lights were just coming on in the walkways and the atmosphere couldn't have been more romantic.

For Sophie she was truly in love for the first time, but with life. Rhia chatted occasionally on the short journey, but on the whole she left Sophie to enjoy her first experience of Venice in silence. Rhia sat savouring her own memories of the first time she had explored this city and made her way like a homing pigeon to the Rialto Bridge. The bridge itself was awash with stalls and crafts and the atmosphere was lively and bustling, but Rhia bypassed the crowds and slowly made her way to a small Trattoria just a little way across from it, where they could appreciate the atmosphere, without the annoyance of fighting a path through the many tourists.

The meal was excellent and the flavours rich. This was all accompanied by a fruity red, Primitivo, the wine Rhia said she had been introduced to by her friends from the Bari region and she had been surprised to find it here so far north. Sophie found herself flushed by the end of the meal and a bit tipsy. Rhia smiled and topped up her water handing her the glass with a wink.

"Best you share the love and drink water also. I don't have the strength to carry you back to the hotel," she said with a smile.

"Good idea, it's strong, isn't it?" Sophie blew her fringe off her face and Rhia laughed.

"You'll get used to it. But it's never good to drink too much when you're travelling, especially if you're alone." Rhia added a warning for future reference to the young naive girl sitting opposite her and tipsy as Sophie was, she took it onboard.

"Shall we have a little walk onto the bridge now its quieter Rhia?"

"Don't see why not" she answered and signalled the waiter. "Il conto per favor."

Rhia handed the young Italian her card and noticed that he had more attention on Sophie than his work. She was going to be beautiful very soon. Once she got a little more life experience, she would be unstoppable.

"Grazie per una serata perfetta." she said as they left the table and made their way slowly to the exit.

"Prego signora e signorina." His polite response was to both, but he only had eyes for Sophie who was oblivious. Gone were the days when Rhia received that kind of attention.

They walked arm in arm through the few lingering tourists on the Bridge and Rhia reminisced about the first visit she had ever made here. It had been a day trip from elsewhere and she had dashed through St Mark's Square to the Rialto Bridge, followed by a sprint to the Bridge of Sighs and just enough time for a quick visit to St Marks which had been covered with scaffolding at the time. The Ducal Palace had to wait for another visit, but she managed to get to the top of the clock tower to see the views. The wonder was short lived but not a disappointment and was worth the panic of getting back to the meet point for her tour by the skin of her teeth. Crazy days…

"You speak fluent Italian!" Sophie said in wonder.

"Not fluent, but it's such a beautiful language that I wanted to learn but I always get a little rusty. It comes back once I've been here a few days. You must try your skills now you've been practising." said Rhia and Sophie shuddered.

"I'm frightened of looking like a fool," she answered.

"No, people appreciate that you try and are generally very helpful. Tomorrow you can do all the talking."

"Oh no don't make me, I'll die of embarrassment!" she cried clinging tight to Rhia's arm and Rhia laughed out loud. Sophie couldn't help but think how lovely she was when her laughter lit up her face. She hoped she could be this good when she reached Rhia's age.

"You won't die my lovely, you will excel, I just know it!" and with that she guided them to a Vaporetto moored nearby and they headed back for the hotel, weary but excited at all that was before them in the coming weeks.

They spent a lovely few days in Venice and then headed for a couple of days in Milan which was a busy city. Rhia took Sophie to a few of her favourite haunts and then making sure she was confident finding her way about she let her explore on her own, giving Rhia time to rest her aching feet. Rhia had told her to visit Romeo and Juliet's balcony and as she walked through the streets alone, she suddenly felt very grown up and assured as her Italian was improving daily and she could now ask basic questions to get by. The shops beckoned as she passed, and she promised herself a little spree on the way back to their hotel. Rhia had told her they were going to the open-air opera in Milan's grand amphitheatre that evening. She wanted to look special and here was definitely the place to find the outfit. The tunnel through to what was a very small courtyard below the balcony was covered in love messages and she stopped to read them fascinated. Italy certainly was the place for romance and its atmosphere was captivating, despite her indifference to the opposite sex.

People were filing along its walls adding their own messages and she felt a little left out, so taking out her pen she wrote 'Thank you Rhia for giving me this x' and was satisfied that she had put some small piece of herself in history.

The shops were an experience as the Italians certainly knew how to dress. She finally found an oyster-coloured satin shift dress that though simple at the front had a low draped back. As she turned in the mirror she breathed a sigh of happiness. "Perfecto" she said to the assistant. Adding long crystal earrings and the most beautiful but impractical pair of shoes and matching bag, she took a deep breath and totted up the bill, it took a quarter of her spending money for the whole holiday and her heart started to race in panic. Rhia had said everyone should have one very expensive outfit in their lifetime, so she guessed this was hers and Rhia wouldn't disapprove.

When she got back to the hotel, she called in on Rhia who was sitting on her small balcony looking down at the crowds in the square below. Laying all her things on Rhia's bed she showed off her purchases with pride. Rhia smiled her approval.

"Lovely!" she said. "You need to hang the dress up and let the creases drop out. The heat will do it naturally."

She walked to her wardrobe and brought out a gossamer shawl embroidered beautifully with small crystals; it couldn't have been more perfect.

"This is just what it needs, and you'll appreciate it when it goes dark and cool later." Sophie gasped with delight.

"Don't you need it?" she asked.

"No, I have my own opera outfit, I wore it here many years ago and incredibly it fits me again as I've lost my middle age spread with age." She went to the wardrobe and brought out a vintage Jasper Conran heavily beaded almost ankle length Indian coat made from a black gauze and satin pants. She laughed as she looked at it.

"I used to wear it with a Madonna style long length bra, but age dictates a little demurer behaviour nowadays as its see through." She brought out a black satin chemise and grimaced," How the mighty are fallen!"

Sophie looked at the beautiful beading on the vintage coat and thought how well preserved it was. They would be an impressive pair she thought and just hoped they hadn't overdone it.

She needn't have worried as they walked across the square towards the amazing amphitheatre where VIPs were mixing with the normal tourists, and no one felt out of place. Rhia had spared no expense with their tickets, and they were led to a comfortable seat just behind the first few rows of chairs where local dignitaries were sitting, along with probable famous faces that Sophie had yet to recognise.

"Much better than my first visit," said Rhia and pointed to the stone steps where people were sat above the stage. "You need two cushions to sit up there, luckily someone warned me the first time and I hired two thank goodness. The opera was several hours long, and I really needed them by the end!"

She took out a black painted fan and started to fan herself gently. The sun was just setting but the volume of bodies in the large open-air amphitheatre was making it warm. Sophie folded her wrap carefully and placed it on her lap. She looked around the massive space and was left in awe. They were seeing Aida, and the set was beyond impressive with obelisks and pyramid. Rhia had told her they were bringing on live horses for the grand parade.

Looking about her, she realised that she was sat with the elite, and she felt insignificant amongst them. When she voiced her feelings to Rhia. The older woman leant in and placed her hand on the young woman's.

"Just remember this. The elite have either worked hard to get where they are or have had it handed to them on a plate, you will find good and bad amongst them. The trick is to realise that they don't know who you are, so you can be whatever you want. Tonight, I suggest that you consider yourself a princess because you certainly look like one and you are equal to them all. One day you will have enough life experience to measure up easily to any of them. You must believe in yourself. The rest will come naturally... Oh look, the lights are dimming!"

CHAPTER FOURTEEN

The weeks went by in a dream of an experience. They went to Rome, which was tiring for Rhia but inspiring for Sophie who's mouth never closed either in excitement or awe at the beautiful and bustling city. Next, they went to Garda, to a stately three-hundred-year-old hotel on the side of the lake close to Malcesine. They arrived in the worst thunderstorm she had ever experienced, but by morning the skies were the clearest blue and the view from their terrace stunning. The waiter at their table the next morning had remarked they were lucky to have arrived when they did. Only storms such as that gave such clarity of view the next day in this mountain region.

They spent a happy week just resting by the pool and sketching. When the need for action arose, they would hop on one of the boats in the harbour and let it take them to the various sites along the lake without walking Rhia to the point of exhaustion. There was no view that wasn't inspiring as the boats made their way up and down and they would lunch in the small harbour side trattorias and wander around the shops and stalls that adorned the colourful streets. Rhia had scheduled their travels well so as not to overtax herself.

The weather was kind to them and by the time they left they were rested and ready for more sightseeing. It had been an easy week that drew the young woman and the elder one so very close with many opportunities for chatting and learning about each other. Rhia told Sophie about her early life and the short-lived marriage she had rushed into as a young woman that soon became jaded, leaving her no option but to divorce. How that divorce had ended a hiatus in Rhia's ambitions, and she had thrown herself into life and career once more retraining as a set and costume designer.

Coming to this very place as a salve for her wounds from a husband who had no ambition or lust for life. It was here she discovered that life could be entrancing, even alone. How could one not be happy amidst such spectacular nature, and she had laughed as she told Sophie the moment that she had realised there was life after marriage.

She had arrived alone and that was how she had wanted to stay, drinking in all this beauty without the distraction of having to be companionable. Avoiding all the well-meaning guests at her hotel, she had found her way to the cable car above Malcesine and when it had let her off at the top of the mountain, she had strode out looking down in awe at the windsurfers on the lake who were now just mere pin pricks. 'How insignificant we were' she had thought and had stood revelling in the sheer magnificence of it all. She had been so captivated by her own internal eloquence as she had mused on the meaning of life when a loud fart had brought her back to earth with a jump. She had turned around in shock to find herself looking at the rear end of one of the cows who were grazing at the top of the mountain. She had laughed out loud and her self-pity had lifted. It had stuck in her memory of the first time, and she had laughed again.

"So, you see, there is no beauty without reality and there is no life with equal amounts of sadness and laughter. I came back, retrained, and had a wonderful few years working in theatre, made some lifelong friends who I don't get to see as often as I should nowadays, but we are all getting old now. I was often poor in those earlier days, but never bored. Life was good and slowly my name started to get out there and I made my way forward in my career and it was really starting to take off when I met Sean on a job..."

She stopped suddenly realising she had got carried away and picked up her coffee cup and finding it empty had called for the waiter to bring them more.

"Who's Sean?" Sophie asked determined not to be deflected. Rhia looked at Sophie and her eyes clouded over with pain.

"He was my love, my nemesis, my cruellest enemy and my saviour all rolled into one. He is the reason for my pain and the instigator of my artistic fame." Sophie wished she had one tenth of Rhia's vocabulary and sat expectantly. Rhia drew a deep breath.

"I met him on a shoot in Liverpool, it was a major break for me, and I was so nervous and very excited. All the crew met up at the studio and Sean was the photographer's assistant. It was just one of those chance meetings where you never expect to see the person again and would be normally too busy to get to know each other well, but there was a row over the content of the ad we were shooting and so we spent two days sitting in a canteen waiting for the wrinkles to be ironed out. By the time we finally got the work done we were the best of friends. Very soon we were lovers and I had thought I had met my soulmate. It took me five painful years to realise that I had taken an irrevocable step towards someone who was not all I believed him to be, and it very nearly destroyed me."

"Oh Rhia, how?"

"He was married of course, and I should have known better, but even in those first few days chatting over numerous coffees he had said his marriage was close to ending and he was only there because of his children. I was naive and too trusting then and took him on face value because he seemed so genuine and caring. Five years later I was broken and waiting to die on a mountain in Switzerland..." She stopped suddenly as her tears had welled up and she realised she was in danger of bringing down the joy of the day so far. "… anyway, I didn't die, I went crazy for a while, Then I travelled until I got my spirit back and started painting on my return. The rest was history!" She had swallowed down her sadness and left Sophie waiting frustratedly for the confidence that she had almost shared.

"But all those years Sophie, what did you do?"

"I waited, as I still am I guess, for the man I thought to be better than he was. He never came...In the end I realised that what I had thought was gentleness turned out to be just weakness and his vivid imagination and creativity which I had loved so much had spilled over into his reality. Unfortunately for me that made him a fantasist without integrity or moral strength. By the end of it all I didn't have any clear idea of who he really was and on discovering the lies I found myself without my soul, looking down on his reality, with no reality of my own. Five wasted years. I had a choice that night and I chose to live… and look at what it has brought me darling girl!" She threw her arm gracefully encompassing the mountains and lake before them and finally cupping the cheek of the shocked girl in front of her with affection.

"Now enough of the past! Five minutes of sadness is enough wasted of any day, especially one as glorious as this. Drink up lovely, the next boat home is in half an hour." She drained her coffee cup and called for the bill leaving Sophie wondering who could have been so callous as to nearly destroy the woman before her who seemed only to want to bring joy to those around her.

The days in Garda came to an end and they flew south to the Amalfi Coast. Here was a more cosmopolitan experience. Sorrento was just waking up for the tourist season and was not as unbearably hot as it would be in a few weeks' time. It made for pleasant journeying by boat down to Positano and Capri and Sophie was careful to ensure Rhia wasn't over-tired. Rhia would not allow Sophie to draw her out about her lost love further that week, but it made the younger woman look at her with new eyes. We often forget our elders have experienced similar dreams and heartbreak and as Sophie had never known a normal existence as a teenager, she was fascinated with this untold mystery and the implications of its tragic romance.

They had hired a personal driver to take them on the final stage of their journey to Puglia as Rhia wanted to look at the countryside along the way. The journey was certainly memorable, and Sophie cringed at the thought of ever having to drive in Italy. They seemed to have a casual disregard for their own lives. It was more like being in a pinball machine. Sophie was much happier when they reached the more rural roads and there was only the odd suicide jockey to contend with.

As they got nearer to the Puglia region, Rhia started to tell Sophie about the round houses that were called 'Trulli' and the history behind them. How they would visit Aberobella, which meant beautiful trees and the largest remaining site of the Trulli houses. They might have a trip shopping to Bari close by to blow the last of their holiday money before returning home she had said. As Rhia spoke with enthusiasm, Sophie kept thinking the name Bari was familiar and then in a flash of clarity she realised that it was in the film that Rhia had been so eager to avoid a few weeks ago.

"How did you find this area Rhia?" She questioned with a purpose.

"It was in a favourite film of mine, and I just decided that I was meant to come, so I did. I was in a very sad strange place at the time and packed a bag and visited several places on some kind of an indiscriminate adventure." There it was, Sophie had been right, and she silently vowed to watch the film again on her return to Josselin.

Rhia continued. "There were certain places that had come up in conversations in my life and I just decided I would follow that path and see what life brought me by visiting them. It brought me a world of new experiences and as I travelled my sadness started to lift. I went to New Zealand, Andalucia in Spain, Malta and finally returned to France where I had spent some wonderful days a couple of years before... I had once had a vivid dream that I was meant to live in a certain place there. I dreamt I walked through an ancient town and remembered the dream so vividly the next morning I even drew the path I walked and the buildings along the route. When I got to France finally and by chance came to Josselin, imagine how I felt when we got out of the car and found that I was in my dream? I still have the original sketch somewhere; I'll show you on my return. My travelling companion laughed at me at the time, but I knew we had come there for a reason. When I had finished my travels elsewhere and felt better, I went back to England and started to prepare for a new life here. It was at that time that I had been painting with my mentor David, incidentally he was the first promoter to Bring Hendrix into Britain."

"Hendrix?" questioned Sophie and Rhia laughed.

"Never mind, before your time. You can Google him. David introduced me to Bertrand at a time where all my emotions were pouring out into my art and something he saw must have resonated with him. Bertrand was just at the height of his fame as a fashionable young art dealer, and he took me on. My paintings started to become known and before I knew it, I was in demand. It was a manic time and emotionally I was not ready for it, as I had not long split from Sean, but I threw myself into the life with a madness born of despair and I became fashionable and sell-able. My painting prices went up and up and I became sought after and wealthy. It was that crazy. The more I tried to hide away, the more they wanted me. I was classed as eccentric… the new Joni Mitchell of the art world!"

Sophie did know of Joni Mitchell since Rhia had converted her to her genius.

"So, you went To France and found your place by the river?" asked Sophie.

"I did indeed, it took me a couple of years for things to settle career wise to settle and then I came back and found a place to build my home."

Piece by piece Sophie was starting to get an idea of what had caused her dear friend to lock herself away for so many years in such solitude. Whether her assumptions were correct was another thing, but from the little Rhia had let slip it appeared she had met this 'Sean' in her early forties just as her career was taking off. The whole episode had affected her severely and she must have had some kind of breakdown and suicide attempt which changed the direction of her life towards art from theatre and media. By the sheerest of chances, she had unwittingly struck lucky and achieved success which had then allowed her to make the move to France. Had the fact that she had been financially able then to work in isolation got her into the habit of the lonely life she had been leading, if so, how sad. She had chosen to remove herself from friends and those that might have pulled her back into normal life.

As the countryside grew more open, Rhia's excitement grew with it and she began to talk about the place they were staying more animatedly. It appeared that all those years ago she had put a pin in the map near Bari and looked for a place to begin her Italian adventure. It had brought her to the undiscovered beauty of Locorotondo, a citadel-based village in the heart of Puglia. She told Sophie how on arriving the first thing she encountered was the scent of Jasmine as her hired car at the time pulled into the drive of Trulli Trito, an exquisite property of seven trulli houses with its own pool set in a vineyard and the nearest thing to heaven she had encountered.

The owners, Carole and Mino had met at Catering school in London, fell in love and Carole had left her life in Wales to start this new life with Mino on his family property here. Slowly they had started to convert the Trulli into a tourist residence. They were the perfect hosts and at the end of ten days' stay, Rhia had rung two of her girlfriends back home and arranged to come back with them the following month.

Since then, she had visited them many times and it was her 'go to' place for peace. She was clearly excited at seeing her friends again as it had been seven years and far too long. The poppies were just coming into bloom and a joy to see as they lined the roads along the way in cheerful red abandon.

As they drew closer, she saw the first of the Trulli houses. An odd one was spotted here and there until eventually they dotted the countryside in clusters that were getting more prolific as they neared their destination. The pictures that Sophie had found on the internet did not do the area justice and by the time they arrived Sophie was already in love with the place.

Turning into the residence, Rhia saw Carole, older than she remembered but still lithe and stylish, her blond hair whiter but her smile still as bright. She was pruning the front of the reception shrubs and when she realised it was them, she waved excitedly and putting down her secateurs, she made her way towards them as they alighted from the car.

"Rhia! Oh, it's been such a long time, how are you?" she asked.

"I'm very well, and you?"

"More grandchildren, more work, but at least the girls are helping, and the wine crop is now established, and you...more success. How do you do it?" she laughed.

"Sheer luck, believe me!" Rhia and the woman embraced and then Carole turned to Sophie.

"This must be the lovely Sophie I have been emailing. Rhia has told me all about you, come, let's get you both settled in and then we'll have a glass of wine and a chat. Il Cotogno ok for you and Sophie next door?"

"But of course. The first villa I ever stayed in."

Sophie could see that this place was very special, it had such soul and beauty that you could not help but bathe in its peace and tranquillity. Sophie couldn't resist a walk round the grounds before she had even unpacked her case. When she came back, she found Carole and Rhia sat with a bottle of red chatting amiably.

"Primitivo?" Rhia held up a third glass and nodded to the bottle.

"Thank you, but just the one and then I must unpack. I've fallen foul of it before!"

"We found a bottle far from home in Venice," Rhia informed Carole with a grin.

"Well, it is going far and wide now, so is Negra Mara, another one that we export from this region."

Sophie pulled up a chair and breathed in the scent of Jasmine. This place washed over you like sinking into a warm perfumed bath,

"You have such a wonderful place here."

"We are very lucky where we live, but it's been hard fought at times, and we are just starting to reap the benefits. Still, it's better than living an ordinary life." She smiled and filled up a glass and handing it to Sophie she raised her own glass.

"To old friends and new,"

"To this wonderful place," said Sophie.

"To life" added Rhia.

They all savoured the wine and Rhia looked at Sophie. How this few weeks had changed her. Her skin now olive brown and her sleek hair falling on beautiful straight shoulders. She was positively blooming. More noticeably, after several weeks of conversing in Italian, the opera's, the concerts, the food, and the art had all given her a confidence and knowledge that had been previously missing. Here was a young, talented, and intelligent woman starting to realise her worth and grow her world. Rhia prayed she would stay with her, at least for a while, to lose her now would be unthinkable. If she went, it would be with Rhia's love and support in the hope that she would always return.

The days they spent with Carole and Mino were elysian and as the time came to leave Sophie was rested and content, knowing that Rhia had enjoyed the company of her friends so much. For now, it was time to return home and use all the influences she had found into her art. She expected Rhia would feel the same. She did, but as she said goodbye to her old friends, she hugged them like it might be the last time. Who would know when they would be next in this magical place, if at all.

As she handed the luggage over to the driver that had come to take them to the airport at Brindisi, she noted they had grown in size, and they were likely going to encounter excess baggage charges. When she mentioned it, Rhia waved her concerns away with a "No matter, we enjoyed spending on them, and we will enjoy wearing them in Paris soon!" Rhia was quiet on the drive and Sophie left her to her thoughts. She was looking forward to seeing Christina and John and Mack would be home in a few short weeks also. The exhibition in Paris was fast approaching and there would be lots for her to do as Rhia's PA. They were going into busy times, and she would have to be on her game.

The house was full of June evening sunshine when they finally opened the door and unloaded the cases. Christina had left them groceries ready for their return and it was with some relief that Rhia slipped her shoes off and padded to the sofa whilst Sophie made them a coffee. Rhia didn't like shoes nowadays as her once slim feet had started to swell with age, and she preferred to go without. Sophie was always telling her off, but she refused to concede and said she'd rather risk a broken toe from going barefoot than suffer old lady shoes.

Evening was drawing on before Sophie had unpacked all their baggage. She made them a sandwich and brought the post in to sort through as she ate. Rhia had her feet up as they had swollen more on the plane and Sophie could see the older woman would be not so long out of bed as she had to wake her from a nap to bring her food.

"What a wonderful time we've had," she said as Sophie made neat piles of things to action tomorrow, and things that could wait. The things that required Rhia's private attention could also wait. It was clear she was travel weary.

"It was; indeed, I feel like my life has gone on a weird path for the better, I can't thank you enough Rhia," answered Sophie.

"No thanks needed; you have set me free to travel once more. I was becoming a little nervous of travelling on my own recently and now we have the world at our feet. We shall be well and truly ready for another outing by the time Paris comes."

Sophie opened an envelope that had the Château Josselin logo on.

"Oh! it's an invitation for you to open the local art exhibition Rhia."

"Oh no, it's not really my thing" came the reply.

"But you must, you live here, and people will respect you for it if you give your time. You are a well-known artist, and it would be a coup for them to have you." Sophie put on her most determined face and Rhia laughed.

"Okay, I will do it, if you will submit some of your art."

"But I've nothing good enough, I'm not ready!"

"No artist is ever ready to show their work... that's the deal, you submit some work and I'll attend..."

"Damn it...OK but you have to help me prepare," she laughed.

"Certainment," smiled Rhia triumphantly.

The June nights were still a little cool after Italy and Sophie put on the heating to air the rooms for a while.

Rhia announced her intention soon after to go to bed. Sophie was tired also, but the journeying home had made her agitated and she wasn't ready to sleep just yet. Making her way to the video shelf she searched for Rhia's film and dimming the lights she settled down to watch it once more with all the new knowledge she had gleaned from the moments Rhia had let down her guard.

As she sat in the light from the flickering screen, she realised now that Eastwood played a photographer, and that Meryl Streep played the married woman. The roles had been reversed. But this time she felt their pain as though it was Rhia's and therefore her own. The short time they had had was measured in days together, but the love had lasted a lifetime and though they had never seen each other again, she had kept his memory in her heart until she was sent his belongings on his death and the book he had dedicated to her. She chose her family over love. Was this what Sean had done? Had Rhia wasted all these years waiting for his return and was he actually dead? So many scenarios. Sophie had eventually to concede that only two people knew the truth and one was absent and the other tight lipped. She went to bed unsatisfied and emotional, sad that her friend and mentor had seemed to have lost her way from what should have been a happy and fulfilled life because of a broken heart.

CHAPTER FIFTEEN

Unbeknown to Sophie, Rhia had pottered quietly from her room in search of some painkillers for her aching feet and stopped dead in her tracks as she heard the familiar dialogue of the film that symbolised her years of quiet grief. She had retreated quickly back to her room, but her heart was racing. Walking over to the window she stood and looked at the dark starlit sky, and for a moment she was lost back in those dark days that had started the slow descent into a temporary madness and was with Sean once more.

1995

They had managed a most blissful four days in France after Sean had met her close to Dover using a bogus job as his excuse to get away. Travelling down to Brittany with just a tent and a couple of sleeping bags and two changes of clothes, they found Josselin and pitched by the river, laying naked in the sun between swims. They wandered round the local villages in the daytime drinking wine and coffee and eating bread and cheese.

The three nights, they spent curled up together by the campfire designing the home and the life they would one day have. Arguing animatedly over the right materials and how they would build it, they would end up making love and any differences would be settled by who was the most dominant at that moment and Sean would usually win. The time passed too quickly and as they packed slowly on the final day ready for the return journey, it was with heavy hearts.

"I'll always remember this place," he had said as they embraced one last time before climbing in the car.

"And I too," she had whispered.

They held hands all the way home as he drove one handed, only letting go to change gear until they had to board the ferry. They returned to find her car at the Leather Bottle and transferred all her things over. One last kiss, one more goodbye... always goodbyes.

The Summer left just as quickly as it had come, and the season began to turn with the colours of the trees. With it there came a slow withering of trust and a growing desperation to return to the wonder of those first few months. It was not to be. By September there were long intense discussions on the phone. He couldn't get free to see her and she sensed he wasn't really trying. Seeing him briefly in a pub close to the M6 for two strained hours after he had finished a shoot in Preston late in the month. They made love in the back of her car behind kennels, hardly romantic. He came quickly and selfishly, which was unlike him, and she received him with the sound of agitated dogs barking to sully the moment and nothing precious to remember. At least she thought so at the time. Fate and its little games were starting to trace her footsteps.

They parted with a slow, pain-ridden kiss on the services, and he left her in the car park with his wife and kids five minutes away. They were going to Edinburgh for a family wedding, and she had driven from London to meet him on route there. Rhia did the decent thing, or maybe the foolish thing and left quickly before they arrived, With the knowledge that she really did not want to see it all laid before her and driven home on this particular day. Instead, she fled, taking herself away quickly, not knowing when the next chance to see him would arise. It was an empty feeling and unrewarding, being the part time partner to a part time married man she thought. The drive home was tedious and emotionally painful. Her head filled with conjured images of domestic bliss, her heart with lead as he drove his family in the opposite direction.

Two days later, as if sensing her disillusion, he phoned her and told her to watch a Clint Eastwood film, The Bridges of Maddison County, the most tragic, subtle, and heartbreaking story of a love affair with no hope. It was a triumph of direction and performance.... He had said it was their story, except in this instance he was Meryl Streep. At the time she had laughed, but he had been serious. She was instructed to watch for the moment where the woman had her hand on the door handle of the family truck and perhaps then Rhia would understand how he felt. So, she sat and watched, and she sobbed brokenly throughout the film, especially at the pain and the poignancy of that moment and the intensity of the unending love it portrayed. Once again, the doubts fled, and she truly believed he loved her. He was creating their story as a grand passion. It was to be a further four years before she realised, he had a talent for doing just that.

Late October she went on a cruise she had promised to her ageing mother now widowed and she had raced across the Grand Bazaar at a stop in Istanbul to buy him the identical bracelet worn by Clint Eastwood in the film. It was a crazy lovers' trick to cross the world just to buy a love token she thought as she rushed through the chaos and bargained for all she was worth. Her goal achieved she returned to the ship; silver band held like a treasure. She couldn't wait to be home and give it to him. She wanted so much to have the word 'Certainty' engraved on the inner edge, again for a quote from their film, but couldn't risk it being seen. He knew it was woven invisibly into the metal and loved the gift saying that was how he felt, "Never more certain." To Rhia, the bracelet symbolised his declaration and the bond. It had been the highlight of a holiday that otherwise was a disaster with bad weather and permanent seasickness and a longing to be home and with him once again.

By the end of November in a complete and shocking reversal, he was certain that they had to end. Lynne was asking questions as friends of hers had mentioned seeing him through the window as they dined at the Leather Bottle pub. He was in the car park, (hopefully, after she had left). Unless they had been hinting to flag up a warning and were keeping the fact that they had seen more. That way they at least could be good friends and cause Lynne to consider where her husband had actually been that day, without totally dropping him in it. Telling a friend her husband was unfaithful never usually received a great reception, however well meant.

The remark had been casual, but the damage done as he said his wife had rung him at work to ask, "and what were you doing in Cobham then?" He told Rhia it *had scared him half to death and after a day of abject misery he had realised that he just couldn't live the lie anymore and jeopardise his family, it was making him ill.*

Receiving only her shocked silence, he continued that he was trying to teach his kids decency and honesty in a crazy world and felt a complete hypocrite. He just could not take the risk. Deep within, she knew it to be true. She had driven a wedge by having expectations that he might care enough to consider making a life with her. Had he but known, she had had her reasons.

The moment he said the words, from a phone box in the suburbs of London, so as not to have the call register on his mobile, something cold settled upon her and she cried silently on the other end as he pleaded with her to talk to him, to say something. 'I'm forty-one and pregnant' seemed hardly the right response as the words gagged in her throat with the shock. Instead, she swallowed them down, placed the phone in the cradle and ran to the bathroom to vomit.

The phone rang and rang repeatedly for ten minutes as she retched until he gave up, a little too soon she thought, and crawling into bed, she curled in a foetal position as the realisation came over her that he was gone. Her gut felt like she had been hit by a basketball as the adrenalin raced through her, A great believer in chakras she knew the solar plexus was where we feel real emotion. The blow had taken her joy and replaced it with a small growing life to fill the void.

She lay in stunned silence, not crying now, yet her mind exploded with conversations, moments stored and the overwhelming knowledge that he could leave her. Nothing made sense, they were so in love. How would she carry his child and not tell him? Eventually she slept, empty with the effects of the shock that had raced through her body that his nervously spoken words had generated. But he had left her and sorted himself and his family out with no regard at all for the pain he had laid at her door. As with most of her life, she was on her own in this.

He rang the next day and offered 'we can still talk to each other?' The triteness of it brought real anger and despair for the first time and she told him in a voice that didn't even sound like her. "All or nothing. Unlike you, I don't do grey half-life," She had spat through tight lips. His voice broke as he tried to persuade her that he was doing it for all the right reasons. Hanging up on him once more, she went back to bed where she stayed for days.

Three months passed and her hair started to fall out daily, even her hairdresser was amazed as she had such strong hair normally. Its texture had completely changed. Friends worried, tried to get her to go out, mistaking her pallor for grief and her weight gain for comfort eating.

For a time, she shunned them all in despair at not being able to hold on to anything precious. For at eighteen weeks old, the small foetus... their child, that she had held in her belly, secret and unannounced not even to her friends, announced itself, in a bloody and painful miscarriage.

There had been no doctors' visits, no funeral, but she couldn't bear to flush the little premature soul, which had been a girl, unceremoniously away. Instead, she took the baby in a small box up into the woods near her studio and created a pyre and there she stood until the fire had burnt away and cooled. Half mad with grief and paralysed from the moment she lit the flames until hours later when she gathered the ashes of her lost child into a small box and walked back to the mill that housed her studio. Putting the box inside a jewelled box and out of sight of visitors, she walked to the bed she had made with pallets and a mattress, lay down and slept. It was the sleep of a deep depression.

A week later he rang. It had only been a short time and yet her life was in tatters to such an extent she could barely speak. Their baby was gone, and it was never likely to happen again, she wanted him to cradle her and tell her everything would be all right. That there would be a house on the slope of a valley in Switzerland and children, his, and theirs to fill it, but she knew it would never happen now.

"I miss you," he had said quietly "Please let's just at least support each other through this," and in a moment of complete despair she agreed. They started to talk, a couple of times a week at first, but she never spoke of the child to him, or anyone. Yet in her heart, the baby had a name... Estelle, named for the stars and the knowledge that their child would have been the most perfect creation cut the loss like a physical pain across her breast. She also had learnt to hold the unrelenting grief of having that precious thing taken from her within and the need to bear it silently, but she allowed herself the comfort and consolation of his voice.

Slowly, painfully, they mended the breach and acknowledged the need for each other, spiritually at least, but for six months there was no mention of the physical. It hovered unspoken in polite over casual conversations which ripped tiny strips off the façade she now called her heart. To talk of sex would be to rekindle and they would be a full relationship again, so he kept away from the subject. This way he could assuage his guilt on both sides yet keep the comfort of her unspoken love.

She started to think he had the best of both worlds. A passionate tragic affair to ease the boredom and a wife and three kids in cosmopolitan normality. Now she truly was the other woman, with nothing real or any thought of a future in exchange for the pain. What remained was like a radio play, performed across the airways with no real substance or growth. An empty fantasy that lasted for several months.

The meetings were few, far between and painful. Always close to breaking the promised boundaries and into the physical but otherwise going nowhere. She bit her lip to keep the friendship intact, it was all she had of him. Maybe...if she let him step back, he may start to realise the unconditionality of a love that was worth having. They were two years in, and Rhia had started to try to rebuild her life and returned to theatre work. She had even tried dating in the hope of a miracle, but only ended up with several disasters and so retreated, avoiding male company entirely.

The longing was as strong as ever. There just wasn't the proximity to make seeing each other easy and so emotions floundered and a depression started to set in with Rhia once more. Still, they carried on like two weary protagonists, neither wanting to give in and walk away.

This carried on into the next year, until in June she had a major theatre job that required her to hire a carpenter. He was good at joinery. "It's a week's work, six hundred quid,'" she said, "Do you want it?"

"I'll take it...It means we can have a week together," he replied. The course was set.

A whole week working together, the set was being built on the floor beneath her studio as it was a 30ft revolve and two tons of staging that had to hold fifty children safely. It meant they may have to work long hours and sleep in the studio until it was done, such were the timescales.

He arrived Monday pm, and when she saw his beautiful, ravaged face and the rucksack and tool bag slung across his back, it took her back to that very first night and she was lost. For the sake of propriety, they stayed on either side of the design board for an hour and talked costings, set changes and structural strength. She only dared to look at him fully as he studied the drawings and noted how his hair was showing more grey.

He glanced up and she smiled "Tea?" She asked and she moved away to put the kettle on and before she knew he had pulled her round and kissed her with a full two years' worth of withheld passion. A mattress scattered with cushions and velvet rugs became their home for the next few hours.

The week was glorious. Her design students worked with them. Lunch would be made for twelve on camping stoves and in microwaves and the work progressed in a party atmosphere. Rhia's heart sang every minute of those few precious days and the students working with them sensed their happiness and it made for the most lighthearted of times. The weather was kind, and every perfect day ended with just the two of them sitting on the fire escape of the studio, glass of wine in hand and just watching the activity below on the river.

The studio was set above a canal and the river ran alongside. The mill was surrounded by woodland and eighty feet up they used to watch the heron swoop round the corner almost close enough to touch, pursued relentlessly by a crow desperate to attack the larger bird. Her good friend in the neighbouring studio always believed that crows were the message-bearers, but she had yet to see what the message was. They were exhausted, dirty, and unbelievably happy. Late evenings they would wash away the dust and spend the remaining hours before the night got too dark making love. Some nights they just collapsed exhausted and curled around each other to sleep instantly.

All too soon Monday loomed and with the growing light in the sky came despair. At dawn he kissed her as he woke. She lay still and watched him dress, lay equally still as she watched him pick up his bags and walked to the door, He turned at the door, looked at her intently and left. As the door closed, she rolled silently over into the fetal position once more filled overwhelmingly with a quiet pain, hoping to lose consciousness in sleep. The idyll was over, and reality came back like a boot in the gut.

At eight am the call came but she missed it, having finally fallen into a deep sleep. The answerphone relayed his message quietly and emotionally. His words filled her equally with love and despair.

"I just wanted to say I got to see another part of you this week, and how you are so respected by your friends and students, and I just wanted to say I miss

you." His voice broke, "So there it is..." The phone clicked and was silent.

Everything reverted to as it was. Rhia worked, came home, slept, woke up and worked more just to erase the loneliness. He had made his bed in her head and had decided he was going to conduct his Sunday morning lie-in there for eternity, or so it seemed.

The phone calls continued, but there was something different now. In her head she knew it would never come to anything, still the idiot gene she must have been possessed of held her fast, hoping for better. One hot evening in July he called, and her heart soared.

"Can you meet me at Watford Gap tomorrow, I'll book a room, I need you," were all the words she needed to hear, and on a thundery, incredibly humid afternoon. The door knocked and she opened it to him. Within seconds they were making love against the wall. 'I should have brought condoms,' he groaned, and she couldn't help but wince at the thought that he had never cared before. Maybe this time would be her swansong and a last chance for a child with him. Even to her it smacked of desperation.

The rain continued and the air cooled as they slept entwined. They woke and ate strawberries, drank wine, and talked of anything and everything rather than what was really happening. Then they slept again and awoke to make love once more with a gentle erotic tenderness as though this time was their last.

She could not have savoured those moments more. Even if she had known that she would have one more meeting two weeks later, where he would lay her down in a wood in Essex and she would receive him as her heart broke in the knowledge that he was leaving to move to Munich.

He had rung her a few days after Watford gap to deliver the bombshell, admitting that he had planned to tell her then, but couldn't bring himself to say the words. She had been struck dumb with the pain once more, whilst a river of tears flowed down her face as he pleaded with her to talk to him. The words wouldn't come, as her heart fractured into a thousand jagged and painful pieces that felt like each shard was fighting through her chest wall with every ragged breath.

He asked her to meet him for lunch in Essex. The walk in the woods would be the last chance they had to be lovers before he emigrated to Germany. As he sat there lost for words and she sat there equally silent, he reached out his hand to take a stray lock of hair from her face and tucked it behind her ear.

"You are more beautiful today than I have ever seen you" was all he had said.

She couldn't help but embrace the words of advice her friend had given. "Let him go with dignity, he'll adore you for it." she had said. Rhia thought that it was her only defence to not to lose her control completely and beg him to stay, so she remained quiet and calm.

"When?" was all she could muster.

"Next month," was his equally quiet answer. His eyes searched hers for emotion and found none. She had it all trapped in her solar plexus, and it felt like white heat searing her from within, but she remained, for his sake and hers, unmoved.

"And how long have you known?" She asked. He looked down uncomfortably and she had her answer…this had been coming for some time.

"A few weeks…I didn't want to upset you."

"But you did anyway," came the quiet answer and the cynic in her realised that he had known, even when he came to help her with the set. He had rekindled the physical side of their relationship knowing he was

going to leave, and she half despised him for his selfishness. As she climbed into her car seat and buckled up, he leaned in and kissed her. Tears started to fall, and he wiped them away.

"Please don't cry darlin," Was all he said, his own eyes full.

She brushed the tears away and started the car. It stalled. After a few awkward minutes where they had to behave normally whilst he gave her a jump start, the engine sputtered to life. He stood silently and watched her leave. A few miles later, sobbing all the way down the motorway, she pulled into a service station and went to the loo having run out of tissues. His lovemaking in the woods had triggered her overdue period. She shrugged resignedly.

'No swansong for you girl' she thought with a quiet bitterness as she looked at her ravaged face in the mirror, oblivious of the curious stares she was attracting ' and no reason for him to come back to you.' It was over.

Sensing her impending decline she realised she should not be alone and opted to spend a week on the east coast with another close girlfriend and her very young children. She pinned on a smile and was determined to move on, but deep in her heart she screamed the pain. Determined to undermine her heartbreak the weather was glorious, and they spent most of the week on the beach at the quiet end and read whilst they kept a watchful eye on the kids. Being young they were just content to run in and out of the water every day and eat beef burgers cooked on a portable barbecue for tea. The peace and family atmosphere and having to deal with normality kept her sane. Her friend watched her and worried.

She had been waiting for the phone call that finally came two weeks after he had left, and she was furious with him for leaving her dangling with no reassurance. Taking the phone in her room, her anger spilled over and they had their first real row. He said he was painting a house in France for a friend to earn some money and that the signal was poor, and he expected her to believe his reasons. 'Bullshit!' she had declared, and things deteriorated fast until she very quickly slammed down the phone.

Her friend looked at her, eyes full of concern when she came back into the lounge. "I know you love him, but you need to end this Rhia, it's making you ill" she had said quietly and firmly.

"I'm way past that" she answered wearily.

Three weeks passed, and she was determined to maintain her silence, but it hurt like hell. The temptation to ring him was great but she knew this time it had to come from him.
It did…

Very early one morning the phone rang…" Hi," he said wearily.

'Is that it?' was her response.

"I'm sorry it's been so long; I've been in hospital…"

Alarm bells started to ring. "What do you mean? Are you ok?"

"I lost it after we had the argument and I hit my eldest son for no real reason… I've never hit my kids…and I smashed the place up I was painting, I ended up in a psychiatric unit on medication, they thought I'd flipped. I had to put right the damage I did, and I've probably lost a good friend, at best he'll never give me work again. I shouldn't have rung, but I just wanted to hear your voice. I miss you babe…"

Rhia couldn't raise her head from the pillows as she physically stalled trying to calm all the conflicting thoughts in her head. That wasn't her Sean, he was gentle and kind.

"Are you ok now?'" She didn't know what else to say under the circumstances.

"Yeah, I guess the pressure valve gave, I'm ok, but I never want to feel that kind of rage again, I'm sorry, I just felt pulled both ways and either way I hurt someone, so I did nothing, and I blew."

The conversation continued and she asked him if they were settled in Munich. He told her they had a flat, it was ok for now till they got somewhere permanent, but they were living on top of each other and there had been no privacy for him to ring till now.

"Where are you now? It's too early for you to be ringing from home?"

"Switzerland… I've been doing a driving job… but if I get work now in England it will be easier to see you as I won't have to go home to London." He continued, his earlier apathy lifting. She didn't quite see how that was going to work, but held back from commenting.

All the time he spoke, Rhia's attention was deepening. He had gone from weary to animated in a few seconds.

Previously he had told her that he had met his wife when he was twenty and she had taken every drug available, a product of her sixty's years. She was ten years older than him, and she had introduced him to the delights of sex fuelled by cocaine. Regular use became a habit and she wondered whether he had snorted something before ringing her as the conversation was so bizarre. Surely not at seven am. She didn't do any drugs herself and felt a bit of a hick at her naiveté. It was still better than being broke and having a messed-up head and body, she thought, as she listened to him talking manically. Come to think of it, he was always sniffing up on the phone, a sure sign of overuse. Why had she never thought of it? She had worked long enough in the media industry to recognise the signs.

"Are you sure you're, ok?" she asked again.

"Sure babe, look I'll ring you in a couple of days, bye darlin." He was gone, leaving her at a loss what to think. She lay in bed a good hour trying to make sense of the conversation, but it just didn't make any sense.

The next phone call took two weeks to come. "Sorry babe, I broke my thumb and couldn't work. Lynne is home and watching me like a hawk for some reason, and I didn't dare chance it."

"How did you break it?" she asked.

"Skiing accident." It tripped off his tongue and then he quickly started to ask her what she had been up to, and she was distracted once more. Only later it crept into her head that she must ask him where he had found the time to go skiing in Munich in early October assuming there was snow so early and then, just as quickly it crept out again and was forgotten.

Christmas came and went and no present materialised or call. It seemed such a small thing, but she was hurt by his lack of care over a time when loved ones were supposed to mean everything to you and her heart died a little. January hit with a blast of severe frost and snow and the odd phone-call came, but they were dwindling more and more. Rhia started to think that this was all too much a waste of her energy. He himself seemed lethargic and depressed, when questioned he would just say 'It's no bed of roses Rhi' and that would be all he offered by way of explanation. Was he coming anytime soon? It appeared not, but his reasons always seemed valid. They were four years in.

Things continued the same for the next few months and Rhia found herself just getting through the days. She had finally accepted that she was in a heavy depression and needed help having already withdrawn from work life and retreated to her studio to paint. With the help of a prescription for antidepressants she blanked out the pain and she found a kind of peace in the creative reclusive life she had fallen into. At least it seemed so to her. Close friends, however, saw something else.

She went out locally with friends, but she couldn't find the motivation to network and source work in theatre or tv. So, the woman who was never without work, spent her days sitting on the fire escape that clung precariously to the side of her studio with a glass of red in one hand and a paintbrush behind her ear.

Her comfortable home was left empty, and she rarely came home from her studio in the mill, preferring to stay where the best memories of him lay. Her only entertainment was music and to watch the winter sun go down on the latest spat between the heron and the crow, as her savings were silently melting into the pot of nostalgia that was all he had left in his wake, money was tight, but she managed.

She painted a large nude from a sketch that she had done whilst anticipating a visit from him once and called it Waiting Woman. As she had put the finishing touches to it, the thought occurred that was all she really was now, a women waiting. All her ambitions were dormant. But the spring was coming, and she had good friends and her art. It was enough for now and so she painted prolifically. One could still paint and conjure him, so that's what she did. The canvas rolled out like a manufacturing line, angry, sensual, spiritual but never joyous. Her mentor David, who was already a known artist, more for his difficult and wild nature in some ways, than his , and who had a studio close by, watched with interest and saw the change in her style. He picked up his phone and dialled.

"Hi Betrand, I have an artist working with me that I think you will love. How about you come over next time you're in town and I'll introduce you."

Rhia had completely panicked when several days later he had said his friend, the extremely choosy agent and acclaimed art critic Bertrand would be arriving next week and to have her work ready for him.

"But I'm not ready. I don't even know what type of artist I am!" she had cried petulantly.

"No artist is ever ready and as for what you are...You are an outsider artist" He had replied, which helped little as she had never formally studied art, just design for theatre. "You paint from in here, from emotion.

That's all that matters," he said, punching the spot above his heart.

Bertrand had arrived the next week, circled the work around her walls slowly and nodded.

"Can I take a couple away with me Rhia? I'd like to show them to some people," he had said with a smile, and she had thought 'What a nice man...so unexpected.'

It was a strange time. Her career as an artist appeared to be on the rise, whilst her personal life was taking a dive, and she really didn't care or consider that life was about to change forever.

Rhia opened her eyes with a jump and the room was dark. She realised her hand was over her heart and she had been somewhere else entirely. For how long, she didn't know, but her feet ached, and she eased herself back into bed praying for sleep to come. 'Hold onto the good' she willed silently to herself to banish the hurt. She looked to the stars through the window, to her little Estelle and she sent her love eternal. A small star twinkled back at her, and she was appeased enough to sleep. Clucy, who had been staying with Christina whilst they travelled and who had not left her side since their return earlier, crept onto the bed and lay close to her feet.

CHAPTER SIXTEEN

Mack stretched in the early morning light and turned over to encircle the waist of the auburn-haired girl he had been seeing for six weeks now. She had been in the pub one night and caught his eye and he had smiled mischievously and raised his glass to her. She had been with a group of students from a drama course who were all quite vocal and very soon he and Connor moved further away to chat where they could be heard. He kept a quiet eye on her, nevertheless. She was tall, slim, and heavy busted with wavy auburn hair, classic Irish features and very pretty in a robust, outdoor way.

Mack had learnt very quickly how successful he could be with the opposite sex and had ventured into several experimental liaisons since returning at new year. Sex was always top of the activity list to a guy of twenty and particularly to Mack as he had been a late starter. The London girls were confident and didn't worry too much about telling him what they were interested in. Mostly he was happy to oblige, but somehow it had never gone further than a couple of days before he lost interest, or he found the girls lacking somehow when he compared them to Sophie. They usually moved on without a problem, occasionally a few harsh words, until Anna.

When first she had approached him, it was to rebuke him for not picking up on her best come on look. She had laughed and thrown her long hair back over her shoulder and said, "I'm off to a club now with my friends, but tomorrow I will be in here and I fully expect you to reciprocate when I throw you my best looks, otherwise I'll lose face." She threw a look towards her companions, "I bet them all I could lure you in within the week. You're Mack, aren't you?"

Mack was taken aback that she knew his name and she laughed. I'm not telepathic...I tapped up your friend here on his way to the loo. Connor had just returned, and a slow smile spread across his features. How did Mack do it, it wasn't as though he was pushy. They just seemed to gravitate to him, not that he wasn't grateful as he had benefited himself from a few friends along for the ride. It had to be a combination of that French accent and his Greek ancestry. He might have to start calling him Adonis the way it was going.

Anna had flounced away with a smile true to her word and left Mack open-mouthed thinking there might be more, but she had left with her friends. Her confidence that he would be there when she returned the next day piqued his interest and instead of 'slobbing out' with a pizza on the Sunday evening, he found himself showering and looking for decent clothes to wear. By the time she came into the pub with her friends, he was propping up the bar watching the door for her arrival which she duly noted with a seductive smile before bending her head to her companions and excusing herself.

"Well, I guess we'd better be finding a table if you're going to tell me all about you so I can consider whether I'm taking you home tonight...and let me tell you I don't say that lightly." She looked him square in the eyes and he felt his body responding with a ripple of sexual awareness threading down his stomach.

"You don't?" he asked, and her eyes opened wide and flirtatiously.

"Oh no, but I reckon you and I have already got something we need to work out of our system, otherwise why are you here,

"I could ask the same of you." he smiled, and she nodded to a corner seat.

"Exactly!" she replied.

They had talked animatedly all evening, getting closer as the drinks kicked in. By ten she reached for her bag and stood up taking him by surprise.

"Well...are you coming then Mack? Never let it be said that I'm not a woman who isn't true to her word."

It took Mack a second for the light to dawn before he stood up slowly, finished his drink and on her cue followed her past the group of her friends who could barely hide their smiles. She had led him by the nose and his reward had been a relentless night of pure unadulterated passion that left him exhausted and wanting more. Not only was she an animal in the bedroom, but she had a quick wit to accompany it and somehow it didn't dwindle as with the others. He really liked her, and she was honest to the point of bluntness, but never cruel, so what wasn't to like. The days turned to weeks and the sex slowed to healthy levels which allowed him to catch up with his coursework. What's more she seemed to like him, and they fell into a comfortable partnership that encompassed all their friends. Life was ok. The only thing he couldn't bring himself to do was tell anyone at home...especially Sophie, not that she cared that way, but it just never felt like the right moment.

In France Sophie was in the throes of final prep for Rhia's show. They would only be there for the four days of the 'get in' and the opening itself but she wanted it to be perfect for Rhia. The last few days she was never off the phone and computer, checking and double checking the catalogues, the literature, and the promotional copies of the book that they had been sent. Rhia had watched her with pride, noting how the young woman was showing signs of being as astute in business and organisation as she was talented with her own art. It was a great apprenticeship for when she was ready to exhibit herself and far from stressed, Rhia let her have the driving seat and just waited to approve what she had arranged with little dissent required. By now Sophie was driving like a natural and it was hard to recognise her as English, such was the polish and serenity she had acquired. Nothing phased her and she had become almost fluent in French by now having had to use it as a necessity every day as Rhia's PA.

Once more the bags were packed, and the dog was off to Christina's to be spoiled. Sophie did one last check before ushering an orange clad Rhia to the car. Wow! She hoped she had one tenth of Rhia's dress sense. The suit was linen, but she had dressed it with brown leather accessories and much to Sophie's delight, comfortable but stylish leather clogs. No broken bones on Paris's streets hopefully. Sophie dressed comfortably in jeans for the drive and was determined not to outshine the main attraction in her own dress choices.

Bertrand met them that evening and kissing them both soundly on each cheek, led them to a table in the Hotel restaurant. He was so delighted with everything that had come to fruition, not to mention his cut of the commission, that the atmosphere was almost giddy, and they drew much attention as the champagne flowed.

The exhibition was well received, and the books had been signed and distributed to all the attendees to promote on their behalf. The rest were already en route to the shops and Sophie couldn't wait to take Rhia in as soon as they were on the shelves. It certainly was a beautiful book, reminiscent in style of the Suzanne Seddon Boulet Goddess books that Rhia had said she loved as a young woman, before she had even considered herself an artist she had told Sophie. The descriptions and poems added to the high gloss images were so important and Sophie was very glad that she had convinced Rhia to insist on their inclusion.

They spent a lovely couple of days setting up the exhibition and thankfully, Bertrand had set up a hospitality station with very comfortable chairs in the heart of the activity to encourage Rhia to sit rather than spend the day on her feet. It worked to a small extent, but Rhia wasn't one to be disengaged from the process. She was very hands on, no doubt down to the years she had spent in theatre as a designer. By the end of the day, she was tired and although she would have died rather than admit it, her body was screaming 'Go to bed!' and she would take herself upstairs insisting that the younger woman stay and enjoy her evening. Sophie would use that time to sit in the hotel lounge and undertake the final marketing on social media for the launch. Bertrand had it covered thoroughly but she wanted to learn for her own sake.

This night they had a light meal in the hotel restaurant, and they had dressed for dinner. Sophie was loath to wander about in Paris late alone dressed to the nines, so she stayed put and ordered just a coffee. Rhia liked her wine, but she had had years to get used to its effect, where Sophie got tipsy if she even sniffed its bouquet. She was deep in Facebook when she was aware a shadow had fallen across her.

"Excuse me, but I am sure I know you?" Came a softly spoken voice in English with a heavy French accent. Sophie looked up to see the man who had tried to join her in the cafe in Josselin last Christmas. She coloured slightly in surprise and put her laptop aside holding out her hand for him to shake. This was a different girl to the one who had fled the cafe. For one she was speaking the language confidently now. Her time with Rhia had been equivalent to an old-fashioned finishing school and she greeted him with poise and a smile. She noted he had reverted to English, so she was pretty sure he knew he had met her and where. She replied in French.

"I believe we may, Josselin wasn't it? What a coincidence." He smiled and took the hand offered and she had to admit there was a little frisson of excitement as he brushed his fingers against her wrist.

"It was indeed, what brings you here?"

"Oh, I'm here on business." 'How grown up I sound' she thought smugly. "...And you?"

He nodded to the seat beside her, obviously worried that she would flee if he took any liberties and waited for her to nod in consent before sitting down. The waiter, on the ball, came to take his order and added another coffee to his gin and tonic on her refusal for anything alcoholic.

"I'm here for an exhibition launch. We have a local artist who is very well known, and I hoped if I came in person, she would open our exhibition at the Châteaux where I am the events manager. I needed a break, so it seemed like a good idea to combine the two. She's a bit of a recluse and difficult I've heard..." He tailed off as a sixth sense warned him of the coincidence of them both being here at the same time. "Are you by any chance here for the same thing?"

Sophie smiled wryly. "I could have saved you the journey, I've just posted Rhia's acceptance with my submission." He looked pained as though he had just shot himself in the foot.

"I'm sorry, I didn't mean to be rude, I meant she was difficult to get hold of..." Sophie laughed.

"No. She is difficult, but in the most charming way. I'm her PA and I adore her, you just have to approach her in the right way, she's very strong willed!"

"Forewarned then." He smiled and reached for the glass the waiter had put down and tipped his glass. "I'm Jacques by the way."

"Sophie." she answered.

"To a successful event then." He lifted his glass taking a sip and then gave her his full attention, which flustered her.

"Indeed...to a successful event." He was far too good looking for his own good...and hers she thought.

The event launch was to be at 7pm the next evening and so after spending a pleasant hour chatting to her very attractive new friend and pumping him for information about the Château's coming exhibition, she announced her intention to retire early as tomorrow was guaranteed to be frantic. As she stood, he stood also.

"Till tomorrow then?" he said and held her offered hand too long for comfort. She felt her colour rise in her cheeks.

"Yes, lovely and thank you for all your advice. I'll get onto it when I get home."

"Sophie, it's been an absolute pleasure," he said and raising her hand to his lips, he turned it and kissed her inner wrist and there it was again, that little thrill that shimmied its way down her stomach.

Sophie took her leave of him and was conscious that he was watching her all the way to the lift. When she turned as the doors closed, he raised his hand, and she was very much aware of herself as a woman at that moment. Was this what normally happened between two people when they flirted with each other? she never had a chance to know. How old was he? twenty-eight? thirty-two? Too old really but incredibly attractive. The lift doors closed, and she looked in the mirror on the ascent to find herself flushed and looking very pretty.

"Not bad then," she murmured to herself with a smile.

"Rhia was sat up in bed perusing the guest list for tomorrow and smiled as she knocked and entered.

"I've just met the guy from the Château. He's here for your exhibition." Her sparkle did not go unmissed.

"What's he like?" asked Rhia.

"He's very dishy!" Sophie giggled and she hadn't had a drink for hours.

"Oh, is he? We'll have to keep an eye on him then, won't we?"

"I certainly will be!" laughed Sophie out loud.

"Naughty girl!"

"I'm off to bed, night Rhia, I'll wake you at eight." She blew her a kiss and Rhia returned the gesture. When the door closed Rhia whispered, "Sweet dreams lovely one, just don't get your heart broken." She set aside her papers and switched off the light.

The following day went by like a blur and Sophie sent Rhia back to the hotel to rest and get ready for the evening's onslaught. She stayed behind until she was sure every aspect was perfect and then she hopped a cab and ran in just in time to wake Rhia with a tray of sandwiches and tea before she ran back to her room to shower and change.

Sophie knew there would be no way they would get a chance to eat anything later despite the buffet. Event organisers never did. Besides knowing her luck, she would spill something down the front of her new halter neck vintage maxi dress that she had found in a boutique near Mon Maître and would look like a fool. Rhia would be hemmed in also and she needed to keep her strength up.

At 6 o'clock they alighted the taxi looking as though they had had all day to prepare. Rhia wore a deep purple satin dress and coat with aubergine accessories. When Sophie had chosen it with her, she had said it was in honour of the Waspi Women back home in Britain who had had their pensions stolen and were fighting for justice. "Not all women are as lucky as me to have been successful in life and these women were fighting for their lives and the futures of their daughters. They had been thrust into poverty by a government who had targeted them and thought they would just go away. They didn't... and we should be behind them. If it were in France, the people would be out on the streets by now in protest. It was to Britain's eternal shame that they had shafted mothers and grandmothers for a cash grab to pay off the banking debacle." She was quite passionate about it and Sophie took note and promised herself to look it up on the internet. Rhia continued.

"Women will never have true equality in Britain till there are as many of them in parliament as men. You must never take life for granted Sophie," she had said. "These corrupt bastards in government will have you at every turn. Women must become political and as an artist you will have a choice to use your art for awareness and good, remember that. My days are numbered but I would like to do something to support them, I just haven't thought what it is as yet." Political or not, the effect of the colour on Rhia, with her white hair was dramatic to say the least. She looked every inch the avant-garde artist that she was. Sophie had never idolised anyone in her life, but Rhia left her in awe, and you would never have put her at nearly seventy as she made her way through the guests greeting each of them personally. She was a trouper.

Sophie had to admit she had one eye on the door for the illusive Jacques but as yet he hadn't appeared. Was she piqued? Maybe… Perhaps he had been delayed? The evening wore on and he was obviously not coming. 'How rude!' she had thought, especially to Rhia who she had just persuaded to attend his poxy exhibition. She was seriously miffed, and her inner dialogue forgot her newfound sophistication, but more insulted for herself if she were honest. Maybe she had got the attraction between them wrong.

The evening was a huge success and Rhia was glowing with all the compliments. Sophie felt proud she had been part of it. They walked into the hotel reception tired but happy when the receptionist hailed them.

"Mme David…I have a message for you." Sophie barely recognised her own name with the French accent and the receptionist called her again.

Handing her an envelope he said. "Monsieur Arbonne asked me to give you this with his apologies." Sophie opened the envelope to find a slip of hotel headed notepaper. His mother had had a heart attack and he had been called home suddenly. Could she please give Rhia his deepest apologies and wished her every success for the evening. He would be in touch on his return to Josselin.

"Oh dear." Sophie said, giving the note to Rhia. She perused it for a moment and smiled at Sophie with mischief in her eyes...

"Not quite the shallow bastard you thought he was earlier perhaps?"

"I didn't...well maybe I did a little." Sophie reddened. Rhia was far too astute.

"Let's have a liqueur and a coffee down here, I'm too excited to go to bed just yet." She made her way to a large comfortable sofa and took up residence. The waiters were there immediately to take their order. There was something to this being a name thought Sophie as she sat down. Rhia put out her hand between them and caught Sophie's. "Thank you for making this evening so special, lovely one. Have you enjoyed it?"

"I have Rhia...so very much."

"Good." She patted Sophie's hand affectionately. "It will be your turn soon...Ah coffee!" she exclaimed seeing the waiter's approach.

CHAPTER SEVENTEEN

The summer was at its zenith and hot once more when Mack packed his bags to finally come home for the holidays. He was going to be there until the last week of August and he was so looking forward to seeing his parents and the peace of home for a while. To say it was reciprocated was an understatement. Christina had cleaned his room, rearranged the furniture in the lounge and gardened till she was ready to drop, such was her excitement at having her boy home. John smiled and remarked that he wished she got this excited when he came home. "I'm lucky if I have a meal prepared!" he teased.

"Cheeky!" she laughed. "I'm used to you going, but I always had Mack for company till now. Thank God I have Rhia and Sophie, it would feel so isolated otherwise without him."

"Have you told Sophie he's bringing a friend?" he asked pointedly.

"Not yet, he only told me Tuesday and I haven't had a chance."

"Is it serious, do you think? He talks to you." John pulled out a chair at the kitchen table and sat down with a coffee.

"Not about this, she's coming here so it's got to be serious on some level." Christina couldn't help but be a little sad. In her heart she had hoped her son would naturally gravitate to Sophie, but it appeared not.

"Well, I suggest you warn her, it's going to be a bit of a surprise to say the least when he turns up with an entourage. Where's she sleeping by the way?"
"His room on a camp bed would be fine, he said."

"It's serious then." John answered wryly.

"I'm worried how Sophie will react, she's been asking when he's home and has said she will do a barbecue at Rhia's to celebrate. What should I say?"

"The truth? That he's bringing a female friend, and she will have time to prepare herself. To dump it on her without warning would be unfair. Besides, surely, he's mentioned her to Sophie, they're in contact often enough." Christina sat down with her husband.

"Do you know, I don't think he has, she would have said something. It's a bit remiss of him don't you think?"

"It's a bit bloke of nearly twenty putting it off until he's no choice more like!" said John "Anyway, it's his life, we can't live it for him. What time is his train tomorrow?"

"No train, they're driving, she has a car apparently. She's staying a few days before heading to meet her parents in the south. That's all I know."

"Independent young woman then, I expect she's running rings round him, like you did with me!" He grinned and took a sip of his coffee as her eyebrows shot skywards.

***

The time since returning from Paris had been frantic for Sophie. There were all the enquiries that had to be answered on Rhia's behalf that she had taken on board. Rhia was tired on the return and letter answering and phone calls were tedious for the older woman who much preferred the painting rather than the business side.

Sophie crammed in as much as she could into the mornings so that she could still find time to paint with Rhia in the afternoons. She was amassing quite a body of work and Rhia had insisted she put some up alongside her own on the walls. If Rhia had worried that Sophie would put too much of her influence into her work, she needn't have. Sophie had developed a unique style of her own, using layers of colourful tissue amidst the paint which was quite unique. When Rhia had questioned her on how she had thought this up her answer was simple... "It just came to me." Rhia had thought that was a good enough explanation for any artist.

The exhibition at the Château was scheduled for just before Christmas as was tradition and it was always a wonderful atmosphere around the town then. It had been a few weeks since Paris and all she had heard of the mysterious Jacques was that his mother had passed. His assistant would be handling correspondence on the exhibition for the next few weeks. Life took over and Sophie only thought of him when the need for information required her to contact his assistant on her own or Rhia's behalf. She had hardly met him for more than an hour. It was only natural other things would take over for him at such a sad time and she would be forgotten, so she let it go. She had so much of her own work holding her interest that really thinking about any romantic ambitions didn't occur.

Sophie was naturally looking forward to her friend's return and she had shopped to stock up for the barbecue. Rhia had smiled when she had produced the idea of building it from some old oven racks and stone from the surrounding areas.

Rhia thought back to the days when she had buried herself in the building of the house and the satisfaction of laying the wall stone by stone. Looks like Sophie was a chip off the old block, and she had watched her bring a few pieces of stone home every day and didn't ask where she got them. She suspected there were a few local walls with gaps nearby. Sophie had bought cement and when the day came to put it all together, she had refused to come in until her project was done. When she did it was eight at night and she looked a sight with cement dust everywhere. Rhia had watched with pride on the terrace as she worked out the design and bit her lip when she wanted to intervene. It was Sophie's project; Rhia had had enough of her own.

The next morning Sophie checked all had dried and laid in the finishing touches and that evening she had lit it just for them to test it out. The two of them had sat in the evening sun as the kebabs Sophie had made sizzled and gave off a delightful aroma, drinking wine and chatting on life in general.

When Christina had said Mack was driving back, Sophie had wondered as he hadn't taken a car. She had called for coffee early in the morning, which was unusual. As they all sat around on the veranda Christina took the plunge.

"I think a girlfriend is giving him a lift and she is staying a few days." Christina gave a pointed look to Rhia, and she acknowledged it with one eyebrow before looking to Sophie who sat very still for a few seconds before responding.

"Oh…I didn't know, he didn't tell me." The silence that followed was enough to tell Christina that it had been a blow. She tried to compensate by telling them she wasn't sure if it was a girlfriend or just a uni buddy. Either way Sophie would have been hurt not to be told. She could see that. After a few seconds Sophie recovered.

"Well, you'll have to invite her to the barbecue of course…7pm tomorrow by the way." She said with a laboured smile, as politeness dictated, she offered.

"Thank you honey, I will, it's very kind of you and I'm very surprised at him for not telling you first." Christina was cross that he had placed her in this position, they would be having words at some opportunity.

"That's ok, we're only friends." Sophie put on a brave face, but they could see she was hurt. Christina hoped that the barbi would break the ice and get them back on a normal footing.

"Fabulous job you did on the barbecue. I could never attempt anything like that, I just have the ideas and John ends up with the work!" Christina's compliment was received with a quiet 'Thank you' and she suspected Sophie was close to tears and she was cross once more with her son for placing her in this position.

Rhia had been sitting quietly till now and then she reached out a hand to squeeze Sophie's reassuringly.

"This girl can do anything she sets her mind to, she's amazing!"

"You'll make me blush Rhia" Sophie had regained her composure, a sign that she was maturing.

"Not at all, well deserved lovely one."

Whatever Sophie was feeling, she covered it well and with grace and they chatted amiably for an hour. As

Christina left the younger woman realised that her reason for coming had been to warn her. Closing the door her face lost its smile. How could Mack have not told her and why? It seemed so cruel.

"You ok?" Rhia had come out of the kitchen to check on her.

"Yes… a bit of a shock and I can't believe he didn't tell me, but I'm not his keeper. Let's hope she's nice!" With that she brushed off any further probing and went to the computer to check the emails. Her stiff back was all Rhia needed to see to back off. Rhia left her to gather her thoughts and went in search of turpentine for her brushes.

Sophie was quiet all day, but Rhia knew this would be expected. Sophie was not a young woman to release her emotions easily. More likely she would hold them in until they blew.

Most of the time she was level headed and was comfortable speaking her truth, which considering the circumstances of her upbringing, was a blessing, she could have been much more damaged. She was very level and forthright in her dealings with Rhia's affairs and that's why she had been given such responsibility so soon. It was natural for her to be upset in this instance.

Mack was her only close friend and she would have had expectations that at least he would confide in her and not leave it to his mother. Rhia was surprised at Mack, she had always found him open and honest, so why hadn't he been so with Sophie? It was pointless to use conjecture. 'What will be, will be,' she mused.

The next day Sophie spent all afternoon preparing for the home coming party, although she felt too hurt to consider it as such. Anyway, it was a party for all those she held dear, and she wanted it to be right. She dressed casually but with care. It had been many months since she had seen Mack and she wanted him to see how she had come forward under Rhia's guidance in knowledge and culture. He was just a little older than her, but they say women mature earlier than men, so they would see.

Christina had returned home and was just preparing a light lunch for them all when John shouted, 'They're here!" and she put down her knife and went to greet them. They were just getting out of the car when Christina reached the drive and John was already hugging his son. A tall statuesque girl with a mass of fiery hair was standing waiting to be introduced and Christina walked over to them. John had released Mack and he turned to his mum a little nervously. She embraced him lovingly but not too 'momsy' so as not to embarrass him.

"Oh, I've missed you so, welcome home darling! Now introduce me to your friend."

Mack put a proprietary arm around the girl's shoulder as he made the introductions. Her name was Anna, and she was a drama student, he had said. Christina kissed her in the way of the French on both cheeks and stepped back to let John greet her also. She was pretty in a wholesome way and certainly confident, that much was evident by her response. No nervousness here, she thought.

Mack stood back and watched his mum quietly, he wasn't stupid, he knew she would be cross with him springing Anna on her without warning, but it had been a last-minute thing from his girlfriend who had a very charming way of boxing him into a corner until she got her way. So, his train ticket had been refunded and he had tanked up her car with the money instead and they were on their way before he had a chance to think it through.

"Come on then, let's get you settled and then by the time you have done that lunch should be ready," said Christina with a brightness she wasn't really feeling. She had wanted her son to herself really and a visitor hadn't been on her list of desirables on his first-time home.

She waited till they got their bags with John's help and then led the way. Stopping at the kitchen to hand them a cold drink to take upstairs whilst they unpacked. She watched them take their things upstairs and noted that this girl was at the opposite end of the spectrum to Sophie physically. She was Athena to Sophie's Aphrodite. She walked back in the kitchen where John joined her. Christina looked at John as he pinched a tomato from her carefully arrange halloumi and grilled pepper salad and she tapped his hand with the back of her knife.

"Do that again and you lose a finger!" Her husband grinned mischievously, and she raised the knife in warning.

"He seems different somehow, he looks different..." She said.

John snuck another small tomato off the plate and popped it in his mouth with the words "He's popped his cherry, course he's different!" He had grinned widely but quickly realised a mother's feelings would be different.

Christina gasped at Johns humour, but her eyes welled with tears as only a mother can, that her son would no longer be her boy. He was a man now and she had to start treating him as such. Always an emotional time for a mother, when you must accept that they have taken a step from your protection and made a life for themselves, good or bad.

"Big softy!" John had said quietly understanding the moment.

"I know, I know, I'll be all right in a minute." she replied as she blinked the tears away.

The lunch was pleasant enough and the dynamics positive. Anna was polite and confident in conversation, if a little pushier than Sophie, but that was not always a bad thing in this world. The times they were changing, and women would need to be strong the way things were going. The world, it seemed, was taking a backwards step in every way, and she was grateful to be in her bubble out here in rural France and not fighting her way daily through the City of London.

Mack was getting on well at Uni and quite happy as he told her where he was at in his studies. His ultimate goal was IT consultancy that would take him round the world, not just confine him to a sectioned off desk in a glass tower somewhere. For that kind of career, you had to be good and so he was studying hard despite Anna's best efforts to distract him. However, he had to admit he was never going to turn into some computer geek with Anna around, she had him out partying and to the cinema and theatre every week for something related to her studies. He had even seen her act in a small role at a local drama studio recently and he had to admit she was good.

He had left Anna having a shower, despite her best efforts to drag him in for a quickie and made his way downstairs. Sex in his digs in London was fine, but his mother's shower was taking the rip a bit, and so he politely declined and came downstairs slightly damp with her efforts. His mum was putting the lunch dishes away. She turned to him, and raised an eyebrow as she spoke quietly.

"So, are you going to tell me why you left it to me to tell Sophie you have a girlfriend?" The disapproval was evident.

"It's not serious mum, and Anna kind of sprang the idea on me when she had decided to join her parents on holiday. I'm sorry, I should have told you, but I didn't see any need. We're just friends really, Anna and I."

"Friends with benefits mmn?" She knew her son was going to experiment, but the girl he was with obviously liked him and she didn't like his dismissing her so easily. He had the grace to blush.

"Anna's pretty fierce and very independent," was his defence.

"Don't kid yourself son. A girl doesn't drive across France with a boy she's not serious about...and what about Sophie, why have you not told her? I could tell how hurt she was, you're supposed to be friends." He sat down at the table embarrassed.

"I really like Sophie mum, I always have, but she's not interested in me. So, what am I supposed to do. Besides I'm away for another two years, it would have been pointless."

Christina put the last of the crockery away. So, her son had been attached to Sophie, she had thought as much and in a way he was right. Two years is a long time in a young man's life and Sophie had been so damaged when she had first arrived. A boyfriend would have been the last thing on the girl's mind.

"You should go over and speak to her this afternoon before we go tonight, break the ice," she said.

"Don't you think it's a little late? Besides, Anna won't be happy with me dashing off and leaving her to see another girl, will she?"

"Up to you." His mum replied in that way that was so annoying when he knew he had been remiss, and she was right.

An hour later and slightly miffed, he was walking up to Rhia's door and pushing it slightly open, he called out to Rhia to warn her of his approach. She was standing at her easel painting thoughtfully. Her strokes on this occasion, small and precise. It was interesting how her style changed with her mood. She had heard her name called and was just finishing her stroke to be able to walk away happy in its completion and greet him.

Wiping her hands on a rag, she held out her arms to embrace him.

"Lovely boy! How are you?" she cried.

"All the better for seeing you Rhia," he replied affectionately, receiving her embrace. She embraced him whilst holding her paint-stained hands away so as not to spoil his clothes.

"Sophie's out in the garden setting up the barbecue area. She was so excited she wanted to celebrate your homecoming." The words spoken with no agenda still made Mack wince internally.

"I'll just nip out and see her," he said, and Rhia gave him a knowing look.

"Yes, you do that. I expect she'll appreciate you coming over on your own."

Mack slipped out through the veranda door to the terrace where Sophie had set up an area for all of them to sit comfortably. She had also set up a long table, that she had dressed with citronella candles and flowers that deter insects to indulge her artistic side. She was making some final adjustments with her head down and hadn't seen his approach and he stood and watched her for a second.

Here wasn't the rosy-faced girl in the woolly hat he had tried to kiss last Christmas, but a young, olive skinned and extremely shapely woman with slender fingers and the glossiest of dark hair falling softly across her beautiful face. The change in her took his breath away. He felt like there was years of difference in her and she bore no resemblance to the young girl he had left behind just a few months ago.

She must have sensed his presence and looked up from her task, colouring slightly as she raised herself up to her full five feet five inches. The table being between them did not help and he had to walk around it to hug her. She reciprocated but there was a stiffness that was not natural to her.

"How are you?" He asked, unsure of how to begin.

"I'm absolutely fine," she replied. Didn't women always say that when they were pissed off, he had heard somewhere.

"I came to apologise," he said, "I should have told you about Anna, but we haven't been seeing each other that long and it didn't seem relevant somehow."

Sophie pushed her hair back over her ears in a nervous gesture that she had always had since he knew her. "Well, it's not as if there's been anything between us but friendship… I'm just a little surprised you couldn't confide in me as a friend. I thought we were that at least." Her voice, though calm, had a little barb in it and he knew she was unhappy with him. He sat down on one of the chairs to watch her finish the table setting as he talked.

She had on a little lemon shift dress that skirted the top of her knees and a matching bandanna in her hair and she looked like an Italian with her tan. The thing that fascinated him were her lips. They were painted a rich deep red and it emphasised their fullness. The effect was dramatic on her and on him and he felt a rising feeling for her once more. For that moment she had completely banished Anna from his mind.

"I am sorry Sophie; Anna is a bit strong willed and as she was driving down to the south to meet her mom and dad, she convinced me to share the drive with her. It was only decided a couple of days ago." He looked directly at her, and she looked directly back, something the old Sophie would not have done previously, and it unnerved him.

"How long have you been with her then?" she asked.

"A few weeks, that's all."

"So long?... And yet you never mentioned her?"

"I know, I just didn't want to upset anyone unnecessarily."

"Don't you think you achieved the opposite effect?" she shot back at him with a forthright look. "It puts your mum in an awkward position. If you had been truthful in the first place, we would have accepted it for what it was."

"Would you really have?" His question probed and Sophie looked down defensively and continued arranging things that were already perfect.

"But of course, we've only ever been friends and I admit it's a blow that we won't be spending our usual times together, but you have a girlfriend now to think of, so we all have to get used to it." Her words were placatory, but her voice gave her hurt away.

It suddenly felt like a blow to Mack also. He had been so looking forward to coming home and falling into his comfortable routine for the summer. Anna being here would change all that and he hadn't really considered the dynamics of her being here on them all. He was already beginning to regret it, but it wasn't Anna's fault and he had to be hospitable now that she was.

"I really am sorry I didn't tell you sooner Sophie..." He was genuinely contrite, and Sophie's face lost a little of its guardedness.

"I know, it's OK," she said. "You'd best tell me all about her, so I don't appear ignorant when you introduce me."

Mack breathed a sigh of relief. Sophie's generous spirit had kicked in and she had forgiven him a little. He couldn't think of anything worse than hurting her feelings. They chatted for half an hour and then he made his excuses as Anna would be on her own and subject to interrogation by his mum. He gave her a quick hug and left her to say his goodbyes to Rhia. Sophie watched him go. He was still Mack but different somehow. She would have to get used to the fact that he was living a different life and there would be influences on him that would change him. Deep down there was a low-level sadness that she could not define. As though something might have been lost forever.

The hot day had cooled sufficiently enough to make the early evening a pleasant one for sitting out. As Christina and John greeted Rhia, Sophie was left to greet Anna and Mack. Sophie had changed into a deep magenta culotte suit which Mack thought was a little over dressed for her. Having said that, he really didn't know the new Sophie, who had gained a sophistication over her travels that had not been there previously. She handled the introductions with grace and a welcoming smile that would have fooled most people, but Mack noticed when Anna was introduced to Rhia, Sophie had watched intently how she had behaved to the older woman.

Sophie was watching Anna; Mack was watching Sophie and unbeknown to them Anna was closely watching them both at every opportunity. This girl bore no resemblance to how Mack had described his timid friend, and she would have to keep a close eye on her. Mack certainly was and it wasn't a good feeling.

Anna had surprised herself, normally she could walk away from most lovers, but here was one who she genuinely had feelings for and her laissez faire temperament had taken a hit as jealousy reared its head as she watched them both laugh and exchange reminisces with his parents and Rhia.

As the week moved on Sophie had been included in outings, some she refused, citing work, often when Mack and Anna were going somewhere alone. She went on the occasional ones where Christina was present, but being a gooseberry was not her style. Anna's body language had left her in no doubt that she considered three a crowd and although she was polite, Sophie sensed she'd rather she wasn't around.

It meant she saw much less of her friend than she had expected. Though it was a blow, she had plenty to fill her days and time passed quickly. She was also undertaking an online marketing course and one in art theory. If Mack had been unhappy at her lack of uptake on his invites, he covered it well and Sophie had no choice but to acknowledge that Anna was an important part of his life. Whether it would remain the case would be something she could not foresee, but for now any feelings she thought she had had for Mack, she reasoned away as a young girl's crush. Anna's strong and confident manner left her under no illusions that she would be a definite adversary if she crossed the line with Mack and so she retreated into her art and found solace there. If Rhia noticed, she didn't say.

CHAPTER EIGHTEEN

Anna stayed ten days and then feeling she had stamped her mark as Mack's partner, she packed ready for the final leg of the journey to La Rochelle where she would stay the rest of the holidays with family. Every day there would be phone calls and texts from her, and Sophie realised she was ensuring she stayed foremost in Mack's mind, just in case. Mack never acknowledged he was with Sophie on these calls if he could get away with it and she understood his reasons. Anna was a strong personality not to be crossed.

Mack had only left it a couple of days before turning up in old, ripped jeans and a tee shirt to undertake the promised garden overhaul, which he felt was long overdue after Anna's visit had delayed him. He soon settled into an easy routine coming and going doing the odd bit here and there. It meant he could be close to Sophie and every day he came more and more to the realisation that Sophie had left him behind in her new sophistication and her maturity. He was in awe. She was still friendly but there was a strength about her and a serenity that fascinated him. Sophie, however, was keeping him at arm's length mentally or otherwise and he wondered if she did feel more than just friendship.

Rhia and Sophie painted that afternoon as Mack strode up and down with the mower and pruned Rhia's Shrubs only where she had allowed, as his knowledge was limited.

"You two ok now?" she asked.

"I guess so, to be honest I must admit it's better now that Anna has left. I don't mean to be awful because she was nice and all that, but I felt under scrutiny every time I had a chat with Mack."

Rhia wiped her palette knife and turned to Sophie. "She obviously thinks a great deal of him, and they get on well enough. I can't help but think he was feeling a little under pressure from her."

"Did you?" Sophie's interest was engaged. "I thought they got on very well, but she just seemed a little loud for him...am I being bitchy? I don't mean to be."

"Yes, you are, but it's OK, I know what you mean...anyway it's his choice who he sees." Rhia smiled and her eyes twinkled with mischief.

"I guess it is," she said sadly, and Rhia felt for her...

The days flew by, and Mack and Sophie were once again comfortable in each other's presence. The five of them, when John was at home, spent leisurely days together. When John took off on a new project, Christina and Mack would spend much of their time over at Rhia's, only returning in the evenings.

This evening Mack and Sophie had been given dog walking duty and a mission to pick plenty of berries along the roadsides as Christina had announced she would be making them into a pie for each household. She stood in Rhia's kitchen where she was now completely at home preparing the pastry and Rhia sat in her armchair with a coffee watching. Rhia loved the company of the woman more of her generation, although there was fifteen years between them. In between painting sessions, they would chat endlessly about life, politics, and work. Always animated and happy, Mack had to admit that though he was enjoying life in London, his heart was here with these three women who he loved each in a different way. Christina would read and cook to allow Sophie and Rhia to paint and Mack to garden, life went by at an easy pace. Rhia insisted on paying him, saying he would need it to help fund his next year.

The sun had descended in the sky as Sophie and Mack pulled the last few berries from the bushes as they had walked Clucy for Rhia. There was a stillness at that time of night that was almost ominous, and the conversation was interspersed with the odd forage in the brambles and accompanied by the odd yelp when a thorn connected. Sophie couldn't help but think how life would be when Mack went back to uni and the thought didn't appeal.

She watched him walk ahead calling the dog behind him every so often. He was more mature and so much more interesting now he had gained confidence in himself. They had both moved on, yet together there was still the same rapport. Sensing her scrutiny, he turned round again and threw a blackberry at her and questioned "What?"

Missing the blackberry completely, she bent to retrieve it and popped it in the bag. "I was just thinking how quiet it's going to be when you go back."

"Thought you'd be glad to see the back of me," he laughed and threw his arm around her shoulder as she caught up.

"Not at all!" she replied, "Although you can be a pain at times." She threw her arm around his waist, and they walked up the road. A few paces on each had grown quiet with a growing awareness that what had seemed natural a few seconds ago had suddenly started to feel intimate somehow. Their walk slowed and the dog had to keep stopping for them to catch up.

"Sophie, you know how much I care about you, but I'm going to be another two years at Uni and then who knows what…I just wanted you to know."

"I know, but it's been hard for me to tell you how I feel because I have had such things in the past I couldn't share with you… Mack?"

His name was a question and he stopped to look at her. She was so lovely and so Sophie he thought to himself. "Will you kiss me, Mack?" she asked very solemnly.

That wasn't what he thought she would ask at all and for a few seconds he floundered. She carried on.

"I don't know how it feels to be kissed, so I don't know how I feel…but I do want to be kissed by you." She was so honest and gentle that she threw him.

"Haven't you ever been kissed before Sophie?" She shivered and looked down.

"Not in any way I'd wanted to be, I want to know what it feels like when it's special."

"And you think I'm special?"

"To me you are..."

It was his undoing and he reached down and touched the lips that were devoid of make up today with his own and they parted against his touch. Without a minute's thought for Anna, he pulled her to him and kissed her gently at first and then as she relaxed against him and her mouth opened, he pulled her tightly against him and kissed her deeply. The kiss was the most perfect and sensuous thing he had ever experienced, and his hands gathered her as close as he could to continue, when they heard a car coming up the lane. The dog barked a warning and they had to break away and flatten themselves against the hedge to keep safe.

As the car's engine faded away into the distance he looked once more at Sophie and then held out a hand for her. She took it with a look he had never seen before. Like someone taking a decision and committing to it and he was awash with feelings once more. They walked home hand in hand and only broke free as they entered the garden.

Christina and Rhia were sitting in the loungers drinking wine and awaiting their return with pastry at the ready. Neither said a word but Rhia was swift to notice Sophie's flushed cheeks and eyes as big as saucers. She also noticed the way Mack couldn't keep his eyes off her. Something had gone on.

The evening went by until at nine when Christina pulled Mack up and announced her intention that he would be driving as she had drunk far too much. Rhia was a bad influence. Rhia laughed but something in her eyes wavered. She hadn't realised she was drinking that much. 'Time to take stock and pull back' she thought. It could be such an easy decline.

1997

The weeks had been ticking by and with only a rare call from Sean, Rhia's emotions took a downwards turn once more. His promised English work and means for them to be together had not materialised. He had told her he was still settling in, in Munich and the work was scarce. Unknown to him she had put her house up for sale with her original intention of moving to France now turning towards a non-too coincidental need to seek work in Munich.

Such was her unhappiness that she had managed to delude herself into thinking that if she were nearer to him, they could somehow resolve this pain and the situation between them.

Her closest friends noticed the desperation and the drinking. This was not the optimistic and happy go lucky woman they had known previously and Colin, one of her best friends of many years had taken to dragging his portly figure up the four flights of mill stairs to her studio, much against his inclination, in order to get her to come out, more so, to go home. By now she had now completely abandoned her lovely house, preferring to closet herself in 'A box of paints,' as Joni Mitchell would have called her studio. The words of the song were poignant for her but in reality, she was 'drinking a case' of something else on a regular basis and it wasn't good.

She didn't accept normal theatre work when offered, using the excuse that she was currently painting. In truth she was. Work poured from her every day as an excuse to close herself in and not think about anything else.

By five she would pick up the first beer and drink enough to convince herself she was having a great time in her prison of choice. Bertrand was happy with the work she sent him, and the money was starting to come in, so she was fine. He was unaware of her behaviour and where once she had been teetering on bankruptcy there was now a steady trickle of art selling. Bertrand wanted her to do an exhibition, but she had put him off so far, preferring her bubble of unreality back in the studio to real life and success.

She wouldn't go out and so everyone came in. They knew there would be a warm welcome in Rhia's studio and there was always a party to be had there and people congregated, friends and wasters alike. The friends kept a protective eye on her, the wasters helping themselves to her hospitality. It was all good natured, but a none too healthy means of escapism for Rhia herself. She had also started smoking weed and there had been a severe drop in her emotional well-being and the drinking didn't help. She was becoming increasingly dependent on its effects to blot out the days.

This particular spring day had been very lovely, and she had produced some quite interesting work and as her phone began to ring, she raised her head from her current task of property hunting in Munich and reached to answer Colin's call.

"Hi hon," she said quite happily for a change.

"Hiya... Where are you?" came Colin's serious response.

"Do I need to tell you?" she quipped.

"The Mill... Rhia, I need you to come home. Hil and I will meet you there." Hilary was another close friend.

"Colin what's the matter?" Her voice started to lose its humour and a cold feeling started to seep into her stomach.

"I need to speak to you, it's urgent and I'm not talking on the phone, you need to come home. Hilary is coming as well."

This was not like Colin and his refusal to discuss only made her feel worse. The thought flashed in that her other close friend Hilary was being brought in for support, it must be bad.

"Is it Sean, has something happened to him?" She had no idea why Colin would know anything about him as he had refused point blank to meet him, disapproving of his married status as he did, but she couldn't think of anything that would require this level of urgency other than her immediate family or Sean.

"I'm not saying anything till you get home." He refused to answer any more questions and she was annoyed because she really did not want to journey home the half hour it would take without a good reason. She sighed exasperatedly and complied.

"Ok, I'm setting off now." she said.

"Meet you at your house" came the grim reply.

Colin was an actor she had met at college and swiftly become best friends with. Their friendship had matured over several years until he was now like a brother to her. He was very rarely serious and so when he followed her in and put the kettle on, insisting they wait till Hilary arrived, she freaked.

"Colin for Christ's sake, just tell me! You're frightening me!" The door knocked and Hilary walked in shortly after.

"Come and sit-down Rhia," he said.

Hil sat down on the sofa with her, and Colin took the armchair opposite.

"You've got to stop this Rhia," was all he said.

"Stop what?" She was getting angry.

"You've got to stop this search for a house in Munich and you have got to stop this ridiculous affair! It's destroying you!"

Rhia lost her resolve to stay calm. "You've made me come home for this? Really?"

"Hear him out Rhia," Hilary said firmly, and Rhia stopped and looked at her. "Just hear him out please!" She was serious and Hilary was rarely firm.

Colin sat forward in the chair. "Look. we all care so much about you, but he's not who you think he is...I spoke to Dawson today. We are all worried about you. It's not just you he's hurting, there are others...You know how we all network... Well Dawson has been working with a makeup artist and she has told him that she was moving to America with her husband soon, to get away from Sean. Her story was virtually the same as yours but unfortunately for her, she got pregnant, and the husband thinks the baby is his. She had been going through a bad patch when she met Sean and fell for the charm. Sean has been pursuing her and she thought he was genuine, just like you did. She was warned off when someone else let her in on the fact that he is a serial womaniser. She doesn't want anything to do with him, she checked it out and it's true. Rhia...He's not in Munich, He's in Switzerland! You are about to give everything up for a liar!"

Colin was flushed with outrage, and he was trying to keep calm. Rhia just sat with her mouth open whilst Hilary looked on, pale and worried. She had been brought in for backup as Colin was seriously worried that Rhia was on the edge.

"You can't mean my Sean? My Sean? You must be mistaken." Nothing made sense. She could hardly breathe.

"Rhia...Check it out, seriously, check it out! He's in Switzerland. I've also checked it out for you, this is the address. He had no intention of staying with you, He's just some kind of indiscriminate game player. You have got to wise up!" He handed her a scrap of paper and she stared at it not really seeing. Something was coming up from her feet and she felt very strange. She hadn't recognised it as an overpowering surge of adrenalin caused by shock and disbelief.

What followed was a blur, she remembered fumbling for her phone and dialling his number...a woman answered. She caught her breath as Colin snatched the phone and clicked the off switch.

"You have got to calm down, this is not the way." She remembered little other than them both pinning her in a corner of the room whilst she screamed out her despair and rage. They held onto her to stop her hurting herself and hugged her whilst she sobbed as only true friends do. The days that followed went by in a haze for her with thoughts going through her head at the speed of a paparazzi's flash with no respite. She dialled DB and he reluctantly confirmed all that Colin *had said. She found a voice somewhere, thanked him and hung up.*

Someone else had his baby whilst her child that was so wanted, was just a handful of ashes. Her friends had no idea of the news they had imparted and its catastrophic effect. She knew deep down that they only wanted the best for her. No, she must go to see this for herself and somehow, she managed to gather enough resolve to book a flight. She hadn't even packed an overnight bag; such was the state of her mind.

Luckily, her bank balance that had for so long taken a dive in her dejection and apathy had now with the grief and anger pouring out onto canvass, taken an upwards turn and enabled her to book a seat at whatever cost. She rang a taxi to the airport and followed some predestined path to her gate, hardly hearing the announcements. She was aware that she was drawing looks but had no idea that she looked so distracted that people were wondering if she was a mental health case.

Climbing the steps she could barely respond to the stewardesses greeting and she missed the warning nod to another stewardess about her state. Others had dozed on the plane but instead she stared blankly out with swollen eyes at the clouds outside the window.

Everything was a blur, she had nothing on her but her passport, credit cards and anything that was fortunate enough to be in her handbag at the time she left. She stumbled into the first hotel close to Zurich airport and falling on the bed was immediately unconscious...and with no thought of food.

On waking in the early dawn, she showered to pass the time before putting on yesterday's clothes once more, paid her bill and walked to the taxi rank. No one was surprised more than the driver when she handed him the address. It was a good fifty miles away and she looked like she didn't care what the cost was.

Her, staring out of the window when he tried to make conversation in broken English, caused the driver no little concern and eventually gave up on Rhia, sensing there was more to this, keeping a nervous eye on her through the rear-view mirror. The taxi wove its way up green valley sides with houses dotted along the way as she was re-running every moment, every promise, every strange occurrence that she had chosen to ignore in her blind love for him.

Rhia thought she was having conversations, but they were all in her head as the driver followed the road upwards in an ominous silence.

The snow was quite thick on the mountains above and somewhere she registered that she had only brought a thin jacket and then the thought was gone. When they finally pulled into the village, she was surprised to find it was part of a ski resort. Something came in her mind about a skiing injury, 'wasn't that what he had said, his thumb...'

"Here we are lady" The taxi driver handed her back the piece of paper and cut the engine.

"Which house is it?" Somehow, she expected him to say it was a mistake...that the address didn't exist. The house he pointed to was a classic Swiss chalet and very pretty. She sat there and just looked until the driver prompted her.

"Are you ok lady? Do you need help?" he asked, and she almost laughed out loud. It would have been hysterical laughter if she had let the sound go. No... she did not need help and 'Thank you' was all she managed to get out as she paid him and slid out of the car.

There was a cafe across the road, and she headed for it fearing if she didn't get a hold of herself, she would run up and hammer on the door opposite. Sitting herself down on the table outside, she shivered in the thin early morning sun. The cafe wasn't long open, and the *owner invited her in to sit where it was warmer, but she thanked him and said she preferred to sit outside.*

She sat with her coffee eyes transfixed on the house, her fingers gripping the cup for its warmth, she searched for something that would make her feel better. It was not to be, as the first thing she noted was the two cars in the drive, one of which was his. Everything she had prayed was a mistake on her friend's behalf was being opened up before her like a film horror plot, slowly unfolding. The viewer was fully aware of what was transpiring and yet too petrified to look away.

She didn't have to wait for long and was only on her second coffee when the door opened, and two children and a woman came out. There was a shrill whistle and there he was...summoning the woman back for a forgotten bag. She ran back up the path as the kids got in the car and he met her halfway. His hand reached out with the bag, and he kissed her goodbye...probably again. Hardly the grey half-life as he had described so often to her when speaking of his home life.

He waved them off and closed the door as she stared fixated on the place he had been standing, looking every inch the man she had trusted and loved with her life. The adrenalin started to pump through her once again and her mouth went so dry she couldn't even swallow.

Her whole head went light, and she had to grip the table to stay upright. How had she been so stupid, so gullible, so completely naive? How could he have led her along for five years and how had she not seen through him? All the little signs she should have noted, the easy lies, the things that hadn't added up. The constant phone calls at first and then later, weeks going by with just the odd phone call to keep her just hooked enough.

The time had gone by so quickly it hadn't seemed like five years. The imbalance in treatment that kept her self-esteem so low. Where had she disappeared to in all that time that her common sense hadn't kicked in.

Somehow, she managed to get to her feet and pay the cafe owner with some semblance of normality. The smallest task but it took all her concentration. Picking up her bag she walked down the cafe steps and towards the house. As it loomed in front of her, she noticed how neat everything was, how cosmopolitan, how perfect. The house they would have built themselves in Switzerland would have been different, more homely, not so stylish. She almost laughed at herself for comparing... what exactly? The reality of the dream? He had fed her dreams and she had built them in her head whilst he had been building his here in reality.

Colin had done his homework. He had said that apparently Sean's wife earned the real money whilst he played at a career, flying around the world assisting his friend with photography shoots and filling in with odd jobs in between like some shoestring playboy.

She climbed the steps onto the veranda and as she stood there too frozen to move nearer, the door opened and he was there in front of her, ashen faced with shock and something else...anger? He had obviously seen her approach. How many months had it been since she'd seen his face? She couldn't say at this moment.

No words came. Instead, she just stood and stared at him, drinking in everything she had thought beautiful about him and seeing it turned to petulant and weak as the scales fell from her eyes, and her life fell in tatters with it.

"You need to leave now!" he said with a nastiness she had never witnessed before. She was rooted to the spot, unable to speak. Her legs started to shake, and the tears started to fall. He sensed he had an in as she was weak and could be persuaded, rather than threatened.

"Please Rhia, you must leave. She will be back from school soon. Book in the hotel, I'll come see you and we'll talk. I'm sorry! Please, she'll never let me see my kids again!" The talk of children triggered something, and her mouth started to move, silently at first but then she found the words.

"You did this for entertainment? And not just to me....?" It was all she could say as she watched him looking beyond her nervously checking that this wasn't being witnessed, rather than concern for anything he had done to the woman standing before him.

Was there actually anything real about him or was it all just a facade? He was a master, and even now he was reverting to the game to find a way to be rid of her. There were no more words, just an overwhelming pain in her chest that stopped her breath. It was though she was seeing him for the first time. He was a narcissist, preying on women in some pathetic game to feed his ego or perhaps fill a gap he couldn't find in his own life. Good God! and his poor wife was funding his adventures. Her tears stopped and she turned away from him.

"Rhia please, book into the hotel babe, we can talk. I'll ring you!"

His voice was cracking in fear now and she stopped dead in her tracks. Turning round she fumbled in her handbag and drew out her phone. Looking straight at him she raised it to shoulder height and then just opened her hand and let it fall to the ground and watched it shatter before turning her back on him.

She had to get away from here somewhere she could breathe. The snow capped mountains above the green valleys beckoned her. Up there he would be just a pinprick, insignificant as he truly deserved to be. This man she had loved with every fibre of her heart was a nothing and her heart now empty because everything in it that had been his was gone.

She put first one foot out and then another, the effort it took for her shaking legs was immense, but she carried on until she found a path at the end of the street that led to the hills and mountains above. She never looked back.

***

At what small moment, insignificant, unnoticed, does the past start to destroy a future. Is it a progression of *moments that we follow relentlessly without regard for what we may bring down upon us? Or is it truly fate – a slight deviation from the norm that sets us on a path of destruction...*

Rhia sat silently and pondered on the thought. Through the thin material of her skirt the damp earth clawed at the flesh of her thighs. She sat in quiet regard as the mountains, calm, majestically, white capped and unbelievably beautiful beckoned her even higher. She had a choice to make... would she make the right one, or become a pawn at the hands of fate, her own destiny?

How does the end of a life start? Is it a slow realisation? A state of panic or just plain tired of the game. What brings someone to the point where it no longer really matters? and they opt for death with an almost que sera attitude. She rested her chin on her hands and her elbows on her knees, lost in the reasoning.

The evening was drawing on, and with it the cold. All she had to do was stand up and walk down the mountain, or not... She looked at the snow dusted roofs of the village below illuminated by a mixture of early streetlights and oncoming sunset, musing on the scenario that was likely being played out right now by those seemingly intelligent and reasoning people living under those nouveau-riche, cuckoo clock homes.

Such games, such twisted and bitter and selfish games. Games with no humanity. Games for the sake of games, from sheer boredom and with no regard for damage done. Revenge without reason. Manipulation for the sake of ego. In short, activity to break the mediocrity of their lives.

It seemed to her that on the whole, people were just facades, and few of them worthy of trust or even simple regard. This much she had learnt now. It had been a slow process. A gradual peeling away of faith, and in its place a growing cynicism and despair. Each small event chipping away at something innocent and beautiful, till all that remained was the woman sitting quietly and still, awaiting the end of her days...

The stillness of the approaching evening crept insidiously over her, and with it the cold intensified. Yet she felt nothing, for a half smile slowly warmed the face that had recently started to line with five years of pain and longing. The veiled but visible sadness that hovered in the once lovely eyes lifted, and it was as though all had been a mere moment that could be easily forgotten, like some small insignificant memory. Wiped away as once more, she sought sanctuary in a place of ancient times and distant music...her eyes sparkled with some overwhelming and joyous emotion...Certainty.

The first opening chords of massive attacks 'teardrop' echoed through her mind like a distorted overture on an ageing piano and she was no longer on the hillside in Switzerland. Breathing deeply and quietly the air of the mountain that would be her last living memory. It was instead the strong musk of his skin she remembered, telling its own story of their lovemaking that she inhaled, tasted. Once more she was seven years ago, on a red wine scented April evening... trembling, mouth on mouth with an intensity of passion that she had thought only soulmates could create...Skin to skin once more...' Immeasurable...what I feel for you...' The words of a poem she had written for him drifted through the memory and she was lost to the present and all its pain.

Rhia awoke in the dark. She was shivering uncontrollably and couldn't move her fingers as they were so cold. Where was Sean? She needed to find him, where was she? It was too dark to see anything in front of her, she could be on a cliff edge. She sobbed with terror. She had no recollection how she had got there, but she knew she had to get back down to the lights below or die. She chose instead to live.

Staggering to her feet, she cautiously put one foot out and stumbled forward as her eyes adjusted to the darkness. For three hours, step by painful step she made her way back down the mountain, sobbing with relief as the stony ground turned to meadow grass and the lights of the village drew nearer. What gave her the strength she did not know; she would never know. For when she fell through the doors of the first open pub, she found she was suffering from exposure and unable to speak. Luckily, she had strapped her bag around her shoulder, and they found her passport.

It must have made the local news, but she knew nothing of it all. She had had a complete breakdown and had been lost to all around her for several days sedated in the local hospital. Every time she woke, she became hysterical. They checked her for signs of assault, but she was unscathed apart from hypothermia and a few scratches from stumbling in the dark. Resigning themselves that it was a mental health case, they kept her in until she resumed some normality. Made local enquiries, but no one knew her. Not even Sean. Finally, they booked her on a flight home where she was received into the arms of her friends, who had been frantic with worry.

They circled the wagons and watched her in shifts fearing she would attempt suicide at the first opportunity. She would not, for she had done much thinking on that mountain side and asked herself many questions. Her conclusion had been to live and not only live well, but to paint and show the world, and Sean, that she was worthy of much more.

This, in her temporary madness, she did with panache and within months her name was becoming known. Bertrand was delighted, but in reality, her celebrity was something that existed in the public eye only, for she shunned everything that wasn't necessary for her climb to success. At the evening's end she would make her excuses and climb into a lonely bed. No more tears were shed until years later when her breakdown and the manic behaviour started to lift. The fact that she was an enigma only added to her intrigue and she was hosted all over the world in exhibitions and at parties, pictured with the most attractive men and personalities listed amongst her friends, she excelled. Occasionally she took a discreet lover, but nothing lasted and if she were honest, her disconnect with emotion was probably the cause.

She maintained this persona for a couple of years until she was established and then she disappeared and made her way to France. Only Bertrand and a few of her oldest and non-famous friends knew where to find her.

There, she started to build the home for herself and the Sean of her imagination. It would be her 'Place of Peace.' A refuge from the madness of her working life and a place to preserve the good memories. Gradually those memories of the man she had loved, took over until no bad remained, and Sean lived on unsullied in her heart and her head.

In every way now she was sane, but in this one thing. In her head she had been unable to accept the truth. That Sean had been a coward, a fantasist, and an abuser of how many women's trust? and likely the ruination of some of their lives also?

Instead, she packaged the gentle caring Sean she had believed in away, to treasure and keep safe. She had nearly died that night on the mountain and yet something in her had fought to go on and she had finally found the strength to stand up and stagger down the mountain for help. Go on she did, with everything bad locked away in a Pandora's box, never to be opened for fear of the destruction it would cause her.

Whilst the rest of her had recovered and she had regained her mental strength and the resolve to live a full life. The part of her that had been his, had retreated to this lonely life in France, to live it with him in her memories.

She had built every stone of that house with love, still believing that the Sean of her imagination would one day come back to the place they had loved, to build their home. That one day, she would be walking on the sunlit stone pavements, and he would be there in front of her.

He had not come...not even when she had been in hospital and the news was all over his village when she had nearly lost her life. He had been too much of a coward to even go to see her and instead had locked himself behind his door, giving his wife all his attention, just in case Rhia recovered and came back to blow his, no bed of roses, half grey world, apart.

She had kept the form of him that she could accept safely locked in the place that she had called home for twenty years. There she had remained venturing out only occasionally, painting her own reality and all the time making excuses for him so that she could go on doing so. With just her dog for company she had only existed...

Until one summer's day, a boy answered her 'unplaced' ad for a gardener. Little by little, that chance meeting had started to awaken her soul and gently trickled the joy and light back into her life. She had been reborn to the blessings of being a mother once more and needed, by a girl child called Sophie.

CHAPTER TWENTY

Mack had thrown Sophie a long look after he had hugged her goodbye. With his mother chatting around them it was hard to exchange any serious words and when they had gone, a quiet descended on the house and Sophie looked to Rhia, her eyes bright with a new feeling. It buzzed around her stomach as she cleared the remains of the evening meal leaving her distracted and vague.

Rhia followed her into the kitchen with the remains of an opened bottle of red. She paused behind Sophie.

"Do you think I'm drinking too much?" The question surprised Sophie and she turned round.

"No... why do you ask?"

"It's just for a while I started drinking heavily. It was years ago but I had no awareness that I was slipping into it." Rhia was serious and Sophie looked at her and smiled.

"Rhia, if you were drinking too much, that bottle in your hand would be empty." Sophie nodded to the half full bottle and Rhia followed her line of sight.

"I guess so, good thinking!" Rhia smiled, but it wasn't reaching her eyes. She helped Sophie with the dishes and then with a kiss on the girl's cheek, she said she was tired and off to bed. As she reached the kitchen door she paused.

"I can't tell you how having you here has changed my life Sophie, I hope you are happy?" Sophie stopped what she was doing and went to hug Rhia.

"Oh Rhia, I'm so happy, you have brought me things that I'd never dreamt I could have. My own mum never bothered much with me, you have been more of a mother to me in this last year than she was in my entire life. I am someone completely new because of you and you are my mum in all but name." Sophie held onto the older woman tightly and poured all her love and affection into the embrace and Rhia's eyes filled with tears.

"Night, lovely one." Was all she could manage; such was her emotion, and she gave the girl one last kiss on the cheek before retiring with Clucy at her heels.

Sophie pottered around, unable to sleep. She took a cup of Earl Grey onto the veranda and sat in the still of the evening. The sounds of the garden at night here always soothed her and she looked up at the trees as she put her cup to her mouth and watched them gently sway in the evening sky. Trees had such energy, she thought, is that why artists have such an affinity with them?. She could still feel Mack's kiss on her lips, and it was the most addictive of feelings. What would tomorrow bring? The thought brought thrills to her stomach. Was this sexual desire, if so, it was nothing like she had felt before. She spent an hour out there musing on this new development in her life. She was becoming an artist and a woman at the same time and life was suddenly a joy to live. In the end she made herself go to bed. She knew Mack would be around tomorrow after his shift at the shop that he had taken up again and she needed to look her best.

She knew him well, and he appeared within an hour of his shift ending to see if she wanted to go into Josselin for a wander. Rhia ushered them out saying she had things to do and to go enjoy the rest of the day, she had Clucy for company. The dog nuzzled her hand as if understanding and settled back down to snooze beside her. She was sixteen now and slowing up and Rhia was acutely aware of how little time they had. Life was so fleeting. Where had the years gone since she had arrived at this plot of land in her camper van and bought herself this pup when life and isolation had made her lonely.

Clucy had followed her up and down, as brick by brick she had built the shell of this house, only giving in to hire contractors when she absolutely had to for safety's sake. They had all thought her mad, but her years of handling crews in theatre building complex sets had stood her in good stead and the French tradesmen had begrudgingly begun to respect the strong woman who worked as hard as them. If any treated her with less than respect she had soon put them in their place. No man would dare come on to her, there was a wall higher than any they were building present in that respect. Clucy nuzzled her hand as if sensing her thoughts were straying to the negative and she patted the dog lovingly.

"Swim time old girl, up you get lazybones."

The dog, understanding her words, raised herself up and started to scurry round the room excited at the prospect of a walk.

Sophie had been driving confidently for some time now and as Mack sat beside her on the journey to town, he had to admit she was better than he. He really must drive more before he went back to Uni for the new academic year. He had three weeks left and only two of those in France. Thoughts of how he would extricate himself from Anna kept creeping in and it wasn't something he relished. Still, today he was with Sophie and though he wasn't free to be with her yet, he sensed that she understood that he soon would be.

As she pulled up in one of the streets across from the Château and manoeuvred them with ease into a space, he couldn't help but stare. When had she become so stunning? Bringing her and Rhia together had certainly been one of his best day's work. As they walked it seemed only natural that he should take her hand and she accepted it shyly with a smile.

"Come on, lunch first I'm starving!" he said as he pulled her in the direction of a favourite cafe in the square.

"Nothing changes." she laughed as he dragged her along.

They spent a pleasant hour bantering as they ate. Underneath the laughter and smiles moved something more potent as each was aware of every little nuance in their body and touch that had once been accepted as casual took on a more sensual meaning. They had been first friends and now the realisation was washing over them that they might soon be lovers and the excitement was intense. They moved closer as they spoke and before the meal was over the temptation was too much and Mack forgot he was in public as the French do so well and kissed her until they were aware they were drawing an audience. Some diners smiled appreciatively of L'Amour, and others were disapproving of a public display. Either way it was time to leave, and Mack paid the bill.

The remainder of the afternoon they wandered round the shops arms around each other's waists stopping occasionally to kiss when the feeling overcame them. Sophie's cheeks were full of colour and eventually as they stopped to rest with a cold drink laying down on the grass facing the Château with the river's edge near to their bare feet. The first moments of real passion crept into their embrace and Mack was very aware that Sophie, if she had not even been kissed may not even be aware of the discomfort he was suffering as his arousal pushed through his jeans to where she pulled him close against her slim hips.

"Sophie, we need to go somewhere, we'll get arrested if we stay here, there's too many tourists, come on!" He pulled her to her feet, and she dusted down the dress that had become creased as they had entwined arms and legs. Without knowing, they naturally drove back to the river behind Rhia's house that they knew so well and found a quiet spot in the trees to walk.

There with the dappled sunlight and the joyous singing of the birds overhead they kissed and caressed and without having full sex Mack used the skills he had learned under Anna's tuition and as Sophie leaned against a tree, he knelt before her raising her dress and sliding her briefs aside to bring her to a violently trembling orgasm. It was enough for now.

The anticipation made them risk more each day until one evening three days later she held him in her hand and guided him to her as they lay naked in the woods on a rug they had brought from home. Mack could not have held back a moment longer, but he stopped as he would have entered her and fumbled in his jeans for a condom.

"No babies just yet" was all he said and then a few seconds later he came back to her, and she moaned, and he cried out in relief as he pushed slowly inside her for the first time. There was no ugliness, just passion and kisses and beauty for Sophie. The past had shattered and gone, and the present was all she felt. She gathered him to her, and the erotic dance began.

CHAPTER TWENTY-ONE

Rhia knew something had gone on. Sophie had too expressive a face not to mirror her feelings, but she chose to watch and wait for Sophie to confide. She prayed that nothing would come to hurt this girl in the way that she had been. She knew also that it was a path only Sophie could tread. All evening the girl was laughing gaily one minute and dreaming the next. Classic signs, and when Mack and Christina had arrived the evening prior, Sophie had lit up like a beacon and Mack watched her hungrily. These two were an item, she could see, and she worried for her girl.

This day Mack had much worse to deal with. For on his return from Rhia's he had walked in through his front door and came face to face with Anna being entertained by his parents. Now he knew why his phone had kept beeping with calls from his mum. He had turned it on silent so he and Sophie wouldn't be disturbed. Sophie hardly used hers and so she usually left it in the office unless she was going out alone. Either way he was screwed as neither his mother nor Anna were looking comfortable.

"Where have you been? I've been calling you for an hour and a half?" said his mother with a tone in her voice.

"Sorry mum, we've been to town. Maybe the signal was bad" He wondered if he looked as guilty as he felt. "I'm sorry Anna, why didn't you tell me you were coming early?"

"Didn't think I needed to ask." she answered, looking at him quizzically. He wanted to say it might have been courteous to his mum but kept his thoughts to himself. By the look on his girlfriend's face, now was not the time and a huge wave of conscience washed over him. His mum stepped in.

"Anyway, you're here now, so perhaps you could get the camp bed out for Anna? I'll look at making us something to eat." His mother wasn't the type to be undiplomatic, but he knew she wasn't happy having this sprung on her.

"Yes, ok mum, I'll do it now." He was so flustered he hadn't even properly greeted Anna and she followed him pointedly up the stairs.

He tidied his room as Anna sat on the bed and waited for something from him. Eventually she became impatient.

"So, you've been with Sophie?" Mack stopped what he was doing and turned to her.

"Yes, I have, in town, shopping and lunch...or should I say lunch and shopping." he amended it quickly as the former would have meant a very late lunch indeed and questions might be asked.

He felt such a shit, he didn't know who he had betrayed the most, so he said as little as possible. Anna wasn't supposed to be here right now. He was going to do the drive back with her and then tell her on his return that they were over. That way it kept all the ill feeling from tainting the last few days with his family. Now what should he do? It hadn't occurred to him to do it by phone yesterday when he spoke to her as he felt that would be wrong. She must have been about to be on her way when they spoke. Why hadn't she told him?

"You could have told me, it's not very fair on mum, she probably had plans for the last few days with me," he said.

"I can always go if you feel that way" Anna was hurt, and he felt even guiltier.

"No, I didn't mean it that way, but a bit of warning might have been wiser. Anyway, how was the journey?" he asked looking for an out. She kicked off her shoes and lay on his bed.

"Good, long but good, how was lunch?" She wasn't backing off.

"Lunch was like it always is in Josselin, good."

She stretched and ran a toe up his thigh provocatively "Fancy dessert, I've missed you baby."

Mack squirmed. What the hell was he going to do? He arranged the camp bed as a means to distract whilst his head frantically sought the solution. Nothing came.

"Not now Anna, with mum up and down. Let's get you settled in and then we can talk."

"I wasn't thinking of talking." she replied and stood up to throw her arms round his neck, coming in for a kiss, which he returned and then gently pushed her away.

"I don't doubt it!" He laughed and pulled her towards the door. "Come on, mum will have made us something to eat by now." She dragged on his hand behind in mock petulance but complied. He knew it would be revisited later and hadn't a clue what to do.

They spent a night with Mack's parents and chatted amiably. Anna's parents had a villa, and it was a regular pilgrimage for her in the holidays. The conversation grew easier with a couple of bottles later. Mack was still no nearer what he should do for the best. Did he stay quiet and wait till they got back to London, that way his parents wouldn't have to deal with the fallout...but then there was Sophie? How did he deal with that? There was no way she would appreciate Anna's arrival and his silence. What should he do? Anna wasn't due for several days, He would have to go back early, that was all there was to it. That way he could get Anna told and be free to commit to Sophie. There was no way he could string it out, it would be disastrous.

Mack tried his best to get to sleep without a reunion with Anna, but she could be very persuasive, especially after a couple of wines and afterwards as she slept snuggled up to him in his small bed, he lay awake and agonised over whether he should tell Sophie first thing and just get him and Anna back to London to do the deed. Either way he felt bad. He finally drifted off, determined to leave with Anna by lunch tomorrow and catch a late-night ferry back into Dover.

The morning opened his eyes to bright sunshine and his mum had gone off shopping by the time he had slipped out of bed so as not to disturb Anna and got downstairs.

John was in his workshop out back working on some robotic control panel and wasn't receptive to Mack's visit. Normally he would have discussed his difficulty with his mother, but he hadn't even told her about him and Sophie, let alone that he was about to end things with Anna. He poured himself a coffee and picked up his phone to dial Sophie, she answered quickly, she must have been at her desk as she never usually carried it about with her.

"Hi you," she breathed her stomach doing little jumps that he had rang her so early and the memory of their lovemaking still fresh.

"Hi you too...look I need to speak to you, are you busy?"

"Nope, not especially. Are you ok?" The question had barely left her lips when she heard Anna's voice in the background who had walked in on him, His voice became wary. "...Is that Anna?" Her tone had altered.

"Yes, she arrived to surprise me yesterday..." Anna snatched the phone from him without warning.

"Hi, is that you Sophie...Hi, yes, I turned up on him without warning, he sulked a bit, but he soon came round with a little persuasion, and we've been catching up if you get my drift. The second time I persuaded him, he definitely came round."

There was no mistaking that Anna was drawing the line in the sand and the implication was clear. It was in her tone that he was hers and Sophie had best back off.

Sophie sat looking at the phone that was in her hand with the words 'second time' ringing in her ears. Her stomach dropped through the floor. Mack had grabbed the phone back and there was a non-too playful tussle at the other end. It was enough for Sophie, she put down the phone and burst into tears. How could he be such a bastard? Was he some kind of sex maniac? Four times in one day! She broke her heart quietly with disappointment, and then got angry.

Picking up her sun hat and a chiffon scarf for her neck, she made her face up and told Rhia she was going to borrow the car if it was all right as she needed a few things from town. It was an excuse and Rhia was not stupid, she saw the red eyes.

"Are you going for long? lovely one?" she asked.

"I might do some outdoor sketching along the Nantes after and I've some things to get, so it might be teatime. Will you be ok?" she asked, and Rhia nodded.

"I'm fine, as long as you're alright?" Sophie looked at Rhia and smiled with a nod. Grabbing her rucksack, she bundled in her sketchpad and pens for authenticity and too upset to speak, she left, leaving Rhia alone to wonder what had caused such a change in the girl's temperament.

Anna was no fool and Mack was not the type to lie easily. His face was red and the fact that Sophie had put the phone down was enough.

"Well, that was interesting?" She said with heavy sarcasm, but within her hurt and anger were rising.

What followed was a huge row that even John heard the worst of from his workshop and he chose to stay out of the way until it quieted down. Christina returned an hour later to Mack packing and Anna sat in the garden with a stony expression. She was obviously very upset. Mack explained awkwardly that they had been having a huge row and he thought it best they returned to London early to sort it out, he would explain later. Sophie was not picking up her phone, so in desperation he jumped in his dad's pickup and went round to find that she was out. Rhia was asking him point blank what had gone on.

Too embarrassed to admit that he had sullied something that had been precious and too upset to explain himself with any clarity. He just asked Rhia to please tell Sophie that he was sorry and that he was having to return to London and would ring her in the morning to explain. Please would she try to understand. None of which seemed coherent.

Rhia's eyebrow raised critically. That didn't sound good and when she passed on his words on Sophie's return, it sounded like a goodbye. Sophie had looked stricken and then headed for the kitchen to make a very noisily prepared meal, which she sat through in silent misery despite Rhia's best attempts to draw her out.

Mack cursed himself for being every kind of a fool on the way back. Why had he placated Anna and let her persuade him into bed? He would have been better biting the bullet and just telling her. If she hadn't sprung herself on him, he would have managed it better, kinder even. What a prat he had been and now everyone would hate him, including his mother when she found out the whole story.

He returned to find Anna packed with her bags by the front door and about to leave without him. He persuaded her to stay whilst he said his goodbyes and would accompany her. Anything else would have been ungentlemanly. Christina tried her best to get them to stay but Anna wasn't having any and in truth now it was out there he just needed to sort it, sooner rather than later He couldn't let her drive back alone and there were things that needed to be said.

The several hours it took them were a mixture of heated argument and surprisingly tears from Anna which made Mack feel ten times worse. He hadn't thought she was so attached to him, but obviously she was. Now what did he do? No, it was best to be straight with her and rip the plaster off quickly.

He told her the absolute truth and that he hoped she would forgive him, he had not intended to hurt anyone. By the time they off-loaded at Dover her face had settled into a grim expression. As they cleared the port. She headed to town and the station and dumped him unceremoniously at the drop off point and screamed off. leaving him an uncomfortable wait in the early hours. He texted and rang Sophie but there was no response, and he was just about as low as he could get. Not even the coffee machine was working. He was left filling the time waiting for the first train to London berating himself for trampling on something entirely beautiful. Sophie was deep and she would never forgive him. 'What a fucking debacle!' he thought.

Sophie cried herself quietly to sleep and even refused to speak of anything to Rhia, it was just too raw. When the phone started ringing near her bed, she clicked it off in panic so as not to wake Rhia and then turned it too silent. As the texts came through, she deleted them. He was dead to her. It was the drama of youth and first love, but it hurt like there would be no end to it. She had felt utterly betrayed and bereft that not only had she lost her new love but the best friend that she loved so dearly. It was devastating.

Rhia knew she would tell her in her own time, so she let her be. The next morning when Sophie appeared fragile and red eyed, Rhia had just embraced her with just the words 'When you are ready my darling girl...' She knew that look far too well.

It took two days for Christina to gain a clear idea of what had happened from Mack, and she shouted at him for being every kind of a fool but then forgave him, knowing that her son was not one to treat people with insensitivity. She believed him when he had told her that it had not been his intention to two-time his girlfriend or hurt Sophie. Christina rang Rhia to explain what had happened in confidence and then came the day after to try to build bridges for him as Sophie was still not responding to his calls. Her words fell on deaf ears and though Sophie said little, it was enough seeing her guarded expression to know her son would not be forgiven easily and in truth, why should the girl forgive him she asked herself. She had hugged Sophie gently as she left.

"Please don't be a stranger. You are like family to us and the one thing I know is that Mack is terribly sorry. It was such a mess, and he made a stupid mistake. He would tell you that himself if you could just speak to him once. We all love you so much Sophie…"

"I know." was the response accompanied by a stray tear and Christina hugged the girl to her and was close to tears herself as she climbed in her car.

CHAPTER TWENTY-TWO

Sophie threw herself into work for a couple of weeks and refused to be drawn on the subject of Mack, staying quiet and working intensely to cover her sadness. All Mack's attempts at trying to build bridges with her received no response, and sadly he started to try less often until he gave up. Eventually the pain receded and a little of her spirit crept back into their days and Rhia was relieved to see her smile once more.

Inwardly Sophie was still a mess but determined to move forward, especially with her art, and she painted with a passion that Rhia recognised as therapy. The exhibition at the Château was approaching fast and she still hadn't decided which three pieces to submit. Eventually she put it to the vote using Christina, John, and Rhia as her judging panel. Her work was bold and colourful and after short listing, she let Rhia advise her on the three that complimented each other.

Mack had apologised to Anna, but they had not renewed the relationship and still stinging from Sophie's rejection, he also threw himself back into his studies and excelled. Connor complained he had gotten boring but would ensure he dragged him out at least once a week… 'to stop him turning into an old maid' he had said. If Mack had any interest in the opposite sex, he didn't show it and preferred to just have a quiet drink with his course mates rather than expand his contacts with more females.

The weeks passed and life went on with the winter approaching fast. This time of year, thrilled and frustrated Rhia equally as the poor weather restricted her wanderings, but when she did, the colours of the new season were particularly splendid and inspired her to paint once more. The garden always started to look a little sad at this time and without Mack it was left to Sophie and Rhia to tackle, which they did in close companionship.

As young as Sophie was, she was starting to understand the beauty of this garden and its hold on Rhia. How could one not feel peace breathing in its sweet, scented air and sensing the gentle sway of the trees. She was twenty this year. Her mother had been married at nineteen, but that was not for her. What was innate within her had drawn her so young to make an escape from an abusive situation and was now pushing her to pursue a potential career that she was passionate about. There was a fire in her belly.

Rhia had recognised that quality and nurtured it in her. This girl would be nobody's victim, as she herself had once been. Her work was exciting and sell-able, all Rhia had to do was work on the persona that would bring her celebrity and success. The marketing would be easy with Bertrand in support and a budget from Rhia. This coming exhibition would allow Sophie to dip her toe in the water and get her used to being critiqued in a fairly unknown environment. There it wouldn't damage her potential too much if she encountered someone who liked to attack new talent. Success was rarely a natural occurrence, once discovered it took hard work and grit to go forward. She was certain that Sophie had what it would take within her.

"Shopping today!" said Rhia, one cold morning at the breakfast table. "And hair! I feel the need for a spa day for us both, my treat." Sophie laughed out loud. Rhia was just one of those spontaneous people regardless of old age and she loved that about her. She had no idea that Rhia was commencing a promotional campaign on her behalf, and she was about to be 'Pygmalion.'

They spent a morning in Ploermel and returned with some interesting outfits that were more Avant-garde than Sophie was used to. They couldn't get in anywhere on short notice, so the next day was spent in the local hair and beauty. Nails, feet, hair. All was done and the chatted happily as they pampered.

"You see my dear…" said Rhia "An artist must learn how to attract attention and maintain it; Image IS everything and don't let them kid you. Even the scruffy ones cultivate theirs carefully, so don't be fooled. You my love, are beautiful, so we will nurture that in an artistic way, and you will wow them. Your confidence will be everything in this so the more we do the more you will have, and confidence brings credibility. We are going to start your climb to the top!" she said emphatically.

"Rhia you are amazing! You leave me standing with your energy," said Sophie, mouth open.

"Nevertheless, that is our task on the run up to this exhibition. We are going to study, cultivate and build you up until you can face any audience and leave them in awe. I will be speaking to Bertrand this week and I am going to set him the task of your development, if you will allow me?" Sophie laughed out loud.

"Do I have a choice?"

"But of course not, lovely one… you should take the deep red nail varnish by the way, it suits your colouring." It was obviously decided.

Rhia watched the new Sophie unfold as the day went on. She had her hair cut simply but a very sharp cut that had a vintage feel whilst allowing her the length to change her style to sleeker by wearing it up. On Rhia's advice she had gone for a deep red henna colour and the transformation once the makeup was on to match was stunning. Gone was the beautiful and natural young girl and in her place was a sophisticated and very stylish femme fatale.

"Wow!" breathed Sophie.

"Wow indeed," echoed Rhia. This was going to be fun.

The days that followed were like a condensed degree course. Rhia took Sophie through all the terminology and styles of art so that she would be able to understand if someone started quoting jargon at her. Following that Rhia announced her intention to visit the Louvre and off they went on the train to Paris for a couple of days for a practical study course.

Of course, Paris wouldn't have been Paris without shopping and yet more dynamic outfits being added to Sophie's wardrobe. When Sophie protested at the money Rhia was spending on her she was waved away with the answer that she was 'investing in her, which, if she were so concerned she could consider it a loan to be repaid when she was established.

Before she could breathe Rhia had them booked on Eurostar to London and the National Gallery and the Tate. Sophie paled when Rhia announced the visit. One because it was near to Mack, but mostly she was frightened to return to England.

"Rhia. I never told you everything. I took my mum's debit card and stole two hundred pounds to get away. They might have reported me." Sophie flushed flame red with guilt and Rhia smiled sympathetically.

"I doubt very much that your stepfather would report anything that might put him under scrutiny, and you are hardly recognisable as the girl I first met. I doubt your mother would know you even if she was standing at your side now. Worry not, we will enjoy this trip, and no, I won't press you to meet up with Mack whilst we're there. It's entirely up to you, but I think you should try to forgive him."

"I'd rather not." Came the answer.

"Then we won't see him." Rhia backed off.

By the run up to the exhibition Sophie was fluent in French and Fine Art. The visits to Paris and London, apart from expanding her knowledge as an artist, added to her growth as an attractive and intelligent young woman. She carried herself with grace and a latent sensual quality that was drawing her lots of male attention, had she but noticed. Rhia took note on her behalf and was proud of her protégé.

From nowhere the calendar turned its page to December and all the shops had a gaiety with their festive décor. Rhia had agreed to a small exhibition of her own work alongside the open exhibition at the Château. Until now Sophie had almost forgotten her short-lived flirtation with its events manager, mainly because someone called Jacqueline had taken over the exhibition prep in his absence and been liaising with them.

The exhibition was to start on the tenth until the twenty-third. It was a yearly tradition and people came from all around the area to the event as part of the run up to the Christmas festivities. Sophie, with Rhia's help had devised her promotional material and had insisted on Sophie having professional photographs done. The person that stared out at her from the contact sheets bore no resemblance to the frightened and sunburnt girl that had limped along the street when Mack had first found her.

This cat-like creature was draped in the shots as an art exhibit herself and could have come from a nineteen fifties Hollywood Annual. Rhia had taken her brief history with them and turned it into a fully-fledged bio. Sophie had read it and laughed.

"This doesn't even sound like me," she said.

"Nonsense, it's all true, we've just over egged on a few details... everyone does it," replied Rhia and she nodded with satisfaction at the results.

"When do we have to go in for this meeting at the Château? Can't you go for me?" Rhia grumbled.

Sophie stood in front of her and all but wagged a finger. "No, it would be rude and anyway you know you like to oversee things yourself. We can do some Christmas Shopping after perhaps?" She knew that would tempt her.

"You know Mack's off travelling Christmas and New Year and won't be coming home," said Rhia watching for Sophie's response. Perhaps Mack had heard they had visited London without contacting him and this was retaliation. How stubborn the young could be when it came to resolving conflict.

"I do, and we've been invited to join Christina and John for Christmas Lunch."

"Would we be going if he were home?" she pressed.

"He's not, so I don't have that dilemma." Sophie's answer was casually thrown back, but Rhia sensed that she was covering something...disappointment? Maybe… it was a sadness and she wished Sophie could see it in her heart to forgive him and allow the friendship back into her life at least.

They parked the car in the Château driveway, something not normally allowed but given Rhia's age and status Sophie had insisted. By the nature of its protected position, the walk up the steps from the river road was just too steep and the road running alongside was quite an incline for an older person. Once up there the views across the Nantes Canal were just spectacular and they couldn't resist a look over the parapets at the town and river below.

Today was one of those crisp November days. Cold but not enough for frost. It was a good thing because Sophie had found Rhia's one fear, slipping. Down to a broken ankle when she had slipped on rotisserie grease outside a shop when she was in her twenties and it never left her, so strange as she was fearless in most things. She linked Rhia's arm for reassurance, and they walked towards the entrance. The Château was much more delicately built on the gardens side, with lawned areas and elegantly laid out shrubs. The riverside whilst beautiful assumed the more imposing facade with its three large turrets facing over the Nantes Canal. Sophie preferred the interior side; it was very pretty and far less severe than the castle-like exterior. Sophie had rung ahead to say they were on the way, and a young woman was waiting in the doorway to greet them when they reached it.

Rhia was snuggled into a long brown wool maxi coat and gloves. With thick army boots preparing herself for the chilly welcome of a castle interior and steps. Sophie had also thought it wise to wrap up herself, choosing a deep burgundy, brown wool maxi dress, and heavy boots in a deep burgundy leather. She teamed it with a huge wool wrap in a muted red. It was an odd combination, but Rhia had said it was just perfect. Why should they be drab just because winter was upon them?

"Good morning, I am Jacqueline. We have spoken on the phone several times. You are Sophie? and you must be

Madame Hart. You are very welcome." The young woman conversed in English as a courtesy to her guest, but Rhia assured her they were both fluent in French and with a smile of 'But of course' dropped into French once more.

If they had worried about being cold, they should not have been, for the Château had the most imposing fireplace that was burning brightly. It was so big that it shared its love from the moment you stepped inside. The interior was so warmly carpeted in a deep Rose, and with the beautiful pieces and exquisite wood carving it shouted comfort.

Jacqueline gave them the obligatory tour and background as she led them through the outside rooms and the exhibition space to discuss how the event would flow. There would be a Christmas Market outside and music and the art exhibition within. Everyone looked forward to it and the exhibition space had been made festive in readiness.

"Cafe?" Jacqueline led them to a comfortable room overlooking the gardens and picked up the internal house phone to summon refreshments. They chatted amiably whilst they waited for the coffee and patisserie to arrive. The girl was beautiful Sophie thought with her dark blonde hair tied back in a clip. She was modern in a formal way, expected of someone who worked in these surroundings. Sophie wondered if Jacques would make an appearance or whether he was still elsewhere.

"Your events manager, we met in Paris, but unfortunately, he was called away. Is he still managing the event?" Sophie couldn't help herself and Rhia smiled and raised one eyebrow ever so slightly.

"Jacques Arbonne? Oui, He will be joining us directly." As she spoke the words, it conjured him, and the door opened. Sophie flushed slightly feeling caught out asking as he stepped inside, and she realised that he still had that effect on her. Rhia's other eyebrow rose a fraction to join the first before she stepped in to relieve Sophie's blushes.

"Monsieur Arbonne, good morning, a pleasure to meet you finally. I was very sorry to hear of your mother's illness, I hope she is on the mend?"

Jacques walked over to them and motioned to stay seated in deference to Rhia's age, but he came over and caught her offered hand in his, giving Rhia his attention with impeccable behaviour. Only when he had conversed briefly with Rhia, did he turn to Sophie and focus his full attention on her.

"...And Sophie, what a pleasure to meet you again. Let's hope this time we will extend our time together; we have been previously...how do you say in English? Jinxed!" He held out his hand and Sophie took it, and he did that little movement again where his thumb brushed her wrist and she shivered inwardly with something she now recognised as a physical response. The moment was broken by the door opening once more and another assistant brought in a tray laden with delights.

"Ah, cafe! Shall we?" he asked and reluctantly and far too slowly did he let go of Sophie's hand before pulling up another comfortable chair and relaxing into it.

Jacqueline poured the coffee and served them whilst Rhia and Jacques discussed the itinerary for the opening day to ensure she was happy. Rhia wasn't completely averse to the charms of this attractive man, and she basked in his attention. Sophie noticed that Jacqueline glanced occasionally at him too, perhaps they were an item? Sophie found herself hoping they were not. She couldn't help but take in his rangy, yet strong physique as he stretched out his legs in black jeans. His only salute to the occasion was a crisp white shirt. His dark hair curled just slightly over the collar, and she found herself drawn to his neck.

For a moment she had a flashback of Mack and herself in the woods when her hands had strung through his strong wavy hair, and she recoiled that the thought had brought her a buzz of excitement in intimate places. She sat up straighter and brushed off the thought, but the buzz stayed with her. Jacques finished his conversation with Rhia and turned to Sophie with a look that clearly demonstrated he had been aware of her interest.

Forty minutes later he excused himself, happy they were conversant with how the event would function in terms of Rhia's guest appearance and he left them to finish at their leisure.
Jacqueline gave them an itinerary each and they left and made their way to the car. Sophie opened the door for Rhia, and she slid in slowly, all the time taking stock of the heightened colour in Sophie's cheeks. As Sophie started the car, Rhia loosened her coat and turned with a smirk to the young woman.

"I see what you mean..." she said. Sophie looked puzzled.

"...About Jacques Arbonne, very attractive!"

Sophie looked at her disapprovingly as she put the key in the ignition and started the engine so as not to have to acknowledge Rhia's probing look.

"Well, you are young and free, what's not to like, but you better get yourself some protection..." Sophie gasped.

"Rhia!"

"Never mind Rhia... I could see you liked him, but you might have competition there. I noticed his assistant wasn't averse either."

Sophie took a deep breath and turned to Rhia. "I don't think I'm ready for another relationship yet after the brief disaster of the first."

"Nonsense girl, I'm talking sex, not love! Nothing wrong with a good, robust sex life." Sophie laughed, quite red by now,

"Enough Rhia! I can't feel my cheeks, I'm so embarrassed!" Rhia sat back, happy with the adjustments to her coat and smiled sweetly.

"Just saying..."

Sophie threw her one last look and started the car.

"You... are very wicked." said Sophie pointedly, but a seed had been planted.

CHAPTER TWENTY – THREE

The day of the Château exhibition approached, and Sophie was nervous and excited in equal measures. Her work had been dropped off with Rhia's several days ago after being framed by Rhia's specialist, and the change in the appearance of her work was dramatic. The frames really did make or break a picture. She had no say in where the work was placed amongst the others submitted, but Rhia in the nicest possible way, had made it quite known that her continued favour was dependent on Sophie's work being featured prominently. Sophie need not have worried because when she arrived, she was thrilled to see it centrally displayed with her marketing literature on a table to the front of it.

Rhia was to come later for the cocktail preview and Christina was bringing her so she wouldn't be overtired. That left Sophie free to network with the other artists and visitors. The atmosphere was building as Sophie meandered around the works on the walls. Rhia's work, having much more value, had a wall to itself safely behind a raised dais that was roped off to protect it from the added 'touchers' and an assistant to watch over it who looked to be taking their job seriously.

Today Sophie had put her hair up in a messy bun as Rhia had presented her with two silver chopstick hair pins fashioned in the shape of brushes as a present for her first exhibition. She stood quietly in red jeans and a draped back black chiffon and cheesecloth top with red embroidery, which she had chosen because it felt festive. Unaware how lovely a picture she looked from behind with her hair pulled up from the nape of her delicate neck as she examined the other artist's work. She became aware of him close behind her before she heard him, and her breath caught in readiness.

"Work of art." he said quietly.

"You think so, I'm not sure. It's a little raw for my taste, but interesting." She stepped back to peruse the large oil and realised he was a lot closer than she thought.

"I'm not talking about the painting." He said with purpose, and she could feel his breath on her neck. She turned round very serenely and looked him directly in the eye. It had taken all her determination, but she held her nerve.

"I expect you are a connoisseur?" It was a statement rather than a question. His face crinkled in an attractive smile, and he had the grace to look slightly uncomfortable for his cheesy remark.

"Ouch! I deserved that… would you like a glass of wine? The hospitality is now open." He motioned her to walk with him to where a festive table had been filled with nibbles and wine. "...Red or white?" he asked.

"Red please." He reached over and snaring two glasses with one hand, he picked up the bottle and proceeded to pour them both one. Passing one to her, he raised his glass.

"To old acquaintances." he smiled, and she smiled back.

"Indeed." she said, pinching one of Rhia's favourite sayings that she used when being enigmatic.

"Your artwork is excellent, and I noted your literature is also of a very high standard. I take it that it is Rhia's patronage?" he asked.

"She is very good to me I..." she faltered, remembering Rhia's instruction that she keep as mysterious as she could. "...I have great admiration for her both as an artist and a person." There, she had deflected that one nicely.

"I can see you have a close bond. I was very happy to see you in my office the other day by the way. It was a great disappointment to me that I was called away just as we were getting to know each other." His words were polite, but his eyes locked with hers in an entirely different conversation.

"It must have been a very sad time for you. I was sorry to hear of your mothers passing. They were very good to hold your job open here for so long." she countered equally politely.

"Thank you, my mother will be greatly missed. She was a beautiful and strong woman. I had a good assistant, so I could work at a distance mostly, and the advantage of being related to the family here helped."

"Ah..." she said, but her head only processed 'good assistant.'

"She's very attractive, your assistant." she said, and he grinned again.

"Yes, she is, do you like her?" Sophie lost her calm for a moment and was flustered.

"Oh no, I'm not gay...I mean." He laughed out loud and they drew the glances of a few people nearby. He sipped his wine and waited for her blush to subside. It was clear he had the edge on her youth.

"I'm sorry, I was just teasing." He looked contrite and she forgave him. 'Who wouldn't' she thought as she took in his black jumper, slim black pants with some gorgeously expensive shoes. Black suited him, and he looked very French.

"No, that's OK, I just haven't decided yet which way I lean…" This time he was the recipient and at his shocked look she leaned in as she sipped her wine smiling wickedly and said "Sorry, just teasing." before she turned and walked away. His wide grin demonstrated his appreciation of her spirit. Christina and Rhia were headed through the door and Sophie made her way over to them and kissed them both.

"What a lovely room! I feel quite festive already!" said Christina as she took in the effort that had been put into the event's Christmas décor.

"It is, isn't it?" replied Sophie, aware Jacques was heading in their direction to welcome his guest. He had impeccable manners but still had a look in his eye for Sophie that said they were not done yet, before taking Rhia away to introduce her to local dignitaries who were arriving. He was very good at being charming, Sophie thought as she watched him go to work. Christmas might just be picking up.

The evening went very well and even Rhia had to admit she'd enjoyed it. The last few stragglers were getting ready to leave, when a hand reached out and pulled Sophie away from the group of people she was with. Jacques pulled her over to a corner.

"Have dinner with me Friday? You know there's something going on between us here." He kept hold of her hand and looked like he wanted to kiss her and for a moment she was frightened he might.

"You're very sure of yourself Mr Arbonne," she admonished.

"Nevertheless… Will you have dinner with me Friday?" His intensity excited her.

Sophie turned her fingers in his hand and brushed his wrist in the same way he had caressed hers previously. How bold was she being?

"I think I might just," she said with a smile that was nearly the undoing of him. He looked down pointedly at her hand in his and then turned the fingers over and raised them to his lips in a caress that then returned to kiss her inner wrist. All this he did so seductively, whilst never taking his eyes from hers. His actions left her in no misunderstanding of his intentions and shuddering she pulled away as her bravery evaporated.

"I'll call you Thursday to arrange," he said.

"You do that," replied Sophie as she turned to rejoin Rhia and Christina who were chatting to the Mayor. She turned her head to see him smile in satisfaction before turning to say his goodbyes to someone and her stomach filled with butterflies. She had made a commitment to a date with an older French man. How cosmopolitan was she!

All the way home she hugged the thought to herself whilst Rhia chatted happily on the success of the evening and the positive comments that Sophie's work had received. Sophie nodded and responded but her stomach was churning with nerves and excitement. How would she deal with a man that was much more ambitious and confident than Mack in his persona. She had better take Rhia's advice on protection as she had the feeling this man would be more persuasive than she could manage with her lack of experience. The thought excited and terrified her at the same time.

Friday came and she had still not told Rhia about her date. Rhia was very much into promoting Sophie over herself presently and as they sat looking at the potential galleries offered by Bertrand to launch her career, she called a halt for coffee and seized the opportunity.

"Rhia, I'm going out tonight...with Jacques, will you be ok?"

"Well, I'm hardly surprised, he couldn't take his eyes off you."

"He is rather gorgeous don't you think?"

"Many men are gorgeous, but is he right for you? That is what you must find out, my sweet, otherwise there lies madness and in that respect I'm well qualified to advise." She sipped her coffee and smiled but there was always a small cloud of pain in her eyes when she referred to past love.

"Any words of advice for a novice?" asked Sophie.

"Enjoy yourself and don't take things too seriously for now. You are young and you will make mistakes, but you have time to put things right if you do. You cannot help who you love Sophie, but you must be damn sure that they love you back. Anything else is a less of a life. Sometimes you will believe they love you, and even they may believe they love you, but if they haven't the strength to honour that love, then walk away or you risk your soul. If you do find the man that has integrity and passion Sophie, hold him close to your heart. But for now, life is yours to grasp with both hands, so go grasp, but be prepared to let go if it's not right for you."

Sophie put her coffee down and took Rhia's hand.

"Can I ask you a serious question Rhia? How did you cope when your heart was broken? I know it was, but you seem so strong, so resilient."

Rhia's breath caught and her eyes filled with tears momentarily until she blinked them away and raised the young woman's hand to her mouth to kiss the palm affectionately.

"You see Sophie, I'm a great believer in the human spirit and that its capacity is endless. To me all things are energy. We are built into physical form from it and when we pass on, we return to it. It's the one thing I try to have faith in, otherwise what is our purpose? Do we live, make endless mistakes, and then just die having learned nothing? There must be something moving forward...and as I don't really believe in a God as such, I must hope that when our time comes, we revert back to pure energy and find the other energy that we were positively attracted to in life. For example, most people love more than one person in life so how do we choose who we find to merge with in spirit. If energy is endless in its capacity, then I believe the body releases us to many different purposes. So perhaps I might find the energy that was positive with my father, another part of me may go to find the part of me that was Sean's and the energy that was his for me might be waiting. The rest of me may be buzzing round this garden in a most benevolent way waiting for the time when it merges with yours. Do you see? If that isn't the case and we do have an afterlife in some form, then how sad if that meant we had to choose and leave people lonely. My way is much better don't you think? Because in this way I never lost him, and even if I must wait for my death and his, the good part of Sean that made me believe in him will be mine. So don't ever be afraid if you sense me when I'm gone, because if I have my way, I'll be pottering around you with a smile in spirit and checking you're keeping my roses pruned!"

"But what about your life, hasn't it been a waste not finding someone else to be with and be happy with?"

"I never wasted my life, Sophie. I filled it with art, close friends, and memories. If I had found someone to fill the place that Sean left, then I would have loved them. For me it just never happened, but I had many good times nevertheless, so nothing was wasted."

"What if I get to the sex part with Jacques and I freeze?" It was obviously a worry Sophie was carrying and she blurted it out.

"Did you freeze with Mack?" Sophie looked taken aback, it was not a comfortable subject.

"No... but Mack was different. I knew him and we grew together and look how wrong I was there!"

"I don't think caring about someone is wrong, lovely one, it was perhaps not the right time, especially with all the confusion around Anna."

"You're telling me! But I don't think it was confusion on Mack's part." Sophie's chin went up and Rhia shrugged and let it be.

"Anyway, this is all new I know, and you will have trigger points Sophie, but that's all they are. Everything else is in the past and you have a choice whether you let them rule your future. You have a right to enjoy your own body and sex with someone else. However, you have to let it happen naturally, in your own time and when you do, enjoy it. What you suffered will not define you as a person. You are bright, beautiful, and strong and it's those traits that will take you forward. You will be able to enjoy a full sex life if you forgive yourself for not being old enough to stop the abuse happening. Consider that back then you were a child, and now you are something entirely different and entitled to find love and happiness."

"Yes, I guess I am." She said adamantly.

"Good, so enjoy your evening and just let me know you're safe and your plans and I'll be fine." Rhia raised her coffee and relaxed back in her chair and was thoughtful. This beautiful young woman always made her take stock.

CHAPTER TWENTY-FOUR

Sophie spent two hours choosing what to wear, she was so agitated that nothing seemed right. Finally, she decided on a black satin halter neck pant suit and a delicate black and silver woollen wrap against the cold. She hoped he wasn't going to make her walk far, or the killer heels would live up to their name. Rhia nodded with a 'very dramatic' as she paraded for her just as the doorbell went. She shot a look of panic to Rhia who laughed.

"Calm down, it's only dinner and you can always get a taxi home if you end up hating him!" she laughed.

Sophie kissed Rhia goodbye quickly, grabbed her evening bag before her courage failed. He looked beautiful in a way that only French men can get away with as he stood with a smile under the porch light. Subtle but incredibly sexy and her stomach flipped once more.

"Hi, pretty lady, are you ready?" He smiled and held out his arm in the direction of his car.

"Yes, thank you." she replied thinking she very much needed a glass of red for this. If she had thought he would leap on her the minute he got her in the car, she was mistaken. He conversed about the feedback from the exhibition, talked of the restaurant's reputation and though his eyes were glancing at her often, he didn't appear a lech and she calmed slightly over the journey.

The restaurant was small and intimate and the food excellent and after a glass of wine she found herself relaxing in his easy company. He was funny in a quirky French way and before long he had her laughing with only a couple of his remarks lost in translation. He told her he had mainly worked in Paris but when the vacancy had come up here, he was ripe for a change of pace for a while. He had bought himself a house looking over the river and was presently having it renovated, his intention to keep it as a base even if work took him further afield in the future.

She was not as open when it came to her turn and instead, she concentrated on her life here and her new ambitions. The evening passed very pleasantly and whether it was a combination of the wine and his company, but she felt quite relaxed.

"So how long will you stay working for Rhia? Till you establish your career?" he asked.

"Oh no! I couldn't leave Rhia; I couldn't even think about it!" she gasped.

"You might have to if you want to make a success of your art."

"I wouldn't dream of it, without Rhia I wouldn't even have my art. I might travel for a few days, but she's done so much for me I would never leave her, she needs me."

"But what about life for you? You can't sacrifice yourself for her. I doubt she'd want you to." He leaned back in his chair and examined her shrewdly. "Do you even know what you want Sophie?"

"I'm learning as I go, I guess, it's been a very intense few months and I'm just trying to keep up. Rhia doesn't let the grass grow under her feet if she wants something, she has a great spirit."

"I expect that's what she sees in you." he said finishing his coffee. "...Shall we?" He summoned the waiter with a light hand and turned back to Sophie whilst he waited for the bill and his eyes locked with hers and his next words were very French.

"You and I will be lovers soon Sophie, but I think for now we will keep this evening for what it has been. I have enjoyed learning about you, and I would invite you home, but I have plastic across my windows and the wind is howling through. So, for now I will try to forget that I can't think of anything other than getting you into my bed. Does that scare you?"

Sophie blushed and swallowed as her stomach leapt over in something that she could only see as anticipation.

"Yes, it does...and how do you know I would be open to that?"

"We both knew we would be lovers since Paris. You felt it and so did I."

"You are twenty-nine and I am twenty..." she started to reply, and he leaned forward across the table.

"So, I will be gentle, and you will want me...I promise." He raised his fingers to her lips and then he ran his hand softly to the side of her face and down her neck till his fingers spread across her breast to brush the satin over the raised nipple beneath. "You see, you want me already."

She was lost for words and overwhelmed with the sensuality of it all when the waiter approached. Jacques resumed his former position and accepted the bill as though it was quite natural to caress a woman intimately in public. He was enjoying the anticipation, and she was awash with feelings she could only just conceive in her naivete.

He paid the bill and placed the wrap around her shoulders carefully as she stood up. Everything was filled with sweet tension, and she felt his hand brush her hip as he guided through the tables to the door and out into the air.

The street was dark, and she was treading carefully on high heels when he took her hand to steady her. They had walked a few paces when he stopped and turned abruptly towards her gathering her in and kissing her passionately. She gasped with shock for a second, but as his tongue invaded her mouth something primaeval came over her and she returned his kiss with equal passion. This was something entirely new and incredibly sexual and she was lost in its addictive quality. She sought his mouth with her own as he would have drawn away and he groaned with the intensity of it, muttering something in French that she couldn't understand as working both lips and fingers together he caressed her neck and breast, and she was lost in a wave of feeling. "I think we might need to go to mine right now and do the best we can!" was all he could manage.

Twenty minutes later he opened the door to his house and through the building rubble to his bedroom overlooking the river which had just been completed. The seconds it took him to undress himself and then her whilst she trembled with something alien to her, seemed an eternity, until he pulled her onto the bed and started a lesson in love that she had yet to learn. Two hours later exhausted she lay in his arms in a different, erotic world. Mack had been an innocent compared to this man.

Suddenly a thought struck, and she gasped and grabbed for her bag near the bed.

"What's the matter Ma Belle?" he murmured half asleep.

"I've just got to message Rhia, she'll worry." She had no idea how tempting she was bending out of the bed to reach for her phone.

"Tell her you'll see her in the morning Cherie," he said as his hand brushed her buttock and then circled her waist as he rolled her towards him with intent.

CHAPTER TWENTY-FIVE

The light started to filter through the trees outside the window when Rhia woke yet again to a dawn that held a slight tinge of loneliness that she had not felt for some time. She had got the message from Sophie and had tried to sleep, but it was broken, and she was awake, but exhausted. She was fully aware that this new relationship for Sophie, though natural, was a potential distraction from the present path. She wondered whether it would be the start of a waning of her career ambitions as romance took over and she had to admit that if so, it would be a great disappointment to her. She had placed so much love into Sophie's development that to lose momentum now would be a blow. She reached down to where Clucy slept by the side of her bed for comfort and the dog's warmth and gently breathing soothed her.

Just as she was inwardly grumbling about insomnia, the curse of old age, too many thoughts and usually all anxious, did her eyes droop, and she finally slept just as the dawn broke. There were dreams of Sean and lovemaking and tears and being cold.

She need not have wasted sleep hours with worry because Sophie was currently extracting herself from Jacques attempts to drag her back to bed with a firm admonishment that they both had a job to go to. She pulled him up and ordered him to brave the kitchen chaos to make coffee whilst she showered. She retrieved her clothes and dressed whilst he showered and went to look out through the long drapes as she sipped her coffee.

She gasped in astonishment when she discovered the narrow mediaeval house that seemed unimposing when they had entered, opened from his bedroom onto a raised terrace built over the river with bi-fold doors to make the most of the wonderful view across to the château on the opposite bank. How beautiful a spot was this in the heart of Josselin.

Jacques strode out of the shower towelling his hair and came to kiss her neck.

"C'est belle, non?"

"Beautiful, what a great view to wake up to," she breathed happily.

"You are a great view to wake up to," he growled pulling her back against him clearly aroused. She pulled free and held up her hand.

"Work Monsieur!" She laughed and he shrugged disappointedly and walked to the wardrobe to pull out his clothes. She watched him dressing, completely absorbed by his strong but slim beauty. Everything was in proportion, and she found herself comparing him to Mack who was similar build but taller. Mack was a different kind of thing she thought. This guy was pure sexuality and she felt excited by him. No, Mack was something else she didn't want to think about.

Jacques dropped her off at the Bungalow by 8.30am and she managed to get the coffee on, shower and change into work clothes before Rhia appeared. She ached, but it was a good ache born of hours of lovemaking. She poured coffee for herself and sat at the table with a pain au chocolat they had stopped at the bakery for, much to the amused eyes of the baker who knew her and had noticed she was still in evening attire. She blushed with the memory and the thought came in that she might have to change to another baker. It amused her and a smile crossed her face.

"I take it that you enjoyed your evening?" Rhia smiled and Sophie felt quite embarrassed as she remembered the previous evening's activities and flushed again. It was obvious that Rhia would know exactly what she had been up to, and she felt like she had the marks of his passion all over her and probably a few on her neck.

She answered briefly in a way that made it clear that she wasn't ready to discuss this new attachment just yet and Rhia poured herself coffee and took it to drink in her winter armchair by the window. It was her place for relaxing when it was too cold to sit on the veranda and the heat from the aga always made it a welcome place. She watched Sophie busy herself around the kitchen and thought that at least the girl was home in time for work and that was a good sign that she had her feet on the ground.

"I must ring Bertrand today. He wants to discuss the timings for this exhibition launch in Paris." said Sophie.

"Very good...I have also been thinking we should look at a holiday for next new year before I get too crotchety to manage it. I would like to go back to New Zealand, and it will be the summer months for them then. Do you think you might be available for it? It's too late to arrange for next month and you have lots of exhibition prep to do for us both so it would be too short notice now," she asked.

"Why wouldn't I be?" Sophie sensed something was troubling Rhia.

"Well, life changes, my sweet. You may be making plans with your young man by then." The penny dropped for Sophie, and she realised where the sudden need for reassurance had come from, and she looked fondly at Rhia and thought she looked weary. 'Bless her, she is worried I'll up and leave on a whim.' She went over and gave her dearest friend an affectionate hug from behind.

"Rhia, let me tell you this. I love my life here with you, and even if things did get serious with Jacques, I would still want to be doing what I am doing now and with you. Don't ever think I would consider changing the ways things are. I am so happy here. New Zealand sounds amazing, can't wait!"

Rhia smiled warmly whilst inside she chided herself for resorting to incentive tactics in her insecurity. Sophie needed to be free to make her own way without feeling obligated to her and she would have to examine the way they moved forward to allow Sophie that freedom for herself and make provision for other support for herself if the need arose.

"Well, we had best start researching our itinerary at some point, we will need a month and I have some friends out there I haven't seen for years. It will be so lovely to spend next New Year with them.

The days leading up to Christmas were filled with a new excitement for Sophie. Not only had she received much praise for her entries into the open exhibition, but she also had a boyfriend who, when he wasn't taking every opportunity to make love to her, was talking to everyone he could about her work. That combined with Bertrand's efforts on her behalf ensured that in the last couple of days before Christmas, life was all but perfect and enquiries were coming in for interviews and publicity shoots to be set up. She glowed with a new confidence and Rhia was happy for her. Jacques had been invited over on Christmas Eve and seemed to be serious about Sophie and Rhia was content for now that she was being treated with respect. The French could be so casual about love and Sophie was new to it all.

Christmas Eve had come and gone so quickly. Christina and John had arrived bearing presents and the news that Mack was in Austria skiing with friends. The announcement stung a little for Sophie, she didn't even know he could ski. Anyway, it was none of her business what he was doing and with who. Jacques chose that moment to arrive, and introductions were made again by Sophie and though she announced him as her friend, it was clear to all in the room that the two of them could barely keep their hands off each other.

Christina watched them talking intimately as the night went on and wished it could have been different. Mack, when she spoke to him had seemed ok on the surface but when she probed it became clear he was not venturing into any romantic involvements just now. Did that mean he was still hung up on Sophie? If so by the look of her this evening, he was in for a bitter disappointment. Hopefully given time they would know if it was serious and if it was, then Mack would have to get used to it, just as Sophie had had to with Anna.

The evening had gone beautifully and was a relaxed but happy atmosphere. Jacques could be utterly charming and amusing and he even engaged with John. Sophie had watched him and had to admit she was a little besotted by him. As if sensing her gaze, he had turned towards her and winked. He was far too attractive for her own good and she knew he could back that up with action. The woman in her craved him and the girl idolised him, all of which he seemed to take in his stride.

He had to go away to family for New Year followed by a freelance job in Paris shortly after so after one last very passionate night together, they had parted company lovingly. Sophie returned to her painting with renewed energy and the colours she used now were rich reds and black. To her they symbolised their lovemaking and the work she produced when she allowed herself to let go and let the painting take her were dramatic. She liked these very much, they symbolised her growing womanhood and sensuality.

Rhia was working on her own pieces in early January, and they painted in companionable silence. The body of work grew, and Rhia knew that in Sophie's case there was a definite growth in her style and skills. However, she was not so happy with her own work and was finding it hard to concentrate. She realised that she was more concerned with her protégé's development than any incentive to paint her own and that was where she should concentrate her energy. Later that day she rang Bertrand.

"I want you to organise a tour of her work Bertrand. Once the launch is over. I want to get her out to as many galleries as we can manage."

"That's a lot of work Rhia." Bertrand had replied cautiously.

"She can handle it."

"I'm thinking about you. It will be tiring." His concern for her welfare was touching but she laughed it off.

"Nonsense! I'm a tough old bird and I'll enjoy seeing her excel."

"Okay, if you say so." He still wasn't sure, but Rhia wasn't one for backing away from a challenge once she had decided. He had found most artists were very self-driven in his experience, but it seemed Rhia was more concerned with launching Sophie's career rather than maintaining her own. Perhaps it was time for her to ease back, she was almost seventy after all. Most artists her age were inclined to bask in their previous glories at this stage of their lives than seek new. Perhaps Rhia was feeling her time to produce was coming to an end. Although her work was still in demand, he recognised that age gave people different priorities and hers had changed. He took note to have that discussion with her at a later date.

A few days later Rhia announced that Bertrand had set up two further exhibitions for Sophie, one in Amsterdam and one in London. That one Sophie particularly cringed at, but Rhia raised a finger and silenced any protest accompanied by the statement that 'she had to face her fears in life to overcome them. Only cowards run away from facing what life had brought to their door. One day she might have to see her mother once more, but when she did, she would be ready.'

In truth Sophie felt ready for anything and when she walked down the street now, it was with the slow sway of a woman content with her life and her own sexuality. She had grown up in the blink of an eye. Nearly coming of age with her twenty first approaching she was beyond her years. How had she come this far so fast.

Had she not been brought under Rhia's patronage the best she could have hoped for was waiting on in some tourist cafe. She would have starved, or worse. Yet here she was, starting to earn her own money, posing for pictures, and making important marketing decisions. Now her own twitter and Instagram account which she had been instructed on the correct use of by an assistant of Bertrand's who emphasised how important it was to choose carefully what she publicised. She was starting to get followers and it was fascinating. Rhia had laughed when she suggested she did the same. 'Hate it all, not for me, I'm too old! You need to be young and glamorous for that.' Sophie had immediately proved her wrong by showing her an eighty-five-year-old fashion icon on Instagram, who was amazing, but she had resisted, and Sophie had had to admit defeat.

"Your ageist" Sophie had told her, and Rhia had laughed out loud.

The first show was on them before she had a chance to prepare herself and it all felt rushed, but Rhia and Bertrand had assured her it was a great success, and the industry was starting to open an eye up to this new talent. Her style had matured, and she was creating some dramatic pieces. London approached and she had gained a little equilibrium back. Christina had announced her intention to attend the opening as she was visiting old friends on a road trip home and John had opted to stay home and dog-sit, which would allow him some undisturbed down time without three women's daily input.

CHAPTER TWENTY-SIX

It was May and a warm one when Rhia and Sophie arrived in London to meet Bertrand at their hotel. It was just by Westminster Bridge and the Millennium Wheel and Sophie never having been on the wheel, convinced them both that it was a good idea. Rhia loved it but Bertrand hugged the sides of the module like an exposed rat until they were safely on the ground once more. He declared it would be his one and only time with great French emphasis.

Jacques was away on business and could not make London and Sophie was disappointed, but he promised Amsterdam would be theirs. Sophie was upset because she wanted to have him with her for support on her home territory. He had told her not to sulk and he would see her very soon and she softened as he promised to make up for his absence several times over when he saw her next. She was pacified and he flew off with a brief kiss and wave.

The doors were opening, and the wine was starting to flow, and Bertrand was whisking her from one VIP guest to another with the charm of a butterfly and the tenacity of a wasp. By the end of the first hour, she had barely touched her wine and had forgotten the names of half the people she had been introduced to.

She craved a quiet corner and noticed Rhia had seated herself and wasn't that Christina? She rushed over to greet her friend and sat herself down to catch up momentarily. The chatter of the crowd was a positive one and she had to lean into Christina to be heard. As she leant forward something familiar caught her eye and she sat up to get a proper look. Two guys were standing looking at her pictures opposite her and she was sure one was… Mack!

He had sensed her at the moment she saw him as he and Connor walked around the exhibits. Christina saw the direction of her stare and put a hand on hers.

"I asked him to come. I hope you don't mind. I thought it was time you two made friends."

Christina looked worried and Sophie knew now was not the time and so she smiled and said, "No you're right, we should." Standing, she walked over to Mack and his companion, at least it wasn't another girl. If he was surprised at her appearance she was certainly taken back by his, He had filled out and it suited him. His hair was longer than before and he obviously hadn't fell into the fashion of beard and ankle strangler pants that the majority of his twenty something's had. In fact, he looked more serious but completely at home with himself and she suddenly felt less confident.

Taking a deep breath, she stood in front of them both and smiled. His friend looked nice, and she greeted him first whilst she got herself together,

"Hi, I'm Sophie, are you a friend of Mack's?"

"For my pains!" he quipped, and she raised an eyebrow wryly as she turned to Mack.

"Hi Mack, how's life?" It was a strange greeting but the best she could do as a knot of anxiety filled the void where she craved food but had been unable to eat. He looked at her and smiled and it felt like old times for a second.

"Life's busy, coming to the end of my course so its full on… and you? Great things I hear."

"Yes, life is madness, but good madness."

"Your boyfriend is not here then?" Obviously, his mother had warned him.

"No, he's away on business." Did she notice a look of relief in his eyes as she spoke. His friend intervened in an awkward moment.

"Your work's fantastic by the way, Mack told me how good you are, but you are really good!" His enthusiasm made her smile and the knowledge that Mack had praised her to his friend, and she softened.

"Have you eaten? there's loads on the buffet, go help yourself and don't be shy. It mostly gets wasted at these things."

"I will and you two can catch up." Before she could react, he was gone, and they were left together. Mack spoke sincerely.

"Is this guy, Jacques, good to you?" he asked.

"Yes, yes he is." she replied surprised at such a forthright question.

"Better than me then?" he said sadly, and she softened.

"Hardly matters now does it?" she said.

"But it does to me Sophie… What I did was stupid, but I panicked and just did the wrong thing. I'm sorry. Please say you'll forgive me. I miss us being friends."

Sophie wanted to rant at him, but something in his face told her he meant every word and she started to forgive him. Besides, what did it matter now, life had moved on and holding a grudge put them all under strain. Sophie's generous nature came to the fore and she smiled and to Mack she was dazzling as she hugged him and whispered "Don't be silly. Come and sit with us and bring your friend. He's loaded enough food on that plate for all of us to share!

He hugged her back and they returned to Christina and Rhia who were trying not to smile too widely. The evening went as well as they'd hoped, and Bertrand came excitedly over towards the end of the evening to whisk Sophie away to meet the owner of a hotel chain. He was looking to buy mass produced prints of her art to theme the rooms of over twenty large hotels. She was overwhelmed at the implications and just smiled and nodded where required as speech was almost beyond her.

The rest of them watched the conversations closely for a hint of what was going on. Rhia knew that this could mean big money from experience and although she sat and smiled, she had everything crossed for a successful negotiation.

Sometime later Bertrand and Sophie returned and by Sophie's wide eyes and Bertrand's beaming smile Rhia was reassured things had gone well.

"Well?" said Rhia in a stage whisper to Bertrand. He pulled up a chair and sat down beside her as Sophie stood behind him steadying her shaking legs by holding onto the back of his chair whilst Bertrand spoke.

"They want a meeting Monday to discuss the rights to reproduce the prints for each of their hotels on four of Sophie's pieces. Even at ten pounds a piece with over twenty large hotels, we could be looking at a minimum of a hundred thousand possibly one hundred and sixty!" Bertrand could hardly contain himself and they all looked around at Sophie in astonishment.

"I think I might need to sit down," she said, and Mack jumped up to offer his seat.

"Wow Sophie! you're on the way!" he whispered as she took the space he vacated. Somebody handed her a glass of red and she took a sip to calm the jitters that were rapidly spreading across her body. Was she under some kind of lucky star? She couldn't comprehend this sudden rocketing of her career. Rhia had said as an agent Bertrand was second to none and tonight, he had proved her point tenfold and had just received the biggest red spot she could have hoped for as an artist, her images licensed.

"Thank you so much Bertrand. I don't know what to say!" Her eyes pooled with tears such was her emotion.

"You're very welcome my dear. Just doing my job for which I will be very well paid." He smiled and patted her hand. "I suggest you go get a few minutes air and then come back in for another circuit around your guest's ma petite."

"Of course, just give me a few minutes to pull myself together."

This was the moment that Sophie's life went into overdrive. She spent a few days in London with Rhia and Mack and his mother joined them on the last day for lunch before she was due to return to France with them. They managed to get through the time amicably and Christina and Rhia said nothing but their eyes across the table was enough to acknowledge that their two favourite people were on the way to patching up their friendship. The exhibition was to remain there for the month and then move on to Amsterdam. Sophie had not yet managed to get there and was quite excited. The goal had been already achieved in the hotel deal and anything else at this moment was a bonus to what was now only required to be a profile building exercise and any other sales would be just icing on the cake.

Once home she relaxed and gained a little normality as her time was taken up with producing more art now that her confidence had had such a massive boost, but deep down she still couldn't believe her luck. Mack texted her a few times and she replied. The ice was broken and now she could look forward to his company in the Summer when his degree had finished whilst he decided his next move. Things all round felt almost normal with the exception that she had a very demanding boyfriend who was all but wearing her out with his attentions. Was his sex drive normal? She was asking herself. It was exhausting.

Rhia pulled out of the Amsterdam exhibition stating tiredness as her reason once she found out that Jacques would be going. Amsterdam was a place for lovers, and she really felt that she shouldn't cramp their style. Sophie tried to persuade her, but she insisted saying it was unfair to keep asking Christina to take Clucy all the time. Bertrand was there to ensure everything flowed as it should, and she would be fine. All she had to do was turn up at the launch, make interesting conversation and the rest of the time would be hers and Jacques.

Sophie, once persuaded, was quite excited at spending a few days with Jacques alone as a couple. They had a marvellous time, drank a little too much, headed for the coffee shops, followed by amazing risqué sex on the balcony of their hotel with no regard for who might be watching. Sophie was mortified the next morning, but Jacques just lit a cigarette and smiled wickedly, saying he had been too drunk to remember so perhaps they should try again in broad daylight and see how it felt sober, laughing out loud at her horrified 'British' reaction. Yes, it was a good thing Rhia had stayed home on this occasion…

Once home she hugged Rhia tightly and recounted all but a few of the delights of her trip and the exhibition. Sophie unpacked her cases and brought out the most beautiful silk scarf and exquisite brooch she had brought as a present for Rhia and the recipient was clearly touched.

"I know it's not much but now I have some money on the way, I wanted to bring you something to show how much I appreciate all you have done for me." Sophie filled up and Rhia came over and hugged her.

"They're truly lovely, thank you my sweet. Now I have a present for you, but it's not arriving for another hour." and with that she clammed up and refused to be drawn.

True to her words the doorbell rang, and Sophie went to open it expecting a parcel of some kind, but instead she found a middle-aged local woman on the doorstep who looked as bemused as her. Rhia came towards them in her painting clothes looking very much like the artist and waived Sophie aside for the woman to enter.

"Sophie, meet Cecile. She is going to be helping with the housework a couple of days a week so we can free you up to do the more important things. She will also house sit whilst we travel so I don't have to worry about Clucy. What do you think?"

"But I can do all that." Sophie was aware she was being rude to the woman in front of them who looked perplexed but thankfully her English wasn't so great.

"No, you can't, lovely one. You will be far too busy sorting mine and your schedules out, if you still want to be my PA that is?"

CHAPTER TWENTY-SEVEN

Sophie was twenty-three years old and at the height of her career. The last two years had brought her much opportunity which she seized with both hands and excelled at. Life had turned hectic very quickly and it became clear to Sophie that Rhia's decision to employ new help was to allow her the freedom to do what she needed to promote herself without the pressure of worrying about Rhia being alone.

Rhia hated to admit it, but she had started to slow down and found it less comfortable to stand and paint, so she had started a new love, writing. She had said it was a natural progression for someone creative. When she could no longer stand to paint for long without her feet swelling, she had needed an outlet for her creativity to keep her sane and Sophie was pleased to see her sharing her creative time by frequently tapping away on her laptop. It allowed her to put her feet up which was something normally alien to Rhia.

Much of the time she now pottered around her garden with Clucy still at her heels and with the help of a newly engaged gardener at Sophie's insistence, she managed to enjoy her time. Roger was an ex-pat from the village in his sixties. It was clear that he thought highly of Rhia and before long they had formed quite a close friendship. It pleased Sophie as she knew now that between Roger, Cecile, who was a godsend and worked like a trojan whilst respecting their privacy and then Christina and John, that Rhia was looked after in her absences, and she felt free to pursue her own life.

They had done the New Zealand tour and it had been magical for Sophie. Starting in Auckland and heading over to Rotorua. Rhia had even convinced Sophie to go on the luge which she had done on her first visit there at forty-seven years old. A very scary half hour later, Sophie emerged exhilarated but convinced that Rhia must have had a death wish to try those things when she herself had been terrified climbing into the cart to hurtle down the hill at breakneck speed. Rhia had said that at that time she probably had a death wish and the trip to New Zealand had been the make-or-break point of her life. Fortunately, the beauty of the country had healed something within her and allowed her to return with a renewed passion for art and life. Sophie hadn't pressed. By now from the snippets that Rhia had told her she knew it was the time just after Sean had left her life and she had been struggling to keep body and soul together.

They had done all the amazing things that were on offer. Heading next to Waitomo and the glow- worm caves. Wellington next, and a journey by boat into Picton through the fiords to the South Island.

Onto the train to travel across the Alps where Sophie and Rhia stood enthralled on the viewing platform as the stunning journey opened before them. The descent, on a rainbow crystal coloured, lupin lined track which left Sophie opened mouthed with its beauty.

Queenstown where Rhia admitted she had intended to do the Bungy but had lost her nerve. Sophie decided she wouldn't even try, thank you very much! So, they had taken the trip across the lake by boat and spent a couple of days sketching the amazing scenery. Then onto Christchurch, which made Rhia sad to see the remnants of all the beautiful things she remembered that were no longer there because of the destruction from the major earthquake. She told Sophie how she was there at the end of her tour, two days before Christmas and she had spent the day walking round the parks and gallery. It had been such a beautiful place that for a while she had considered returning there to live but had been convinced it was too far for her ambitions, by Bertrand and she had heeded his advice.

Finally, the trip that Rhia awaited most of all to the Glaciers where she had once walked through a track in the forest to climb to the top of the cliff and the viewing platform over the glacier. 'That,' said Rhia, 'Had been the moment that she healed herself. It had taken her four hours walking alone and she had to wade through a rocky stream and risk slipping and being alone and injured to make it the last five hundred yards, but she did it. She had almost given up when a young couple and the only people she had seen all day waded through with the ease of the young and so she had mentally given herself a kick up the backside and stepped into the icy water. When she reached the small viewing platform and looked down at the magnitude and beauty of Fox Glacier with people just pinpricks at its base. She knew she had found her place of peace and that people and all the harm they brought each other were insignificant compared to nature.' That was the moment she returned to be herself once more. All else before had just been a manic blur.

This time Rhia had suggested that they take the helicopter flight onto the Glacier as she wasn't up to the seven-hour return walk that nearly killed her last time! Equally exhilarating but less tiring, she added. From the top of the glacier, she stood on the ice very cautiously and bravely, thought Sophie. She looked out to the cliff opposite, and a smile settled quietly on her face at the remembrance of what she had achieved that day, twenty odd years before. 'Enough now' Rhia had thought. She was revisiting her previous pain and examining her life journey one last time.

Once finished there, they travelled by coach through the Homer Tunnel and came out from stark white mountains to the lush green warmth of the Marlborough Sound, stunning. After that they flew back to Auckland for a very happy few days with Rhia's old friends. It seemed that trip had been enough for Rhia, she had achieved the last challenge she had set herself and appeared content then to return to her tranquil house and the people that loved her.

Sophie worried about Rhia's health, but she was now in her seventies, and it was natural that Rhia would slow down. Since their return from New Zealand, she had told Bertrand to downscale her exhibitions and concentrate on Sophie. Bertrand had done so without argument, recognising that Rhia was right to do so.

Tomorrow Sophie was going away for a few days Skiing in Austria with Jacques. They had been passing like ships in the night recently with Jacques working in

Paris and she jumping about on various promos, so she was looking forward to their time together.

Rhia had insisted she go as she deserved a break and besides, she was now over-run with company and Clucy would fill the gaps. Sophie packed her case excited to have this time to rebuild the bond with Jacques that they had lost a little recently with all the comings and goings. She had taken a day out at the spa to pamper herself and was starting to anticipate the romance of the trip with time to really make love and be together as a true couple.

Roger was digging the rose beds just outside her window and she waved to him as she checked over her hand luggage and he raised a hand in return. She was really pleased Rhia had a new friend. It was just a pity she hadn't found him when she was younger, they might have ended up together. Still, it was lovely to see them chatting and laughing all the time. He was a good man who had moved to France and then been widowed, and so Rhia was as good for him as he was for her.

Thinking she heard something, a cry perhaps, she paused in her packing and listened for a second. The next time she heard the wail she needed no second bidding and dropped everything and ran in the direction of the sound. Rhia was on her knees on the kitchen floor beside Clucy who was making a strange howling sound and burying her head into the corner of the room. Rhia raised stricken eyes to Sophie.

"She started behaving strangely and then just fell down in the corner...Oh my baby, mummies here!"

Sophie dropped to her knees beside her, and it was clear that the old dog had suffered some kind of stroke. Her eyes filled with tears as Rhia sobbed beside the dog, she had had for her only company for a lifetime it seemed. Who had never faltered in her devotion to Rhia and Rhia to her. The loss didn't bear thinking about. She jumped back up.

"Stay with her, Rhia." She ran to the door and screamed "Roger come quick!" and he appeared almost instantly knowing it was not a natural occurrence.

"I think the dogs had a stroke. Can you wrap her up and I'll get the car? We need to get her straight to the vet."

"I'll drive, my estate cars bigger! You get Rhia and the dog... and your phone, to let the vet know we are coming!" He instructed quickly and shot off to bring the car to the front of the house.

When Sophie returned to Rhia, she was cradling her dog in her arms like a child all the time crooning to her. It was the most heartbreaking moment she had ever witnessed in her life. Bringing a blanket, she gently took her from Rhia and wrapped her up.

"Get a coat Rhia, it's cool today. I'll carry her to the car, and you can have her back then." Rhia struggled to her feet and went to grab a coat for them both as Sophie carried the heavy dog to the car who was all the heavier for being barely conscious. Rhia sat in the back seat and Sophie placed her in Rhia's waiting arms and then climbing in beside her she supported the dogs' legs, and they held her together for the journey into town.

Once there, Roger jumped out and took the dog from Rhia and carried her inside to the waiting vet, who examined her beloved Clucy.

"She has had a massive stroke Mme Hart; it would be kinder now to put her to sleep." The words he spoke sent shocks though both their hearts and Rhia sobbed brokenly for the dog she loved as Sophie comforted her. Rhia nodded, unable to speak and the vet quickly prepared the injection.
Rhia bent down to kiss her beloved companion and whispered,

"You wait for me now. No more swimming till I get there my darling girl..." Clucy was breathing, but barely but her glazed eyes looked towards Rhia's as if she understood. Seconds later she was gone, and it felt like something momentous had happened from which they would never recover. They quietly wrapped the dog up once more and Roger took her from the table with eyes full of tears himself. The journey home was so painful, with Rhia sat cradling her pet in silence and shock.

Once home Roger offered to dig the grave and Rhia told Sophie to show him a spot by the swing. The whole time they waited Rhia just sat with the dog on her lap, a world of pain in her eyes as the tears just streamed down her face and she struggled not to sob out loud. Sophie brought them both a sweet tea for the shock and insisted she drink some. She sipped a couple of times and then started to talk.

"She was my saviour you see. There was a time I lost my mind for a while and even though I recovered, for a couple of years there were times when the madness was just under the surface. When I got Clucy, she pulled me back from the brink of suicide a couple of times. I had lost a baby you see, and my faith in love and people in general and I retreated here to France. Sean never knew and I didn't want him too, so I brought my baby girl's ashes here and placed them in the cradle on the swing. Clucy came along and

became my only true companion and she loved me unconditionally. She was the child to me that I could never have, until you. I could not leave her uncared for, so I made myself go on, a day at a time until the days got easier. She has spent her whole lifetime devoted to me and I don't think my heart will ever mend from this…"

A broken sob forced its way through her tightly clenched lips, and she held the dog closer and kissed her. Sophie cried with her and together they sat arms around each other and the dog when Roger quietly entered.

The dog was buried in her blanket and with her favourite toy and Roger respectfully left them to say their goodbyes. Rhia took some of the seeds from the Forget me nots that had just finished blooming and scattered them over the soil left bare.

"I won't be too long, my darling girl." She whispered and brushed her hand on the flower cradle to rock the swing that hovered alongside the grave. Sophie thought her own heart would burst with the pain as she took in all that Rhia had told her. The box held the ashes of a child. No wonder she had been so upset when Mack had moved it that time. She helped her dearest friend to her feet and together they walked back inside, hand in hand.

Sophie made her drink sweet tea, as the last had gone cold and Rhia sat silently in her grief looking out of the veranda window to her garden. For the first time Sophie thought she looked like a frail old lady, and it frightened her.

She went to her room and picked up the phone to call Jacques to explain what had happened. He was busy packing at home and as excited as she had been. She recounted all that happened today as her voice cracked with emotion. She thought Jacques would fully understand why she had to cancel their trip but with typical French bluntness he replied that Rhia would be ok, there were others around to help and it was only a dog for God's sake. It was not what she expected to hear from him.

"It's not just a dog, Jacques, she'd been her only companion for years!" she replied shocked.

"More fool her then, for locking herself away!" It was an unkind thing to say, and she recoiled horrified.

"That's a terrible thing to say!"

"Well, what do you expect, that woman has you all running around after her!" Obviously he was upset, but this was uncalled for.

"Jacques I know you're upset but I'm sorry I can't leave her, she has been so good to me, and I will not go skiing whilst she is heartbroken, so perhaps you should go without me I'm sorry."

"That's your last word on it?"

"I'm sorry but yes."

"Merde!" The phone went down with a bang, and she was left holding it to her ear in shock at his temper.

.

CHAPTER TWENTY-EIGHT

It was an awful few days for Sophie. Too proud to call Jacques, she had let it fester. Angry at his lack of concern for the distress of another human being and the lack of understanding that he could not see just how much Rhia had supported Sophie, and that she deserved their care at this time. She hadn't told Rhia they had argued because part of her hadn't wanted to admit how unfeeling he had been at that moment in his disappointment.

Rhia had been too withdrawn in her own grief for her usual astute observation to kick in and Sophie preferred it that way. There had been no messages from him, and she was deeply upset. She had weakened and rang his phone once and it had rung internationally, so it looked like he had gone on holiday alone and she was shocked that he had done so.

Rhia herself worried Sophie most of all. For though she smiled and responded to Sophie's conversations and attempts to cheer her, there was something going on behind the eyes that Sophie could not fathom, and it frightened her. She said as much to Christina.

Each day that week Rhia sat in her armchair by the veranda door looking quietly out at her garden to where her dog and child lay at rest. Even Christina couldn't tempt her out despite her best efforts, and they had just about given up when on the seventh day, she rose from her chair and declared that she was going to paint. Sophie couldn't have been more relieved.

When Sophie took her coffee later, she couldn't help but notice she was laying on the base lines for a portrait of her dog.

"I need to see her little face," was all she said, and Sophie nodded, not sure whether to be worried again. At least she was on her feet and painting with a passion. Sophie knew that was how Rhia got her feelings out, displayed for all in blatant secrecy on the canvas.

A couple of days later the phone rang and when she picked it up, a quietly spoken Jacques was on the line.

"I'm sorry for being such a shit." he said in his most endearing voice. "I was just so disappointed, and I really miss you."

"Did you enjoy your break?" she replied, with a non-too disguised tone.

"I enjoyed the break from work, but not from you. Can we talk?"

Sophie paused for a moment before agreeing, In truth she wasn't sure how she felt about him at this moment. She had thought they were solid, but this last week had brought its doubts.

That evening she kissed Rhia goodnight and headed out to meet him, having insisted on driving herself as she didn't want any risk of not returning at a decent hour for Rhia's sake. She didn't want her to be alone right now, especially knowing now how reliant Rhia had been on her dog in earlier days when she had been suicidal.

They met for dinner at their usual restaurant, and he apologised profusely. Little by little she softened as the night progressed, but not enough to be persuaded home with him. He had the wisdom not to push her at this moment and he reluctantly backed off with just a single passionate kiss that she couldn't help but respond to before climbing into her car.

She looked in on Rhia who had gone to bed and seemed asleep. Sophie came right to her bedside just in case and Rhia opened her eyes and smiled.

"Still here…" she said with a wry smile as if she knew Sophie's thoughts.

"Night then." she answered, relieved a little of Rhia's sharp wit had returned.

After that evening Rhia's days got better, and she was up early and painting. Roger was back gardening after leaving them for a week out of respect. The April sun was shining beautifully today and worked its magic in luring Rhia out onto the veranda with her coffee where she sat and chatted quietly with him.

She was thrilled, but emotional, when he presented her with a beautiful memorial plaque he had carved for Clucy. It just read 'Woman's Best Friend – Clucy Dog.' They spent an hour placing it in the garden and though Rhia shed a few tears, she carried on afterwards with her day and Sophie breathed a sigh of relief that she might be over the worst.

Christina and John came later that week to say they were in the process of buying a small farm that they were going to renovate for themselves. They would keep the cottage to eventually convert to a holiday rental. Mack had continued onto a Master's degree and was due to finish in June. He would be coming home then to help with the building renovations whilst he searched for work. Christina was obviously thrilled, and Sophie was pleased he was coming home, with just a couple of reservations as to whether they could fall back into the close friendship they had had before it all fell apart.

The days moved on and back into a normal rhythm and Sophie felt free to return to work once more. She lasted a week before Jacques persuaded her back into his bed and their relationship seemed to be the better for it, certainly he seemed more serious about her now and made every effort to make up for his earlier lapse. Rhia always welcomed him warmly, but Sophie couldn't help but feel that the older woman had one eye firmly on his behaviour and it made her uncomfortable. One morning after Jacques had called by, she asked her outright.

"Do you like Jacques Rhia?"

"What's not to like?" Rhia smiled mischievously.

"You know what I mean...I get the feeling you don't quite trust him."

Rhia paused from her writing and looked up over the spectacles she was now forced to wear. She looked like a glamorous Miss Marple.

"Well, he's a man and he's French. It's a blessing and a curse I expect. No, my sweet, I like him well enough, but you are always my first concern and if he ever hurt you, I'd just have him killed, so worry not." She grinned and looked back down at her work as Sophie snorted with amusement and returned to hers.

Sophie was now very popular in the art print world and was making a good regular living, but she craved recognition as a serious artist and was always working towards that aim. Rhia was content to mentor her alongside working for herself when the mood took her. She was noticeably less driven these days and just had short bursts standing at the easel. Sophie had suggested sitting down to paint, but Rhia had replied that she could not paint unless her whole body was free to move. It showed in her work that she was constrained, and Sophie could relate to this and let it be.

The weather was gradually creeping towards a feeling of summer and Rhia ventured out more to sit in the garden and write. On the days Roger arrived, she would work alongside him, but Sophie knew how much she missed Clucy and had suggested getting another dog, but Rhia had been adamant. She was too old to take on a new responsibility and a dog was for life.

Sophie was working on pieces for a new exhibition in Amsterdam once more and Jacques was coming with her again for the opening. She had the feeling that he had something up his sleeve and wondered if he was getting ready to propose as he had been very up and down recently.

The thought unsettled her as she had the feeling that he would become more possessive than he already was. She didn't want to fight him over maintaining aspects of her career. Theirs was a very sexual relationship and he constantly sought reassurance of her feelings physically, not that she was averse. They had an exciting and passionate sex life, yet sometimes she wished she had a little less intensity and more ease of relationship in companionship terms. Could she maintain this intensity long term, she wasn't sure.

Jacques was very French when it came to love. He was very dominant, and he expected that she would go along with all his choices, both sexual and social and overall, she did. It was all very exciting, but there was just something that she craved that seemed to be missing. It was the easiness she found around Rhia,

Christina, and John and in fact with Mack when they had been close.

Perhaps it was a cultural thing and British people were just more casual and at ease, she didn't know, but she wished some of that would be present in their life as a couple. She felt under pressure to be the best dressed, the sexiest, the most successful and that felt great on the whole when she achieved it, but some days she just wanted to be Sophie with him. That was something she wasn't sure would entirely impress him.

She decided to speak to Rhia about it and when she had, Rhia had become thoughtful before responding.

"Sex is great Sophie, but in the end if you commit to each other completely, then that's a long time not to be yourself and you need to be very sure. There's only one way to deal with it and that's to deal with it. Speak to him about how you feel and see how he responds."

"I will, I think Rhia, it's bothering me, so I need to."

Feeling there was no time like the present and on her way to town anyway, she decided to call in to the Château and take him to lunch and bring it up in a less intense environment. He would then have to talk rather than persuade her into bed to distract her questions as he had a habit of doing.

Used to visiting him at work often, she rang the bell and the housekeeper answered and let her in. His car was outside so unless he had gone out with a client he would be hereabouts about somewhere. She walked into his office to find it empty and seeing his computer on, she dropped into an armchair to await his or his assistants return from whatever they must be doing elsewhere.

It took just seconds as the silence of the room surrounded her to start to pick up a muffled noise and she listened intently. A few seconds later the shock ran through her solar plexus as she recognised the noise as a woman crying out in sexual pleasure. It was coming from the events store through a door at the back of the office. Raising herself to her feet on unsteady legs she quietly walked over to the crack in the partially opened door and listened intently for a few seconds as the blood drained from her face. She had heard enough.

Slowly opening the door so as not to give them warning she stood wide-eyed with shock. His very pretty assistant Jacqueline was lay with her back arching in ecstasy and her skirt up over her waist, briefs cast aside, as Jacques was holding her buttock with one hand, his face buried deep between her legs bringing her to orgasm as she pulled him in further hands entwined in his hair. His other hand was fumbling with his own zip in readiness to enter her. She waited quietly, long enough to see him slide his jeans down with absolute intent and crawl back up the woman to kiss her as he thrust himself within her. Sophie had seen enough. It couldn't have been worse if they had been having full sex when she walked in. It was the intimacy of the oral sex that brought it home to her and she was outraged and betrayed. She walked a couple of steps forwards and placing a boot on his backside she pushed him further onto his assistant.

"Perhaps you could use a little help, you absolute bastard!" she said through gritted teeth as he collapsed on top of his lover with a cry of pain and surprise. The woman also gasped in shock and started to push him off as Sophie turned and with as much grace as she could muster, walked out of the office. She could hear him cursing and struggling to his feet in a barely controlled argument with his amour who was trying to get him to stay with her. She heard enough to know that the woman was besotted with him, like her, and desperate to keep him. Obviously, this was not a new affair from what was being said.

She reached her car and climbed in as he ran across the car park to her. He tried to wrench the door open, but she had hit the lock just in the nick of time.

"Sophie, don't be stupid, it's just sex!" The words resonated with her, and she paused looking down and took a breath before turning towards him once more. Winding the window down, just enough to be heard, she spoke angrily.

"Well, I guess that's all right then because I've just realised that's exactly what we are!"

"Cherie wait, let me explain!" He had pushed the glass down on the window. It was clear he was not happy at being found out and his face was red with embarrassment and anger. Sophie, despite that her mouth had dried with shock, found the words that suddenly came naturally to her as an ex-Londoner.

"Not interested you prick! So, in a quaint British saying "DO ONE!" She spat the words out vehemently and with that she turned on the ignition, engaged the gear and spun off not worrying at that moment if she had actually ran over his feet. She drove home recklessly at first, such was her anger, but by the time she had got through the front door she was shaking and as Rhia saw her stricken face and held out her arms, she fell into them sobbing uncontrollably.

Rhia let her cry it out and then sat her down and dried her tears. At least she had someone who knew this feeling intimately and she cradled her like a mother as Sophie cried out her pain and betrayal in broken sentences.

"There, there, lovely one. Men can be such bastards, but you will rise again and there will be better to come, I promise you."

"But you never found anyone Rhia, what if I'm alone?"

"It was my choice, Sophie; I had the chances, but I preferred it this way. There will be someone for you my sweet. I promise."

CHAPTER TWENTY-NINE

Sophie was distraught for several days and would burst into tears on a regular basis and Rhia was always there to quietly comfort her. She would lay in bed at night examining just how she felt about Jacques and whether it was a broken heart or a dented pride. She couldn't quite make up her mind. This was the first time she had to face blatant infidelity and the image of him burned on the back of her eyes as he pleasured another woman.

The disaster with Mack was naive by comparison and she had long since put that to bed. Knowing it to be the innocence of first love and not really a grown-up affair for either of them. At least now on his short visits home for the last couple of years their friendship had found its path again and although they didn't talk all the time, they were in contact.

No, she was surviving the heartbreak and each day she felt a little better. Whatever it had been it was over for her and in truth he hadn't even bothered to pursue her. She expected he had settled for the bird in hand.

Christina and John were due to take over the new property any day now and they were beyond excited. For Christina especially as it gave her the opportunity to have ducks and anything else that crossed her path that needed love. Sophie had laughed out loud and said perhaps she should design into her plans an outside stable for waifs and strays found on the road, just in case.

Two days later they had the keys and the first thing they did was pick up Rhia and Sophie to show them their new project and their future home. They had even elicited a promise from Roger to help with some of the landscaping and light manual. As they arrived that day, Sophie gasped at the work before them, but they seemed un-phased by it. In fact, they couldn't wait.

"Mack will be home soon so we can crack on with it more then. This week we're just sorting out the crap," said Christina.

John was a particularly talented designer when he wasn't doing robotics and the plans he had for the place were amazing. This was to be their forever home, he enthused, where grandchildren could come to visit and live, if necessary, with independent space for all. Christina shot him a pointed look and he blustered for a few seconds realising his blunder. Sophie smiled as she turned away, bless them they were so kind.

"I can help as well." she said.

"Great!" grinned Christina, we'll hold you to that."

So, it was a week later that Sophie and Christina were covered in dust and gingerly pulling off the old French paper and hoping that the wall didn't follow it when they heard a loud knock on the door jam.

"Hiya mum." Mack said, leaning against the doorway grinning.

Christina dropped her scraper and went over to hug him tightly.

"Hello son! We weren't expecting you for a few days, what a lovely surprise!" she said. He smiled over his mother's shoulder as she clung to him.

"Hi Soph!"

"Hi Mack," she smiled genuinely and then blushed as she became aware of what a sight she was.

"I dropped my stuff off at home before coming here, so do you need a hand here?"

"Not in your good clothes love. No, we'll stop now for today and go home to celebrate your return. Oh no! I've not been shopping, what will we eat?" Christina stood aghast and Sophie intervened.

"Look we have a freezer full at Rhia's, she'd love to see you, so why don't you get Mack settled in and I'll make us a meal for seven pm?"

Christina beamed "Would you mind, that would be lovely. I can sort out his room and have a shower then. Are you sure?"

"Absolutely, Rhia will be thrilled, and it's a lovely day, we'll eat out in the garden.

Sophie jumped in her car, half of her relieved to be able to go home and clean up before seeing Mack again. He looked so handsome and strong that he must have been training. She reprimanded herself for gushing. The past four years had matured him, and he had a quiet confidence that, added to his mop of curls and friendly face that made him so appealing.

She rushed in to impart the good news to Rhia and then dashed to the kitchen to pull salmon out of the freezer to defrost before heading for the shower. Rhia sat in the kitchen and smiled. Mack was home, the girl had brightened visibly. There was hope yet…

The weeks that followed were like a rebirth for all of them. Mack would come and sit with Rhia and Sophie some evenings and often Roger would join them, as he was now working on the farmhouse with them as a labourer. Christina and John would often work on, shooing Mack off to Rhia's. If he didn't know better, he would have said something was afoot.

Other days the five of them would work on the building restoration and Rhia would be on hospitality duty and make tea and juice. It was an exhausting task made light hearted by a happy family atmosphere and Sophie felt better that she could finally repay Christina and John for all their kindness when she had first arrived. She and Mack grew closer each day until they were completely natural in each other's company.

At the end of summer, Rhia threw a curveball and said that as they had worked so hard, how about a holiday to Puglia for them all.

"Oh please, say yes! It's so fabulous, you'll love it!" pleaded Sophie to Christina. As Mack had not started searching for work yet having stayed on preferring to help his father with the huge workload, that was really the work of a younger man. He looked to his mother, who nodded.

"We've all worked so hard, we could do with a holiday, but won't it be very hot at the moment?" she asked.

"It will just be starting to cool off and the residence might be quieter. Let's do it!" said Rhia with a sparkle in her eyes that Sophie hadn't seen that bright for quite some time.

The first thing that hit them all was the scent of Jasmine, just as Sophie had said it would. The bright Puglian sunshine was bouncing off the light stone of the trulli walls as Carole showed them to their rooms and the atmosphere was every bit as sweet as she remembered on her first visit.

Sophie dragged Mack down to show them the kidney shaped pool at the bottom of the winding terrace. The only thing missing was the summer poppies that peppered everywhere with their gay red abandon earlier in the year. The end of summer had still the bougainvillaea growing up the walls of the house in white and magenta and the gardens were awash with scent and colour.

An hour in they were all splashing like children in the pool, except for Rhia who sat and watched them in a large hat and kaftan with a smile on her face and a glass of Carole's best offering in her hand.

Mino cooked for them that evening and the meal was exquisite. He brought them the canapés to start with basil leaf in tempura batter which he insisted they try.

"Oh my! These are delicious." cried Sophie and she made Mack try. It was such a beautiful evening and Carole and Mino's family joined them, and the atmosphere was festive.

Rhia shooed them off on Mino's scooter the next day and Sophie took Mack to Locorotondo to show him the beautiful small citadel on the hill that looked like a wedding cake. Rhia had preferred to rest and chat with Christina and John who were not so desperate to site see immediately, and who were finally giving in to exhaustion of the last few weeks renovations.

Sophie took Mack on to Aberobella, and they sat in a cafe on the hillside above the town in the shade of the trees it was known for. They looked down on the honey pot houses all around them and it was another world. Sophie sighed as she looked out across the landscape and sipped her drink. Mack sat back in his chair, his strong legs stretching out as he watched her. She bore no resemblance to the girl he had once known. Her hair now sun-streaked and caramel drifted across her shoulders that were bare and he couldn't help but let his eyes wander to the shadow of her cleavage, where once his lips had traced their way.

He was still head over heels in love with her, he knew it and he was pretty sure she did too. There hadn't been anyone else for him. The occasional adventure with a college colleague but that was all. He could never bring himself to commit to anyone else. It was time.

"Sophie, do you know how much I actually love you?" he asked solemnly, and she flinched.

"I don't know if I'm ready for declarations of love Mac. I don't even know what it is..."

"Well can we start with just making love?" she flushed at his question and her eyes went to his as her lips trembled.

"I'm not sure if I can bear being hurt again." She answered.

"I'm not Jacques," he replied.

"I wasn't talking about Jacques," she said.

"I promise you Sophie. I will never again do anything that will knowingly hurt you. Before I was just a kid. I'm not a kid anymore.

Just one year later they were back in Puglia, standing in a Bonsai Garden just a stone's throw from Carole and Mino's residence. It was the most beautiful place to exchange wedding vows and with just the closest of their friends stood beside them. Under the shade of the three-hundred-year-old fir tree that sang gently to them as its branches caught the wind and the sunlight trickled through.

Mack and Sophie were the first two non-nationals to marry there. The Mayor looked resplendent in his sash as he performed the ceremony with pride. He had allowed Carole to interpret the service for them and it was a perfect blend of spiritual and formality. At the front as their witness, Rhia sat and watched her most beautiful, adopted child passed into someone else's care. It was a moment that could have broken her, but instead she rejoiced as she saw only love reflected in each of their eyes as they spoke their words with absolute sincerity. All she had ever wanted was a happy ending for the ones who had brought her a new beginning. She was content.

CHAPTER THIRTY

A bright full moon shone through the windows and across Rhia's bed as she lay awake in the early hours. She always refused to close the drapes believing that. if she sent her thoughts through the stars that they would somehow find their way to one that had always held her heart fast. Just like Feisel in the Disney cartoon she thought distractedly.

'Today has been a good day Sean.' She spoke in silent words to the man she had lost so many years ago.

She had watched with pride today as Sophie, confident and so very beautiful, conversed with the guests at the opening of her first big show, and how she had answered all the questions that would normally have been coming Rhia's way with ease, looking occasionally over to Rhia to exchange a knowing smile. Rhia returned it with a mother's pride. It didn't matter to Rhia that she hadn't born this young woman herself. She felt every bit of love for her that a mother should. Sophie was becoming a chip off the old block. Confidence, business savvy and kindness, she had everything that Rhia would have wished for her. That and a husband that let her be herself but adored her and was his own man.

Mack was a consultant in IT now working in Robotics operations programming. They parted, did their own thing, and returned to each other in between work to play like children. They were saving hard to buy their own house and Rhia had encouraged them to stay with her to give them a head start which they had done happily.

Mack had sat protectively at Rhia's side that evening, worried that she would be overtired with the number of people attending who might make a beeline for the more famous artist. In truth she was, but it was a happy tired, and she wanted so much to support and witness Sophie's triumph. She had had a small stroke some months ago, and though she was fully recovered both Sophie and Mack worried for her. They were her pride and joy and for all intents and purposes, she was the mother they had very much chosen her to be.

As she looked once more to the stars beyond her window, she thought she heard Clucy padding around her bed and her hand strayed to the side as the spirit of her beloved dog nuzzled her fingers and her breath stilled with surprise.

"It's ok old girl, I know."

Throwing back the covers, she rose slowly to stretch her aching bones and after reaching to switch on the bedside light, she walked to her desk and sitting down, she reached for pen and paper and commenced writing. When she had finished, she slipped the pages into an envelope and wrote Sophie's name with all the tenderness of a mother writing to her child for the last time.

She looked inside the drawer and pulled out the manuscript that she had finally completed. This was her story, the one that she had never told them in its entirety. It had been a work of pain and a work of love equally. It didn't matter to her that it be published. She just wanted it to be written. That she Rhiannon Hart had loved and lived and for Sophie to know her truth, that her life had held a purpose, despite everything and that purpose was to nurture Sophie to be the woman she now was. Placing the envelope on top of the manuscript she looked once more to the window and out onto the garden.

Rising again, she pulled on a robe, stepped into some comfortable shoes and silently opening the door, she made her way to the living room. Sophie and Mack always left a lamp on in there and as she slowly savoured each of the paintings upon the walls, which were now a mixture of both hers and Sophie's, she smiled with quiet satisfaction. On through the kitchen, she quietly pushed open the doors and stepped out onto the veranda where she paused briefly to inhale all the scents of the night garden. The dog followed unseen.

The palest of light was pushing up over the horizon and it was enough to walk without stumbling as she made her way through the garden, pausing to smell the odd rose or the jasmine which was always her very favourite scent. The dog paused also, waiting, and sniffing the air.

She continued towards the narrow path to the swing and brushed her fingers once more across the faded words... 'Certainty,' before giving the swing one last push to rock gently the ashes of the girl child she had never been allowed to bring into the world before she moved onwards.

The river was full when she reached the shallow pebble banks and she reached down to stroke the sleek red coat of Clucy who stood quietly by her side, ever faithful even in spirit. She had been her companion through much sadness and now she was here once more for this final moment.

"One last swim, old girl, it's been a while," she said to no one in particular as she shrugged out of her robe. She had kept on her nightdress for dignity on this occasion and her shoes for comfort. She never had gotten used to the discomfort of those pebbles underfoot and she walked with care. The water rose up to her waist and she paused to pull the band from her plait and combed out her hair through her delicate artist's fingers, still paint stained as they had ever been from the first day she had met him. Clucy was circling her silently as she allowed herself to dip her shoulders under the water to get used to the cold.

The current was pulling more than usual, and she stood and took one look back towards the bank where she saw herself and Sean laughing and naked once more, splashing through the shallows till they reached her side. They didn't see her of course, beings' energy from another time...They were too in love and as they waded past her, so close that she could almost reach out to them. Gasping with the shock of the cold water, they instinctively clung to each other for warmth and then she watched one last memory as he caressed her face and kissed her. The passion took over and she broke free from his kiss, and she floated back in the water, her hair undulating about her head like a dandelion clock. Her eyes sent him an unspoken message as she wrapped her thighs around his waist intimately. Catching her hips in his hands he gently pulled her towards him to make love.

Rhia mirrored the memory and for a second, she thought she felt the brush of his fingers on her face as her head lay back in the water and her hair rose to entwine in them. Had he gone before her and was he now waiting just a little ways downstream to gather in his arms once more?

She opened her eyes to the beauty of the trees silhouetted in the dawning sky above. Birds were starting to sing their morning greetings and with it the musical babble of water over stone would be the last thing she would hear. For only a moment there was fear until she opened herself up to all of nature's beauty and to him, only him. Her heart, her soul and now her body flowed to meet him, and she let the river take her willingly…

CHAPTER THIRTY-ONE

Sophie read the letter once more with trembling fingers.

My Darling Sophie,

What to say to you at this moment that will make your pain any less or help you understand my actions.

You were the daughter I was never able to have, but if I had had the choice of the most special child, she would have been you.

You see my sweet and talented girl; I have been on the longest walk that started many years ago and I have to tell you that I am tired now and ready to leave this life. Please don't be angry with me, it was something I always planned to do when my bones got too old.

I have had some strange times and some sad times, but this last few years, brief as they were, watching and helping you and Mack reach your true potential have been the most exquisitely peaceful and rewarding for me. It has been a quiet and abiding joy. I am seventy-six and it is enough for me.

I had only intended to stay until I lost my beloved Clucy dog, but your arrival threw somewhat of a spanner in the works for me and I knew I had a few more steps on my journey still to tread to see you safe.

I have lived over two decades in this house and as beautiful as it was here, I had made it my prison. You and Mack came and breathed life and youth back into it and a new purpose for me to stay a while longer for.

You see, I was never as strong as you, lovely one. When life threw adversity at me, I chose to build these walls around me, perhaps as a penance or a retreat, I will never quite know, but instead of protecting me it held me captive. You on the other hand fought off everything that was thrown at you with your lion's heart and sought something new and good.

I couldn't find the strength to break the bonds that held me fast to a memory and move on, and so I chose to live the best life I could, mainly in solitude in these last few years, at least until you lovely young people crashed my very lonely party and lit up life with my love for you.

As weak as Sean was, I could never quite believe that he was as cruel as it had all seemed. Perhaps he was, and I am a fool, but the initial beauty at the start of it held me so fast and I could not break the chains of my love for him. I made the best life I could without him. I certainly have still fulfilled all my creative dreams and had many good and loyal friends along the way, so it was not all sadness believe me. However, I was always drawn back to this house and by this river because I built him into every stone. I have no regrets for the path I have taken, for it led me to you and it brought me the much truer love that I deserved, one of family in my later life.

When I step into the river today, it will be my final swim with him. I never told you, but he and I spent a glorious four days camping here before it all fell apart. We swam as lovers in that river, and it is where I have always found my greatest peace. It's all in the book. I will never be without him whilst I am there. The water will be his arms and the sky his kiss. Perhaps when I wake on the other side, that small part of his spirit that remained with me will be there to meet me. I now know my Clucy will be waiting as I will be waiting one day for you, my dearest girl. If and when they find me, I would ask this one thing, that my ashes be taken back to the river once more.

Don't grieve too much for me, for I will already be at peace. Death is but a moment, and I didn't want to end my life weak and dependent on someone else for my basic needs. I wanted to end it strong, determined and loved... and on a creative high. Helping you become the beautiful and fulfilled young woman you are now, has been a delight and an honour, and if I can be allowed some credit, my greatest piece of art.

Live your life true to yourself. Never let it depend wholly on another but love yourself and others around you with strength and loyalty, even through adversity. Most of all be the best you can be, for I see creative greatness in you and that takes a determination which you have in abundance. Never let that go and you will always do well.

Tell Mack and his family and Roger that they brought me such happiness and friendship in my final years. Shed your tears for a while and then promise me not to linger in grief. Be thankful and happy for me, for I had you and that means I left this life loved and fulfilled.

My walk is over now, but I hope I have helped lay a wonderful path before you. Yours has only just begun and I am so excited and proud for you.

All my love, Rhiannon.

Sophie folded the letter and placed it back in its envelope. She had read it again and again over the last few days. Drying her tears she picked up the urn which contained Rhia's ashes. It seemed a small container for such a big personality, and she held it to her as though Rhia would reach through it to comfort her. She had had some of the ashes put in a small jewel coloured bottle that she had painted herself to bury in the planter on the swing so that part of her would rest with her child. The rest she now held in her hands. She thought that Rhia would have wanted that.

Rhia, the woman who had never once questioned her decency but instead had opened her heart and her life to a girl who she knew so little of. She had taken her on trust and in doing so had become the mother she had never really had. The loss seemed unspeakable at this moment, but she knew Rhia had taught her well.

Opening the door of Rhia's bedroom she walked towards the large Cre-angel painting that Rhia had loved so much where Mack, Christina, John, and Roger waited silently for her. Mack stretched out a hand and placed it on her shoulder as he saw her reddened eyes.

"Are you ready?" he asked.

"Yes, I am," she smiled bravely. "She made me ready, you know."

"I know," he replied.

Clutching the urn to her, she stepped through onto the veranda into all the autumn glory of what would always be known to her and the family to come as 'Rhia's Garden' and the place she was always destined to be. She knew Rhia would be smiling as she watched.

THE END

If you have enjoyed my book. Please share and review it on Amazon, Facebook or Goodreads as a new author needs all the help they can get.

Many Thanks

Dee Kearney

Find me at www.deekearney.com
Facebook: Dee Kearney Author
Twitter: @deekearney3

Other books by the author

Children of May - Family Saga spanning one hundred years

Open Hand - Thriller

Naverworld - Children's Fantasy

9 781916 390058